S0-ABO-634

"Why are you afraid of me?"

At Michael's question, Cheri felt flowers of ice blooming deep within her. Lying very still, she tried to quiet her thumping heart, still her racing fears.

"Do you want to talk about it?" he persisted.

"No." *He knows there's something wrong. Oh, God.* The only sound in the room was the soft popping of the fire, the gentle roar of the ocean outside. She felt Michael's fingers move up her neck, into her hair, where they gently massaged her head. Her tension seemed a living thing. Slowly, ever so slowly, she started to relax against him.

With great effort, Cheri raised her head and looked at him. He was lying back, his eyes almost closed. She swallowed, then slid her body up his and touched his cheek with her fingers. Before she lost her courage, she brought her mouth down over his.

ABOUT THE AUTHOR

Elda Minger came to writing via a circuitous route. Throughout the years she has worked in several bookstores, cleaned houses in Beverly Hills, been an usher in theaters, sang for money on Hollywood Boulevard, and even appeared in two movies. Born and now residing again in Hollywood, Elda has lived in many locations, including Italy.

Books by Elda Minger

HARLEQUIN AMERICAN ROMANCE

12—UNTAMED HEART
95—ANOTHER CHANCE AT HEAVEN
106—TOUCHED BY LOVE

These books may be available at your local bookseller.

Don't miss any of our special offers. Write to us at the following address for information on our newest releases.

Harlequin Reader Service
P.O. Box 52040, Phoenix, AZ 85072-2040
Canadian address: P.O. Box 2800, Postal Station A,
5170 Yonge St., Willowdale, Ont. M2N 6J3

Touched by Love

ELDA MINGER

Harlequin Books

TORONTO • NEW YORK • LONDON
AMSTERDAM • PARIS • SYDNEY • HAMBURG
STOCKHOLM • ATHENS • TOKYO • MILAN

Published June 1985

First printing April 1985

ISBN 0-373-16106-9

Copyright © 1985 by Elda Minger. All rights reserved.
Philippine copyright 1985. Australian copyright 1985.
Except for use in any review, the reproduction or utilization of
this work in whole or in part in any form by any electronic,
mechanical or other means, now known or hereafter invented,
including xerography, photocopying and recording, or in any
information storage or retrieval system, is forbidden without
the permission of the publisher, Harlequin Enterprises Limited,
225 Duncan Mill Road, Don Mills, Ontario, Canada M3B 3K9.

All the characters in this book have no existence outside the
imagination of the author and have no relation whatsoever to
anyone bearing the same name or names. They are not even
distantly inspired by any individual known or unknown to the
author, and all the incidents are pure invention.

The Harlequin trademarks, consisting of the words
HARLEQUIN AMERICAN ROMANCE, HARLEQUIN
AMERICAN ROMANCES, and the portrayal of a Harlequin,
are trademarks of Harlequin Enterprises Limited; the portrayal
of a Harlequin is registered in the United States Patent and
Trademark Office and in the Canada Trade Marks Office.

Printed in Canada

Chapter One

"Go right on inside, Mr. Stone. You're on the guest list."

Michael nodded his appreciation at the woman seated by the door, then walked quickly inside. The club looked like hundreds of others in Los Angeles—smoky, filled to capacity, with small tables and chairs crowded around the stage. People were talking, a gentle murmur swelling to fill the small space.

The only difference was the particular band. *And this one might make a difference.* Tough Cookie. He'd received their demo in the mail and had given the tape thirty seconds to make him sit up and take notice.

He had. Crystal-clear vocals, crisp arrangements, catchy melodies. The tape had caught his attention—now he wondered if the band would.

Ordering a beer from the bar, he chose one of the tables in back, preferring to remain as inconspicuous as possible. He tried not to meet anyone's eyes as he sat. Los Angeles was full of people who wanted to live out the American Dream. He had the power to make those dreams reality—but only if the person was outstanding to begin with.

Lights dimmed, the spots on the stage grew brighter. Then a young man performed a quick introuction. Michael leaned back in his chair and waited.

The woman who walked onstage caught his attention with her first step. Dressed completely in black, with high heels and in tight leather pants, she exuded a cocky sexuality as she strutted to the mike and checked her stand. The other women filed onstage, silent, checking their instruments, playing a few chords. Then, with a count from the drummer, the show began.

Nothing on the demo could have prepared Michael for the electricity the band generated live. He took it all in, watched each member carefully. But it was their lead singer, the woman dressed in black, who caught and held his attention.

The hot lights reflected back the red highlights in her dark-brown hair. He couldn't tell what color her eyes were. She had a slender figure, was of average height. But the power packed into her voice made her size inconsequential.

She had it all. Straight to the top, Michael thought as he took another sip of beer. He followed his instincts as much as possible, and they'd rarely failed him. This group couldn't miss. Why weren't they already working with someone?

The first set over, the band members walked offstage. Michael set his beer down, then got up and walked over to the door to one side of the small stage.

He wanted a closer look.

After a short break, the band returned. He watched them carefully now, especially the lead singer as she took her mike off the stand and checked it once again. She looked out over the audience, her expression as haughty as a queen's. Untouchable. Slowly, her glance encompassed the entire club, moving inexorably toward him.

When their eyes met, he didn't look away. Blue. Her eyes were blue. Dark blue, like a dusky sky. They had a startled look for just an instant as she met his gaze, seemed wide open and vulnerable.

The impact shot through his body, centering deep in his soul. It was as if he sensed the missing half of his personality, and a feeling of relief, of elation, washed over him.

The expression in her eyes altered subtly, becoming guarded. Suddenly he saw his knowledge reflected back toward him, and it seemed for a moment that the intensity of her gaze lit up the smoky, dim club.

People's voices, laughter and conversation all died away for the space of—it could have only been a few seconds. They stared at each other, caught in a private exchange, and neither could look away. Then the drummer clicked her drumsticks, started another song, and the singer looked quickly away, back over the rest of the audience. Her hand was shaking as she held the mike to her lips.

As sound and sight came quickly back to him, Michael realized he'd almost reached toward her with his hand, the connection between them had been that urgent. That strong. And as he leaned back inside the doorway and prepared to watch the second set, he knew he'd been touched by something as irreversible as the tides.

"GOD, HE HAS TERRIFIC BUNS."

"He's really cute! Did you see him leaning by the door after the second set?"

"I wouldn't kick him out of bed for eating crackers."

Cheri tried to ignore the conversation flowing around her in the cramped dressing room. She concentrated on removing her stage makeup. After smoothing a thin layer of cold cream on her face, she reached for a tissue, then glanced up at the rippled, cracked mirror.

Studying her reflection, she wiped off the last traces

of foundation and plum-colored blush. Taking another tissue, she closed one eye and began to remove her eyeshadow.

She started when she felt someone touch her arm, then opened her eye. The cream made her tear, but she recognized Rachel, Tough Cookie's bass player. Her best friend.

"He wants to see us afterward. When will you be ready?"

Cheri kept her face turned toward the mirror, avoided Rachel's eyes. "I'm not going."

Her friend sat down on a stool, shifting uncomfortably on the torn plastic seat. "Why not?"

"I don't feel well."

"You sounded fine onstage."

"I'm tired."

"Too tired to meet Michael Stone? You've got to be kidding!"

"Rachel, I have to work tomorrow. I've been late too many times to oversleep. I'm sure anything Mr. Stone has to say to me he can say to you." Cheri smiled, trying to soften the words. "Besides, I trust you to represent me."

"Okay." Rachel paused, a frown on her usually sunny face. Cheri knew she hadn't heard the last of this discussion. "But what if he wants to meet you?" Rachel asked, lowering her voice so the three other women in the dressing room couldn't hear her. "You carry the band through a lot of songs. What do I say if he asks why you aren't with us?"

"Tell him the truth." Cheri leaned over and picked up her blue canvas tote bag, then pushed her long bangs out of her eyes. "Look, I can meet him later this week. But I just can't tonight."

She was aware of Rachel's intense scrutiny for a long moment. Cheri busied herself with collecting her makeup and jamming it into her bag. When her friend finally spoke, her voice was almost inaudible against the excited chatter in the dressing room.

"All right. We'll talk in the morning."

CHERI WONDERED later that evening just what she'd accomplished by staying home. She was too keyed up to sleep, too restless after performing.

They'd been good tonight. She knew it, had felt it in the audience response, in the energy the band had projected onstage. The crowd had called them back after their last set was over to play a few more songs, and they had exited to enthusiastic clapping and whistling. It couldn't have been a better night for a prospective manager to come to see them.

But she hadn't wanted to meet Michael Stone. Cheri had watched him surreptitiously from the wings between sets, had studied the man as if he were some sort of alien species. What she'd seen had impressed and frightened her.

She'd only been able to amass the most fleeting impression. Tall and dark, he had an air of knowing what he wanted and how to go about getting it. When he'd stared at her, she'd had the fleetest impression, the quickest feeling of—of what? She stared at the ceiling. *He's going to change your life. One way or another.* She hadn't needed to stay after and talk to him—she knew he was going to manage the band. Cheri played life by instinct. It was rare she was wrong.

Buffy, her dog, stirred against the red-and-white patchwork quilt. Cheri reached down and scratched soft, spaniel ears. The dog sighed and curled into a tighter ball.

It seemed quiet tonight, after all the noise at the club. Cheri closed her eyes and thought about the man she'd seen. As she tried to fall asleep, the clock radio played classical music soothingly in the background. Her bedside lamp was set on its lowest setting, bathing the room in soft light.

He'd sign them, and if they followed his standard procedure, he'd take their band, Tough Cookie, straight to the top of the rock world within three years.

Michael Stone's management meant stardom.

Her thoughts were interrupted as she heard Rachel's van pull into the driveway in back of the house. Realizing the futility of sleep, Cheri decided to help her friend carry in the equipment.

She pulled on an old pair of jeans and a T-shirt, then let herself out the back door of the small stucco house.

"Hi," she called out softly.

"Hi yourself." Rachel uncoiled her lanky body from behind the wheel. When she stood next to Cheri, it was as if they were comic opposites—Mutt and Jeff. Cheri had often wished she were more like Rachel in looks and temperament. Her roommate, tall and blond, seemed to sail through life with a solid self-confidence that amazed Cheri. Though Rachel did nothing to make her feel insignificant, sometimes Cheri couldn't help feeling exactly that way. Everything about her seemed average: her height, her long dark-brown hair and blue eyes. Her facial features. Though Rachel gave her many encouraging talks, Cheri felt like a pale shadow next to her lively roommate, even though she adored her.

Cheri approached the back of the van as Rachel opened it and began to help, pulling out amplifiers, speakers and what seemed like miles of electrical cord.

"How did it go?" Suddenly she was ashamed of her refusal to stay after and meet Michael Stone.

"He wants to meet you."

"Besides that."

"He seems interested."

"In the band?" She'd known it all along.

"Yeah, but—" Rachel grabbed the case of her bass guitar, pulled it out of the van, and slammed the door of the vehicle. She caught her breath. "He seemed interested in you."

"Oh." Cheri bent her head and picked up a coil of cords. She knew that was why she'd run. She didn't want him looking at her too closely. She'd seen him leaning by the door and had wondered why he'd been watching her so intently.

Now she knew her instincts had been right.

"He was really nice about it. He asked me questions about you—and took us all out for coffee afterward."

"Coffee would have kept me up all night," she replied. "It's a good thing I didn't go." As soon as the words were out of her mouth, Cheri realized she was trying to convince herself she'd been right to leave early. But now, talking with Rachel, her earlier anxiety seemed ridiculous. What could have happened, with the other women there?

"You're up now, so what's the difference?" They laughed and, shouldering equipment, started toward the back door.

Though Cheri had hoped the subject of Michael would be dropped, Rachel talked about him while she washed her face and prepared for bed.

"It's almost three in the morning, I don't want to hear any more about him!" Cheri pounded her pillow in frustration and pulled it around her ears. The gesture was childish, yet comforting. She felt the mattress dip and knew Rachel had come to sit down.

"Listen to me a minute."

Cheri sat up in bed and put her arms around her knees.

"He's a really nice guy."

"I *know* that, that's all you've said since—"

"I think he could be good for you."

Cheri felt her eyes widen, sensed her heartbeat speeding up. How could she explain to Rachel she didn't want a relationship with any man—including Michael Stone? She'd have to be crazy to be involved with someone like him. The emotional and physical demands—she didn't want it. Not now. Maybe never.

She tried to offset the seriousness of the conversation with humor. "Are you trying to tell me I should sleep my way to the top?"

"Not at all. All I'm saying is if a man like Michael Stone asked questions about me—" Rachel held up her hand as Cheri started to interrupt. "If he seemed interested in me, I'd go for it."

"Thank you, mother."

"PICKFAIR BOOKSTORE, Hollywood Boulevard. Can I help you?" Cheri cradled the phone between her shoulder and ear, her hands busily stacking books.

"You want what? I'm sorry, we sold out of *To Tame My Love* this morning. The author was on the Donahue show. We can order you a copy from the warehouse. It'll take eight to ten days." She glanced around quickly, dismayed by the sudden crowd surrounding the information desk. The woman on the phone couldn't wait eight to ten days. Irritated, Cheri made up her mind for her. "All right, then, you might try another bookstore in the city. Thank you."

She turned away from the phone, ready to greet the next customer. The smile on her face froze in place as she looked up into a pair of soft dark-brown eyes.

"Cheri?" Michael Stone.

She nodded her head. Patrick Hunt, the day manager, glanced at her with an annoyed expression on his face. Realizing she was taking too much time to respond, Cheri quickly composed herself.

"Can I help you with something?"

He caught on fast, after a quick look at her boss. "Yes. I'd like to see a book in the music section."

Once out of earshot of the main desk, he extended his hand. "Michael Stone."

After a second's hesitation, she took it. "Cheri Bradley." His fingers felt warm and rough with slight calluses. Not the hands of an executive.

"I enjoyed the show last night."

"Thank you."

"You're very good."

She couldn't help smiling. "Thank you."

"I'd like to manage your band."

She took a deep breath. "I think we'd like that."

He started to laugh, a deep sound that warmed her inside.

"That's different. Usually people are quite *sure* they want me to manage them."

"I guess I'm different, then." Cheri noticed Patrick was heading toward them, and she took a huge, coffee-table book off the top shelf. "This is our best book on Broadway musicals. It makes a terrific present."

He responded immediately. "My sister would really like it. But I had something more expensive in mind."

Cheri had to bite her lip to keep from laughing. She could picture Patrick's face lighting up at the thought of the store making more money. As her manager walked away toward the paperback room, she whispered, "That was terrific."

"You give me good opening lines."

She couldn't believe it. *This* was Michael Stone? No wonder Rachel had enjoyed her evening with him. He had a distinct talent for drawing people out, putting them at ease. Cheri usually had a difficult time talking with men, but she wasn't as nervous around Michael. He didn't try to move close to her or "accidentally" touch her. His expression seemed open and honest. Different. She was used to being careful on the boulevard walking to and from work. So many men had the attitude that if you were out on the sidewalk you were fair game for their verbal assaults. She'd thought Michael might be similar—like so many of the managers she'd met before.

But he wasn't.

As she studied him, Cheri suddenly realized she was staring. Averting her gaze, she straightened a book, then glanced at the floor. Remembering what Rachel had told her the other night, she felt embarrassment staining her face; her skin felt hot and prickly. Michael Stone, interested in her? Rachel had to be fantasizing again.

She hated being self-conscious with him, wished they could have continued laughing and joking as before. But her feelings wouldn't obey her thoughts.

"We can't talk here." Michael had obviously noticed her discomfort, but attributed it to another source. Relieved, Cheri glanced back up at him. His eyes were gently encouraging. She swallowed.

"True." She shifted the large book in her arm, held it in front of her like a shield. Then, realizing what she was doing, she put it back up on the shelf.

"When do you finish work?" he asked.

"In an hour and a half. At six."

"Are you doing anything tonight?"

She glanced nervously away from him, then back. "No."

He reached into the back pocket of his jeans and pulled out a business card. "Call me at the office when you get home. If I can get out at a reasonable time, I'd like to take you out to dinner tonight. To discuss business." When she didn't answer, he added, "I didn't see you last night, and I like to get to know everyone in a band before I decide to take them on."

She nodded, then smiled. His eyes were so warm, his face so open.

"I'll call you," she said quietly, knowing she would.

"Good." The word was so soft it was almost a caress. He looked at her for a long moment, and Cheri had the strangest sensation he was looking inside her, seeing her in a way most people didn't attempt to.

"Line two is on hold!" Patrick's exasperated voice cut into the silence.

Michael quickly scanned the bookshelf and pulled down a thick paperback biography of Beethoven. "Fantastic. I'll take it! My sister will love this." He approached the main desk, Cheri walking behind him. She couldn't help looking at his body, at the firm masculine lines. He didn't look like most of the managers she'd met. He looked...wonderful.

Michael slapped the book down on the counter by Patrick's register. Someone else picked up the phone, so Cheri was able to watch him as he made his purchase. As Patrick rang him up and Michael got out his checkbook, he remarked, "I have to compliment you on the personal service in this store."

Patrick remained silent, but a tight little smile played around the corners of his mouth.

At six that evening, Cheri was the first to punch out.

"Hot date?" Patrick's low voice was sarcastic.

Cheri jumped, then whirled to face him, her breath coming out in a little gasp. "You scared me!"

He seemed to be studying her, and in that instant Cheri felt a rush of pity and silent understanding for her manager. Patrick had always reminded her of a sullen child, with his soft, round body and thin blond hair. His blue eyes were pale and watery, his mouth set in a grim line.

He seemed to be a man who had given up on his dreams, who lived his life on a very practical, uninspiring level.

Don't let me become like him, she thought as she reached for her sweater and bag.

"I'll see you tomorrow, Patrick."

"Don't be late." He turned away from her and she watched the familiar hunch of his shoulders. Then, remembering Michael, she walked quickly down the center aisle of the brightly lit bookstore and out into the cool evening air.

She jogged home, expertly dodging street performers, mimes and musicians. Once she turned off the boulevard and headed up the slight incline toward her house, she slowed her pace.

Though she was still walking briskly up the sidewalk, her thoughts drifted to the evening ahead. Michael would pick her up and—what would she wear? She had almost decided on a particular outfit when she remembered the way the house had looked that morning. Neither she nor Rachel were the best housekeepers.

Tucking her bag more firmly underneath her arm, she broke into a run.

Once at home, she stood in the middle of the living room. What now? Buffy ran around her legs, a flash of black-and-tan fur attached to a warm pink tongue. She knelt and scratched the little dog's ears.

Michael had asked her to call him at his office. All the self-confidence she'd displayed in her earlier daydreams evaporated. He would be expecting her call. She dug into her pants pocket and took out the business card, then reached for the phone.

It rang only once before he picked up. "Hello?"

"Mr. Stone?" Her voice sounded thin and weak to her ears.

"Cheri? You're home?"

"I just walked in. What time should I be ready?"

"I can't leave the office for another hour. Is eight too late for you to eat dinner?"

She glanced around the cluttered living room. At least she'd have time to clear up the worst of it. "No, that's fine."

"I'll leave the office at seven-thirty."

"Fine." Cheri tried to inject a note of casual self-confidence into her voice. Actually, she wasn't doing too badly.

"See you soon." He hung up.

It was only later she wondered how he'd found out where she lived.

BY SEVEN-THIRTY, Cheri was relaxing in a tub of peach-scented bubbles. The dishes were done. The beds were made. All the albums were inside their jackets, and the stereo and bookshelves had been quickly dusted. She'd run the vacuum over the rug and quickly mopped the kitchen floor. Guitars, cords and amplifiers had been stuffed in the back of her closet or carted out to the garage.

"Not that I want him to get the wrong impression," she said to the pair of mournful doggy eyes staring at her.

Buffy barked and ran up to the edge of the tub. She put one feathery paw on the porcelain rim.

"No, you don't! Down!" Buffy obeyed sheepishly, rolling over on her back and waving her paws in the air. "Silly girl." Cheri sank back in the bubbles and tried to relax.

Just what impression *did* she want to give Michael? Her last-minute cleaning would have been done for anyone. She wouldn't have wanted Patrick to walk in on that confusion. And the bubbles were simply to get rid of the smells of furniture polish and Ajax.

She was surprised to find herself looking forward to seeing Michael. He put her at ease in a way most men didn't. If she could just keep things light. She had been all right with him in the bookstore. Until she'd thought about what Rachel had said.

She pulled out the plug with her toes, then leaned back into the water and sighed. They could be friends, she was sure of it. Michael would manage the band. Everything would be perfect.

You could never give him anything more than that, a tiny voice inside nagged her. She pushed the thought away just as she heard a knock at the door.

Was he here already? How long had she soaked in the tub? Groaning, Cheri stood up quickly and reached for the white terry robe hanging on the back of the door. Wrapping it snugly around her wet, naked body, she stepped out of the tub and padded into the living room.

Buffy was barking excitedly and scratching at the door, determined to make a new friend. Cheri laced her fingers through the dog's collar and opened the door, keeping the chain latched.

Michael Stone. Dressed in black denim jeans and a dark shirt and jacket. With a bouquet of white daisies in his hands. The sight of the flowers disarmed her.

Still slightly nervous, she blurted out, "I'm running a little late."

He smiled easily. "I'm early."

Buffy was straining against her hold, obviously wanting to get close enough to smell this fascinating stranger. Cheri closed the door, unhooked the chain, then opened the door and stood back.

His presence filled the room, a quiet, unassuming strength. Cheri let Buffy go, then tightened the belt of her robe. She gestured toward the bathroom.

"I was just getting out of the tub."

"I'm sorry I interrupted you." He set the daisies down on the coffee table, then shrugged out of his jacket and placed it on the couch. Buffy jumped all around him, her toenails clicking on the hardwood floor.

"Take your time." He knelt down and patted Buffy's head. "Hi, girl."

Cheri watched him. In any other circumstances, she would have been afraid of being alone with a man. Especially in just a bathrobe.

But he was different.

"Listen, I'm really sorry." The words rushed out of her mouth, breathy and apologetic. "There's wine in the fridge, and you can put on an album. I'll be out as soon as I can."

"Don't hurry." He sat down on the couch and an ecstatic Buffy jumped up with him.

"Buffy, down!" Cheri felt mortified.

Buffy stayed on the couch, her tail wagging so hard her hindquarters were wiggling with it. She barked sharply, once.

"It's okay. I have a dog myself." Michael scratched the little dog's head and she closed her eyes and edged toward him.

"She'll get hair on your clothes."

"They'll wash."

Cheri smiled, some of the tension leaving her body. She liked him. "I'll be back in a second."

She finished dressing in record time, drying off quickly and pulling on the clothes she'd selected—dressy black denim jeans and a black-and-silver sweater. *We'll match.* She took extra care with her makeup, a pretty plum gloss and blush, and outlined her eyes with a blue-gray shadow, then lots of mascara.

Studying herself quickly in the mirror, she was satisfied. She looked more like the woman he'd seen onstage.

Michael stood up as she walked in. He had been studying the living room and scratching Buffy's head.

"I hope she wasn't a pest."

"No. Just curious."

As her eyes quickly scanned the room, Cheri saw the daisies lying on the coffee table. How could she have left them there? He must think her terribly rude. Flushing, she picked them up and held them against her cheek for an instant, feeling the tiny petals against her skin. "Thank you, Mr. Stone. They're lovely." Retreating to the kitchen, she filled a vase with water and arranged the flowers inside.

How did other women make it look so effortless? Rachel would have struck up an easy conversation by now. Yet here she was with him, and they seemed stiff and forced with each other.

Maybe once you get outside. Walking back into the living room, she took her trench coat down from the coat rack. February weather in Los Angeles was tricky, and the weatherman had predicted rain tonight.

"Let me help you." Michael was behind her before she realized it. He reached for her wrap and held it. She hesitated, then turned into the coat. He helped her ease her arms into the sleeves.

But then he reached to free her hair from the confines of her collar.

Cheri jerked her head away in an action so instinctive she was powerless to stop it.

He hesitated for a second, then dropped his hands. Cheri stood still, her back toward him. The house was so quiet she could hear the clock ticking in the kitchen. She willed the moment to pass, then turned to face him with a false, uncomfortable smile on her lips.

Michael was staring out the front window, his hands in the pockets of his jeans. As if nothing had happened.

Once outside, they walked to Michael's car. The red Ferrari gleamed softly under the streetlight. He opened the door for her but didn't offer to help her inside.

As Michael walked around to the driver's side, Cheri studied him covertly. Rachel would consider Michael short, but anyone under six feet two was short to her. Cheri guessed him to be five eleven. He had broad shoulders and a firmly muscled body. He had to work out. You didn't get a body like that from sitting behind a desk.

His door clicked open and she looked out her window. She didn't want him to catch her staring.

Once he was settled inside and they had pulled away from the curb, he spoke softly. "What type of food do you like?"

"I'm not fussy."

"What do you like?"

"Everything. Italian, Chinese, hamburgers..."

"Fellini's?"

"Sure, I've been there."

The restaurant was crowded for a weekday night, so as soon as Michael gave his name to the hostess, he guided Cheri to a table in the large bar. Originally a small, intimate restaurant, Fellini's had undergone expansion in the past year, and Cheri was sorry. No longer a small, little-known place, now it was huge, bustling and crowded. Conversation droned in the background, along with the clinking of glasses and the electronic sounds of a video game. A wide-screen television set dominated one whole corner of the spacious bar.

"You liked it better before, didn't you?" Michael's voice was soft, breaking into her thoughts.

"Yes, I— How did you know?"

"Your eyes gave you away." He laughed. "I'm not psychic. You have a very expressive face."

Their cocktail waitress arrived, dressed in a short black dress, black tights and spike heels. Her white-blond hair was pulled back off her face and fell in a long braid down her back.

"I'll have a Heineken. Cheri?" Michael smiled encouragingly.

"White wine."

The waitress reeled off several names.

"Just the house wine."

They settled back into their chairs and looked at each other. Cheri felt one of her hands curl into a tense fist. *Think of something to say.*

She was saved when Michael asked her a question.

"How did you start singing?"

She took a deep breath. "My grandmother always had a piano. When I was five, I heard her singing and playing. I climbed up on the bench with her and began to sing a harmony. She thought it was terrific and decided I should have lessons."

"What do your parents think?"

She was prepared for this question; her emotions had been carefully schooled. "They're dead."

"I'm sorry."

"It was a long time ago."

"How old were you?"

She glanced down at the table, ran her finger along the smooth surface. "Thirteen."

"It must have been hard."

"It was."

"Who raised you?"

"My grandmother. When she died, I moved here."

His dark eyes were thoughtful, and again Cheri had the sensation he was looking beyond the surface, deep inside her. The thought made her uncomfortable. He seemed to sense her upset feelings, and she was sure he consciously changed the subject.

"How did you meet Rachel? She's quite a character."

Relieved by the change in conversation, Cheri replied quickly, "She was a sales rep for a publisher. We used to talk when she came into the bookstore where I work. Once we found out we were both interested in music that was it."

"How long have you lived together?"

"Three years."

The waitress arrived with their drinks. They were silent for a short time while each took a sip, then Michael set his beer down and leaned back, looking at her.

"How old are you?"

"Twenty-six."

"You seem younger."

"Why?" Cheri found herself asking questions she didn't usually ask. But she wanted to know what he thought of her.

"I don't know. There's a touch of naiveté about you."

"Is that good or bad?" She took another sip of her wine.

"I like it."

Cheri decided to launch some questions of her own. Usually she wasn't so curious about men, but she found she wanted to know more about Michael.

"How old are you?"

He seemed surprised. "Why do you ask?"

She could feel the laughter bubbling behind her words. "I just like to get to know someone before I sign on with them."

He laughed then, and she was delighted she could tease him this way. Determined to keep this new light feeling between them, she pressed her point.

"Well?"

"I'm thirty-two."

"Awfully young to be running the kind of empire you have."

"My father handed over the firm when he had his second heart attack." His face tightened slightly, and his dark eyes clouded over. The look on his face told her several things: he loved his father, took his responsibilities seriously, and was a man whose emotions ran very deep.

Cheri was surprised at the intensity of feeling Michael generated inside her. For a split second, she envied him his family. What was it like, to be close to people like that?

"I'm sorry. I didn't mean to tease you." And she found she regretted causing him any pain, if only in memory.

"Hey." He reached for her hand, covered it with his own. "You didn't know. It's okay."

She controlled the urge to pull away, let him touch her for a few seconds before gently disengaging her hand. Cheri was surprised to find she didn't dislike the feel of his warm fingers, his strong, square hands.

The waitress came by and told them their table was ready, so they picked up their drinks and followed her into the other, smaller room.

This was the section Cheri remembered from the restaurant's older days. Rough wood paneling, Italian movie posters and local artists' works were displayed on the walls, and huge philodendrons hung from macrame planters. The booths were dark and private, the individual tables made of oak with ceramic trivets built into the tops.

But it was the food that had first attracted Cheri to Fellini's. As she slid into her side of the booth, the air was warm and filled with the scent of spices. Earthy basil, pungent rosemary, spicy oregano. And the ever-present cinnamon spicing the coffee. Fellini's was known for simple, uncomplicated food, mostly Italian and French country cooking.

As she looked across the table at Michael, she was glad to be sharing a favorite place with him.

"You like it here, don't you?"

"Rachel brought me here when I first met her. I loved it. If I find something I like, it's kind of hard to make me change."

"That's encouraging." His voice still sounded gently teasing, but there was an underlying seriousness to his words.

She was prevented from saying anything more as their waitress arrived and took their order. Once she left, Michael launched another round of questions.

"What do you want out of the band?"

She thought for a moment before she spoke, realizing the importance of her answer. Keeping her eyes on the blue-and-white ceramic trivet in the center of the table, she spoke softly. "I want a chance to do good work. With my songs. With my voice." She glanced up at him, relieved to find he was listening carefully. There weren't many people who took the band seriously, so it felt strange having Michael ask her these questions. "I want to stretch myself." She looked back down at her hands. "I'm not making too much sense, am I?"

"You're doing fine. Keep going."

"I guess it all comes down to trying to communicate with people, to make them feel what you feel. I'm not very good at expressing this. That's really all there is."

"That's fine."

She took another deep breath, deciding to risk all and simply tell him how she felt. "You're not at all like I thought you'd be."

His eyebrows arched up slightly, but he remained silent.

"From everything I read, I thought you'd be pushy and obnoxious—I mean, more forceful, more impatient."

"I know what you mean. Don't be embarrassed."

"It's just that we met so many promoters who were...awful."

He nodded.

"I like you, Mr. Stone. I really do."

He smiled then, and Cheri didn't even notice when their waitress set down their food.

Chapter Two

Their meal was almost over when Cheri thought to ask about a contract.

Dinner had been excellent. Both of them had ordered pasta and a salad, then finished with pecan pie and coffee. Relaxed and at ease with Michael, Cheri brought up her question.

Michael took a sip of his coffee before he answered. "I don't work with a contract. I find that if an artist likes the work I'm doing, he or she usually has no qualms about continuing to work with me."

"You mean we don't sign anything?" It seemed strange that such a tenuous thread would connect them professionally.

"You'll be signing contracts with other people soon. A record company, for instance. And I want you to have a good contract lawyer who has nothing to do with me or my company. That's only common sense. But there won't be any papers between you and me."

"Aren't you scared you'll get burned?" She could scarcely believe he was trusting her this much.

"If an artist burns me, then he's probably not worth working with in the long run. All it boils down to is a matter of trust between two parties."

She took another sip of her coffee. "Have you ever been taken advantage of?"

"Not very often. The odds are against it when you give someone good management. So much of the time, people in the music business don't know what they're doing. There's a lot of misunderstanding that comes out of ignorance. But deliberate deception? It doesn't happen very often."

"Oh." All at once, Cheri realized how little she knew about the music business. Her business. She felt as if she were embarking on a long journey without directions.

He must have noticed the look on her face. "Don't worry. You're hiring me to see you through the whole mess."

"Is it a mess?"

He laughed. "I shouldn't have put it like that. Yes, in some ways. There are people in the business for the wrong reasons. There's a lot of money to be made. Don't look so frightened. I'll see you get through it all right."

They lingered over coffee until their waitress gave them the bill. It was only then Cheri realized the restaurant was closing.

The drive home was silent, each lost in private thought. Buffy met them at the door, ready for her evening walk.

"You don't have to stay," Cheri told Michael quickly. It was late; she was sure he had a full day at the office the next day.

"You shouldn't be walking alone this time of night." He matched his pace to hers as Buffy raced ahead, her ears streaming out behind her. It felt pleasant to have him walking beside her. Cheri was surprised. The typical image of a sleazy agent-manager came to mind so easily, but Michael had broken through every stereotype.

She walked slowly, enjoying the feel of being taken care of.

They walked farther than she usually did, listening to the gentle murmur of traffic, enjoying the cool evening air, the night sounds of the city. Cheri found herself regretful when she turned back toward the house, whistling gently for the reluctant Buffy.

Cheri hesitated by the front door. She wanted to tell Michael how much she'd enjoyed their evening together. His thoughtfulness touched her.

"I had a wonderful time tonight, Mr. Stone." The words sounded so inadequate compared to how she felt. It was rare she enjoyed a man's company. This evening had given her some perspective on how it could have been. If things in her life had been different.

"So did I." A light breeze ruffled his dark, straight hair, lifting it away from his face. A handsome, masculine face, with a firm jaw and dark, sensual eyes. A face she had trusted instinctively.

She stood on the doorstep a moment longer, wondering what to do. Surely he wasn't going to kiss her good night? This had been a business meeting. Then why was he looking at her so strangely? She studied the front of his shirt, not sure what to do.

"Cheri?" At the sound of her name, she looked up into his eyes. She couldn't read his expression.

"I haven't been completely honest with you." His words came out in a rush, as if he were saying things he had no control over. "I could have called you on the phone or arranged to have you come down to my office. I wanted...I wanted to see you."

It took a moment for the words to sink in, they were so unexpected.

"Don't be afraid of me," he whispered. "Please." And then, with instinctive clarity, she knew he was going to kiss her. She stood very still as he took her chin gently between his thumb and forefinger and turned her face slowly toward his. In the instant before he kissed her, when she knew he was about to, she felt a small flare of excitement. It surprised and frightened her. Cheri could barely breathe.

His lips covered hers gently, with none of the force, none of the intimate coercion usually reserved for a first kiss. It was a sweet kiss, a deep kiss, a kiss so full of feeling that when his lips left hers she kept her eyes closed, savoring the moment.

When she opened them, he was watching her, a crooked smile on his face. The look, slightly uncertain, touched her heart.

"Did you like it?"

She nodded, not trusting herself to speak.

He caught her hand, brought it up to his mouth and kissed her palm. "I like you, Cheri."

"I like you, too."

"Can I see you Saturday? We could go to a movie."

"Okay."

"Could you do me one more favor?" he asked.

Slowly, she nodded.

"Call me Michael. I hate this Mr. Stone business."

She was silent. How had this happened in the space of seconds? *You're out of control.*

"Michael," he urged softly.

Her lips formed the word, and her voice sounded soft after the deep tones of his. "Michael."

He kissed her again, quickly this time, then stepped back. "Okay." Then he turned and started down the drive.

She watched him walk to his car, her arms hugged around her against the chill evening. But the memory of his kiss warmed her.

DRIVING HOME THAT NIGHT, Michael wondered what she was scared of.

How would you feel if Gina were trying to make a living in the business? he asked himself, putting his younger sister in Cheri's place. It was a rough world—especially for a woman. That could account for part of the reticence he sensed in Cheri.

But it was something else. When he'd helped her with her coat—after she'd pulled away, he'd been careful not to touch her for the rest of the evening. It had been an effort, because it was the exact opposite of what he'd wanted to do.

Admit it. If she'd let you, you'd have spent the night with her.

Yet within minutes of their dinner date, he'd known she was—reluctant. Shy. Vulnerable.

Those eyes. She got you with those eyes. He could still remember the way he'd felt last night in the club. As if she'd cast out a net with that look, thrown it over him and started to draw him closer. But it was a mutual thing—he *wanted* to be close to her.

Maybe because you're a manager. Maybe she's being very careful. He couldn't fault her there. It was going to be difficult—managing her and becoming personally involved. He knew some people had private rules they never violated—don't get involved with a client.

He'd never followed any rules but his own.

So you'll see her Saturday, and the Saturday after that, and you'll get to the bottom of all her feelings sooner or later.

He smiled as he thought of the expression on her face just after he'd kissed her. She'd been surprised. He'd felt her response, the tiniest flare. It had made him feel supremely masculine, confident in his ability to make her happy. To make her want to be with him.

He'd take things slow and easy. They'd talk out any problems.

It's taken a long time. He hadn't felt this way about a

woman in almost three years. After Nancy—there hadn't been any feeling left for so long. It was a relief to discover his emotions were still intact, that he could do more than negotiate a deal.

The Ferrari moved swiftly over the freeway as he headed toward home.

"So, DID HE KISS YOU good night?" Rachel asked the next morning.

Cheri didn't even have to answer. She knew the truth was all over her face.

"I knew it, I knew it! Lucky girl! What was it like?"

"It was ... very sweet."

"Sweet! Michael Stone! Are you crazy or what?"

Cheri laughed. "He's a very sweet man."

Rachel expelled a long breath and reached for another doughnut. "That's not the word I'd use, but whatever makes you happy."

"Rachel." Cheri leaned forward and touched her roommate's hand. "Will you answer a question for me?"

"Sure."

"Why do you think he likes me?"

Rachel sat back in the sunny yellow kitchen, propping her long legs up on another chair. "Well, you were certainly hot stuff the first night he saw us perform."

"Yeah, but that's not really me." Cheri sipped her herbal tea and glanced at the clock above the stove. She didn't want Rachel to be late for work.

"It's a part of you."

"But not the main part."

"What are you afraid of?"

"I guess ..." Cheri paused, looking down at her mug. "Maybe I'm scared because he'll see the real me and not be all that thrilled."

"He liked you last night all right."

"He just met me last night."

"He'll like you fine. Wait till Ria finds out. She really has the hots for him." Ria played lead guitar for the band, and her infatuations were legendary.

"No, Rachel. I...please don't tell anyone yet. I don't want anyone in the band to know but you."

"Come on, Cheri. All anyone has to do is look at the way you'll be reacting to each other and that'll be the end of that!"

"No, I really want it this way. Please."

"All right." But Rachel didn't sound convinced.

After her friend left for work, Cheri did the dishes and put on one of Tough Cookie's tapes. She had to start working up some new material for the band.

She was in the middle of the fifth time through a particular song when Buffy pushed a wet nose into her face. Cheri took off her headphones.

"What is it, Buff-puff?"

Almost in response to her question, she heard a knock at the front door. She got up to answer it, but first peered through the peephole. A young boy stood in front, a package in his arms.

Opening the door, she took it from him, immediately recognizing the raised gold lettering on the box. Flowers from Beverly Hills. Setting the package down on the small table by the door, she tipped the delivery boy, thanked him, then closed the door and stared at the package as if it were alive.

After a minute, she took the box into the kitchen and opened it. Against a background of dark-green ferns, the dozen blood-red roses were startlingly beautiful. Perfect buds, not a single one marred.

She knew before she opened the card who they were from. Reaching underneath the small flap with her nail, she slit it open. His handwriting was strong and assured. *"Because I enjoyed last night so very much. Michael."*

As if in slow motion, Cheri took a vase down from the kitchen cupboard and arranged the flowers in it. Carrying it into her bedroom, she set it on her dresser.

They were gorgeous. Their fragrant scent began to fill the small house. Against the cream colored stucco wall, the color brought the room alive. Such beautiful flowers. Blood-red. The color of passion.

Cheri lay down on her bed. There could be only one outcome in a relationship with Michael. Passionate flowers from a passionate man. She shivered slightly, then reached down and pulled the crocheted afghan up from the foot of her bed and tucked it around her.

It was hard to reconcile the man with his image. She had heard other musicians gossip about how ruthless Michael was in getting the very best for his stable of clients. Just last month all anyone could talk about was the deal he'd pulled off for one of the agency's newest groups, Bad Boy. Yet she also knew Michael was honest, fair and sensitive. He had a reputation for really listening to the people he represented, for making sure the dream didn't go sour when it was actually realized. Most rock acts would pick him as first choice for management, because Michael Stone was the best.

But it was frightening to be in a similar situation in an affair of the heart. Her instincts told her his passions ran deeper in love.

Love. How could anyone love someone so soon? But she had let him kiss her. And had agreed to see him again.

When Rachel came home that evening, Cheri had dinner ready, as well as her plan of attack. As she dished up the homemade chicken soup, she decided to come straight to the point.

"Rachel?"

"Hmm?" Her roommate was thumbing through the mail, and didn't look too pleased. She threw a pile of bills onto the table.

"Tell me everything you know about Michael Stone."

Rachel glanced up from her seat at the small round table in the corner of the kitchen. "The bug has bitten you bad."

"I just want to know." Cheri placed a bowl of soup on a flowered place mat. "Be careful, it's hot."

"I don't blame you. If it was me, I'd be over the moon."

"Has he ever been married?"

"Nope. He came awful close one time. Remember that model, the blonde, on that TV show?"

"No."

"You know, the one who was on the cover of *Newsweek* a few years ago, the article on California actresses?"

"Oh. Yeah, I remember." *She was gorgeous.* "What happened?" Cheri tried to make her voice sound casual.

"They were all set to get married, and she died. She was rushed to the hospital one night. I think there was something wrong internally. I'm not sure. They tried to save her, but they couldn't."

Cheri stood perfectly still by the stove. Michael? Easygoing Michael? Who teased her, asked her about her life? She suddenly realized how little she knew about him.

"He comes from a really tough family. His father ran the agency until he retired." Rachel sampled the soup, then nodded her head appreciatively. "It's good, Cheri. Anyway, I think his family has a house in Malibu. And somewhere else."

Cheri sat down at the table, across from Rachel.

After Rachel took a few more spoonfuls of soup, she continued.

"He's only thirty-two. I know it's young for as far as he's gone, but his father handed him the agency when he was twenty-eight. There were a few rough years, but he's made it work." She wrinkled her nose. "Do you have new perfume on or something? It smells like roses."

"Look in my bedroom."

When Rachel sauntered out a minute later and leaned against the kitchen door frame, she had an enormous grin on her face.

"I'd say you're not the only one who's been bit."

THURSDAY NIGHT REHEARSAL was held in the garage. Michael had phoned Cheri at work two days before to let her know he would be coming to the last half of rehearsal to make some suggestions about their material.

It was the usual practice for a manager to work with his clients until he felt they were ready to play out in public. Michael had told Rachel he thought Tough Cookie needed more original material, so Cheri had been working overtime at her rented piano, playing with melodies and lyrics, and polishing older songs. She hoped he would be pleased with the results.

Ria, their lead guitar player, arrived first. Of medium height, Ria had a voluptuous figure that never gave way to being fat. Her hair was the color of a newly minted penny, her eyes a deep green. Cheri admired her friend's unusual coloring as well as her skill with her guitar. Ria's solos added to Tough Cookie's appeal.

Ria chattered on and on about Michael, what she thought of him. He was a hunk. He was smart. She was going to make a play for him.

Cheri couldn't have told Ria anything if she'd wanted to. She attempted to break into the conversation several times, but Ria kept chattering away, and it became apparent to Cheri that she needed to hear herself talk—about herself.

And Cheri didn't want to share any of the details of her dinner with Michael. Though the two women worked in the band together, they weren't close.

Michelle, their keyboard player, arrived soon after, and the silent tension Cheri sensed was broken. A slightly built, thin girl with pale-brown hair and wire-rimmed glasses, Michelle was easily the quietest of the group. She drifted in and out of rehearsals, content simply to play her keyboards.

By the time Rachel arrived with Patti, their drummer, rehearsal was running late.

Patti fell into step beside Cheri as the five women entered the garage converted into a studio. A friend of Rachel's from high school, Patti had been the last member to join Tough Cookie, but Cheri often thought her the most crucial. A band was only as good as its drummer. Patti, with her short dark hair and sparkling blue eyes, could be counted on to keep the band on an even beat both musically and emotionally. She was the first to crack a joke to relieve tension, the first to cut through the murk and get to the heart of any problem.

"Did you finally meet Michael?" she asked Cheri.

Cheri nodded, hoping her eyes weren't giving her away. She had thought of him too much since their dinner over the weekend.

"What did you think of him?" Patti always made sure each woman had a voice in the band's direction. She and Rachel, by virtue of their personalities, were the unofficial leaders of Tough Cookie. Cheri had major responsibilities in writing melodies and lyrics, and Michelle was content with the status quo. Ria was simply too volatile to be trusted with responsibility.

"I think he's terrific."

"Aside from *that*." Patti laughed.

Cheri could feel herself blushing. "No, I think he'll be terrific for the band. He seems very sure of where we should be heading."

Patti nodded, pleased.

None of the women could have afforded the cost of a rehearsal studio on top of their rents, especially in Los Angeles. Finding this house had been a godsend. Cheri, Rachel and Patti had spent several weekends painting and renovating until the garage had been transformed into a decent rehearsal space. Enormous speakers, amplifiers, a PA board and other pieces of equipment stayed permanently in the garage unless the band played out. Each woman was responsible for bringing her own instrument.

They had also done an extensive job of soundproofing, a necessity due to the frequent scheduling of late-night rehearsals. The neighborhood was composed mostly of older people living in apartment buildings, or up-and-coming performers.

Cheri had cleaned up the studio the minute she arrived home, anticipating Michael's visit. Trying to make the garage look like less of a madhouse, she'd retrieved broken strings and guitar picks, and had stacked up the music magazines. She had also brought out a comfortable chair for Michael.

"Let's work on the problem stuff first and save a good number for when Michael gets here," Rachel suggested.

"Good idea." Cheri loaded a cassette into the tape deck. "I messed around with this song today and came up with a new hook. What do you think?"

Sound filled the studio space as they listened to the clear vocals, complemented by delicate counterpoint on the piano.

"I like it," Rachel said at last.

"Nice, Cheri," Patti said.

Michelle nodded and even Ria agreed.

Cheri let out her breath, relieved they weren't going to start rehearsal with a disagreement. "Let's get going."

Two hours into the rehearsal, Cheri saw Michael come inside the garage. They had left the side door unlocked for him and he entered unobtrusively. Cheri continued to sing, focusing her eyes on a spot above him.

But she couldn't keep from looking at him. He seemed tired. This must have been a long day for him. Undoubtedly he went to the office early; to have to come to a late-night rehearsal was wearing. She saw him take the chair she'd set out for him, stretch out his long legs and close his eyes.

Their next song was a ballad, a slow, soothing song. Warmed up, Cheri sang to him, trying her best to reach out to him, relax him with the sound of her voice.

They took a break afterward. Cheri kept her distance from Michael, wary to mix their personal and professional lives. But she noticed Ria standing close to him, leaning her well-rounded body into his as she emphasized a point. Cheri looked away, irritation flaring inside her.

"Jealous?" Rachel whispered.

She shook her head, then relented. "A little." The feelings she had for Michael were still so new. So different. Half the time she didn't know what to do with them.

Afterward, as Ria, Michelle and Patti were packing their instruments, Michael motioned Cheri over toward him.

When she stood next to him, he lowered his voice. "I'm starving. Do you want to get something to eat?"

She nodded, glancing nervously at the others. Ra-

chel, in the corner, gave her the thumbs-up sign. Cheri
frowned.

Once inside Michael's car, she began to relax. Out of
sight of the others, she felt as if she could be herself
with him.

"This isn't going to work if you're this nervous."

She sighed. "I guess not."

"I want to be able to see you and manage your career—at the same time."

"I know. It's just that... if I were one of the others, I
could see how she might resent it." She wasn't telling
him the complete truth, and she knew it. The thought
of a relationship with Michael still frightened her. Now
more than ever, because of feelings starting to grow
within her.

"As long as we feel okay about it, it's no one else's
business." He stated his decision quickly and cleanly.
Cheri was beginning to realize this was one of Michael's greatest assets as a businessman. He wasn't
afraid to make difficult decisions.

"Michael." She turned to face him in the car as it
moved swiftly over the dark city streets. "Just so long
as our business meetings deal with business. I don't
want any special treatment."

He glanced at her quickly, then returned his attention to the road. "The special treatment I have in mind
for you couldn't possibly be done with others around."

She caught her breath. *Too fast, too fast.*

"Scared?" His voice was gentle.

"A little." How strange that, unlike other men, Michael made her want to open up and admit to her true
feelings.

"I am, too."

"You are?" She studied his strong profile, the high
forehead, firm jawline, well-defined cheekbones. "I
don't believe you."

"Cheri." He reached for her hand. "I'm old enough that when I see what I want, I go after it. I don't want anyone or anything to spoil what we have."

"What do we have?" She wanted to hear him define it.

"The only thing I know is that when I first saw you, I couldn't take my eyes off you. I wanted to get you away from the others and be alone with you as soon as possible."

"Michael—"

"I wanted to ask you out, to talk to you. Get to know you."

"But I'm not the woman you see onstage."

"I know. You're better."

She took a deep breath. "Then we can be friends?" She tested the water gently.

"Is that what you want?"

She was silent. Unsure.

He pulled the Ferrari over to the side of the road and found a parking space.

"Cheri." The look in his eyes was full of a longing so intense she had to glance away. "I think I want quite a bit more than that."

"I'm not sure." She bit her lip. How could she possibly tell him? How did you tell a man you were terrified of the physical demands of an intimate relationship? Cheri wasn't even sure if she was capable—there were emotional scars so deep she was scared to examine them.

"I'll never do anything to hurt you."

She wanted to believe Michael, had never wanted anything so badly in her entire life.

"How can you be so damn sure?" Her voice broke. She looked away, out her window toward a darkened apartment building. Michael was touching her emotionally in a way she wasn't sure she wanted to be touched.

"Because I want you to trust me." He paused. "Be- cause you'll trust me enough to tell me if I'm going too fast for you."

Wishing silently, frantically, that she were more adept, more sophisticated, Cheri leaned her forehead against the closed window.

"You're going too fast right now." The words were barely a whisper.

He was silent for a moment, then he covered her hand with his. "Touché." Starting up the car, he drove on to the restaurant in silence.

Chapter Three

Michael was as good as his word. He took Cheri to Westwood Village Saturday night to see a movie. He let her choose the film, and she opted for a romantic comedy. He didn't put his arm around her, didn't try to touch her except for when their fingers bumped inside the container of popcorn.

She was aware of him throughout the movie, each time he shifted position, each time he moved his hand in the direction of the popcorn. Cheri tried not to look at him, not wanting Michael to see how self-conscious she was.

At the end of the film the comedy took a bittersweet turn, and Cheri was surprised when Michael handed her a paper napkin to wipe away her tears. She blew her nose as elegantly as possible, though she knew when the lights went up she'd look like hell. Why was it the heroines in romantic comedies looked terrific when they cried? Another difference between life and art.

Once they were inside Michael's Ferrari, he drove west on Sunset Boulevard until they reached the Pacific. Moonlight dancing over the ocean was the only light in a blackness that stretched as far as the eye could see. Cheri preferred silently studying Michael's profile to the ocean or the restaurants and parking lots dotting the beach.

It wasn't until they'd been driving for a while and were gliding smoothly past walls of pastel stucco fences and garage doors belonging to houses right on the beach that she spoke.

"Where are we going?" Strange, he had her in his car again—this time so far from home—and yet she trusted him implicitly.

"I thought I'd take you to my parents' home."

"They live on the ocean?"

He nodded. "My grandfather bought the property when Malibu was still considered a cow town. There's a great view of the ocean from the balcony."

He turned smoothly off Pacific Coast Highway, then guided the sports car carefully into one of the driveways.

Cheri had driven through Malibu on the way up the coast—she'd never really explored the area. The houses she could make out in the darkness seemed incredibly beautiful—wood and glass and stucco creations, with large windows reflecting the moonlight, like large, colorful birds perched on the edge of the world. There were lights in several windows, and Cheri looked inside, curious about the sort of people who would live there.

Michael pulled up to a garage and the door automatically opened. The red Ferrari glided inside and the door began to slide back over them, cutting them off from the cool sea air. There were no other cars in the garage.

"I thought your parents would be home." Though she had been uneasy at the thought of meeting Mr. and Mrs. Stone, Cheri had a split second of unease as she thought of why Michael might have wanted to bring her there, out to an empty house overlooking the ocean.

He held out his hand and she grasped it, allowing him to pull her gently out of the car and to his side.

"Do you mind?" He was watching her expression, as if he would find his answer there.

"No."

"That didn't sound too sure."

"No, it's fine."

"Trust me?" His eyes were watching her. Waiting.

"I'm probably insane, but I do."

He smiled, and Cheri was glad she'd broken the strange, tense moment. He took her hand and led her out of the garage into what had to be the kitchen. She didn't have time to see anything until they were standing in the living room and Michael turned on a lamp by one of the low sofas next to a fireplace. She watched him as he took off his jacket and ran his fingers through his hair.

"Would you like a fire?"

She sat down on the couch. The room was exquisite. She had seen similar furniture in shops along Robertson Boulevard while window-shopping, and knew with sudden clarity that wealth of this sort was something completely out of her realm of experience. It made her nervous. But she couldn't show Michael that.

"I'd love one."

Michael knelt down in front of the fireplace and began to assemble a fire. Cheri took quick, covert glances around the room. Done in seashore colors, the decor was restful and subtle. Blues, greens and beiges—the overall effect was lovely. Someone cared enough to have made this house more than a showplace. It was a home.

The fire began to bloom under Michael's ministrations. Cheri sat back a little farther on the couch, trying to relax. She loved to watch the muscles in Michael's back bunch and unbunch underneath his cotton shirt. He had rolled up the sleeves, and the dark hair on his arms contrasted with his lightly tanned skin.

He spends too much time indoors. He works too hard. The thought surprised her, the sudden realization that she cared about Michael, what he did, how he felt. Cheri decided she wanted to make an effort to ensure the rest of the evening was a success.

"Can I do anything?"

"I'm sure there's a bottle of wine in the kitchen. Why don't you bring it in here with two glasses?"

She retraced her steps to the kitchen easily. But when she returned, the living room was in darkness except for the light from the fire. Squinting her eyes, she located Michael lying down on the couch.

A seduction scene? Cheri felt a sudden tightening in her stomach until she remembered what Michael had said. *Because you'll trust me enough to tell me if I'm going too fast for you.* But how long could any man put up with her hesitations?

Approaching him cautiously, she set the glasses down on the coffee table, then the wine. "I couldn't find a corkscrew."

"I'll get it." He was off the couch in one lithe movement, then disappeared down the hall.

Cheri stared at the fire, watching the shimmering waves of pure heat lick around the fragrant wood. What did Michael have planned for tonight?

When he returned, she noticed the bag of marshmallows in his hand.

"Michael!"

He laughed. "Fires on the beach are frowned upon, so I thought we'd do our roasting in here." He held out two delicate skewers. "How do you like your marshmallows?"

"Lightly browned. You?"

"I never have the patience. I burn them and eat the inside raw."

She smiled. "I'll make one for you."

"How domestic." She saw the teasing glint in his eyes as he lay down on the couch.

With her back to him, her skewer in the fire, she heard him uncork the wine and pour two glasses.

"Michael?"

"Hmm?"

"This is really nice."

"I just wanted to get you to myself somewhere besides the car. My legs were getting cramped."

Cheri laughed, some of the tightness leaving her chest. Michael leaned over and handed her a glass of wine. She took a sip, enjoying the taste and scent. Sensations were so clear: the warmth from the fire, the taste of the wine, the smell of the lightly roasting marshmallow. She was happy.

After a few minutes of comfortable silence, Cheri called out, "The first one's done."

"You take it. I'll claim the next one."

She ate it off the stick, enjoying the feel of the soft, warm sweet in her mouth. Then she threaded on the second, keeping her back to him. *But how long can a person toast marshmallows?*

When the second one was ready, she stood up and walked back to the couch. Michael looked as if he had fallen asleep. She smiled down at him, enjoying the luxury of studying his face in repose. He looked more relaxed, less intense. She wondered what he'd looked like as a little boy.

Only the slight glitter of his eyes let her know he was still awake. "I like to look at you looking at me," he said softly.

She glanced down at the skewer in her hand, self-conscious with him. Needing to do something, she sat down on the couch, next to his chest.

"Open your mouth."

He obliged. She fed him the marshmallow, then

laughed at the exaggeratedly ecstatic expression on his face. Cheri was about to pull her hand away and wipe it on her jeans when he caught her wrist. Guiding it gently toward his mouth, he licked the remains off her fingers.

Cheri closed her eyes for a second as uneasy feelings flooded her body.

"C'mere." He took her other hand and eased her gently toward him.

"Michael..." She tried to keep her fear from showing in her voice.

"I just want to hold you. Maybe kiss you."

She couldn't stop him. For just a split second, her body seemed to have a will of its own, seemed to yearn to be against his and feel complete.

Once she was lying beside him, he threaded his fingers through her hair and cupped her face. "Don't be afraid of me."

"Michael." Her voice sounded thick, and it hurt to push it past her tight throat. "Why are you doing this? I feel like you're on a mercy mission."

"That's a strange way of putting it." His voice was soft, the only other sound the rattle and hiss of the fire.

She pressed her point. "There are so many women who wouldn't put you through this." Cheri couldn't believe the words coming out of her mouth, what she was actually saying to him. Part of her wanted Michael close. But another part wanted to push him away, violently, and start her life again as if he'd never been involved in it.

His eyes were dark and soft as they held hers. "But you've overlooked the most important thing."

"What?"

"I don't want any other woman. I want you."

Why? But before she could think any further, he exerted the gentlest pressure on her head and brought her lips to his. This time the kiss was soft but insistent. Cheri tried to relax, tried to simply go with the feelings he seemed to pull effortlessly from her body. It was easier than she'd thought. She kissed him back, tentatively. Her hands fluttered awkwardly for a moment; then she put them on his shoulders, then around his neck.

His lips were gentle, slowly evoking deep feelings. When he broke the kiss, she sighed against his mouth and could feel the beginnings of his smile against her own.

"Okay?"

"Yeah."

He played with a strand of her hair, then brought her head down against his shoulder in a comforting gesture. She could feel the warmth of his skin, hear the steady, rapid beating of his heart. His arms stayed around her, strong and soothing.

"Cheri?"

"Hmm?"

"Why are you afraid of me?"

She felt flowers of ice blooming deep within her. Lying very still, she tried to quiet her thumping heart, still her racing fears.

"Do you want to talk about it?"

"No." *He knows there's something wrong. Oh, God.* The only sound in the room was the soft popping of the fire, the gentle roar of the ocean outside. She felt his fingers move up along her neck, into her hair, where they gently massaged her head. Her tension seemed a living thing. Slowly, ever so slowly, she started to relax against him.

With the greatest amount of effort, Cheri raised her head and looked at Michael. He was lying back, his eyes almost closed. She swallowed, then slid her body up his and touched his cheek with her fingers. Before she lost her courage, she brought her mouth down over his.

He was surprised, she could tell by the sudden tensing of his body. But his arms moved around her waist, pressing her against him, holding her close. He started to kiss her back, and she consciously relaxed her mouth, letting him explore the inner sweetness. He took possession gently, as if they had all the time in the world for this one kiss.

Go on, a tiny inner voice urged. *Show him you're not afraid.* She moved her hand to his chest, gently unbuttoned the front of his shirt and slipped her fingers inside. The warmth of his skin surprised her, almost seemed to burn her palm. She touched the hard wall of muscle, slowly unbuttoning more, until she lifted her body slightly and gently touched his hard, firm stomach.

He broke the kiss suddenly, exhaling sharply, laying his head back against the couch.

Not wanting the moment to stop, she ran her hand up his shoulder and started to ease his shirt off. He caught her hand.

"Cheri—"

"No, it's okay." When she saw the doubtful look on his face, she continued, "I want to."

He sat up then, and she moved slightly away from him on the couch as he quickly divested himself of his shirt. His chest seemed darker in the firelight; the smooth muscles rippled with every movement. The sight of such masculine power frightened her for just an instant, but then he reached for her and she felt herself sliding against him, entering a whirlpool of pure sensation.

They were side by side now, the firelight to her back as she looked at him. Michael studied her for a long moment, then kissed her again, slowly, gently. Cheri touched his hair, caressed his face, explored his shoulders, chest, arms. She wanted him to feel as if he were the most desirable man on earth.

When fear rose to choke her, she opened her eyes and reassured herself. *Michael.* As if she were someone separate from this act of love, she watched the way his face tightened with desire, the way his body tensed. His hands were still gentle, but the pressure against her skin had increased ever so slightly.

She knew he was keeping his hands carefully on the small of her back in an effort not to frighten her. Wanting to please him, she took his arm and tugged gently. When she caught his hand, she moved slightly away from him and slipped it inside the V neck of her sweater, over her lace-covered breast, over her rapidly beating heart.

He stopped kissing her, pulled away from her and remained perfectly still. His hand could have been made of marble. Michael was touching her, but not really.

"Cheri?"

She brought his hand up to her mouth and kissed the rough fingers, then placed them back over her breast.

"Michael, I..." The rest of the sentence formed in her brain so quickly she didn't have time to repress it. *I care for you.* How could the feeling have come this quickly, in just a week's time? How could it be that this man had raced to the heart of her deepest emotions? She knew intuitively that anything he did would be right, that she could put herself in his hands as if she were a bow and arrow; he would never draw her hard enough to break her. That power was solely in her own hands.

She blurted the words out before she had a chance to become scared of her new feelings.

"Michael, I care for you...so much." It came out

barely a whisper. He had to lean close to catch her words.

The change in his face was miraculous. A softening of his features, then a rush of joy. He gathered her into his arms, his lips pressed against her temple.

"I care for you, too." Where her revelations had brought joy, his words were frightening in their intensity. "I never thought I'd be able to feel this way again."

She remembered the story Rachel had told her, but kept silent.

"When I first saw you onstage, I couldn't believe how powerfully you attracted me. I tried to ignore it, because it's always been my experience that the singer is never like her stage persona. But then I met you, and..." His breath escaped in a satisfied sigh. "You were perfect. Absolutely perfect."

That one word was her undoing. *Perfect? Oh, no.* She felt quick tears fill her eyes but blinked them back.

"I knew you were frightened, but I blamed myself. I suppose I did come on too strong."

She nodded, her chin moving against his neck. And she realized nothing in her world would ever be the same after this night.

"HOME SO EARLY?" Rachel glanced at the kitchen clock. It was a little after three.

Cheri had made no attempt to hide her flushed face, her disheveled hair. She and Michael had said good-bye on the front porch for twenty minutes before he had finally walked down the drive to his car.

"All right, I won't pry. But just think about how much money you could make. 'My Wild Night with Michael Stone.' The *National Enquirer* would eat it up."

Cheri started to laugh as she reached for the hot cocoa mix. "Promise me you won't phone and give them the inside track."

Rachel laughed. "Hey, kiddo, it's good to see you smiling."

It was fun, sitting at the kitchen table with her roommate and reliving the evening. Though she left out the more intimate details, Cheri managed to convey the depth of feeling that had passed between them.

"He's crazy about you. It's obvious. By the way, Ria called tonight about the rehearsal schedule. She started on her whole trip about Michael, and I told her he'd asked you to a movie tonight."

Cheri poured the hot milk into two mugs and stirred the cocoa up from the bottom.

"Hey, she had to know sooner or later. And better she should hear it from me than find out at rehearsal. She can be nasty at times, but she'll get over it."

"She'll hate my guts," Cheri said quietly.

"Let her quit."

Cheri set the mugs down on the kitchen table and pulled up a chair. "But this was what I was afraid of. That things would go wrong with the band."

"*You* have nothing to worry about. *We* can always get a new guitarist."

"PICKFAIR BOOKSTORE, please hold—Rachel? What's up?" Cheri glanced quickly around the crowded bookstore to make sure Patrick was nowhere within earshot.

"You'll never believe this! When do you take lunch?"

"In half an hour. Why?"

"Promise me you'll come home. I'll have a sandwich ready."

"What's going on?"

"Just come home, then I'll explain." She hung up.

Within the hour, Rachel greeted her at the door of their house. "Walk into your bedroom."

Cheri could barely open the door. Balloons filled every corner—pink, silver, light blue, white and purple. They bumped and jostled as she tried to ease the door farther open, and Buffy ran around Cheri's legs, barking at the strange sight.

Cheri couldn't stop smiling. "Was there a card?"

"Right here."

She opened it quickly, scanning the firm, masculine scrawl. *"I hope you like balloons as much as I do. Love, Michael."*

"The big M, huh?"

She nodded.

"Balloons, flowers—the guy's got class. Well, sit down and eat your sandwich."

After the last plate was cleared away, Cheri glanced up at her roommate.

"Rachel, I want to ask you something. Do you have the number of that woman doctor out in the valley?"

"It was the balloons that finally got to you, right?"

Cheri could feel her cheeks burning. "I'm still not sure. I just...I want to be prepared in case anything happens."

"Hey, I'm not funning you—I think you're being wise. I'll write down her number. She's usually booked pretty far in advance, so tell the receptionist you're a friend of mine and maybe she'll be able to get you an earlier appointment."

"CAN I ASK you a question?"

Dr. Hanby smiled down at Cheri. Rachel had been right. She was a kind woman, efficient and warm with her patients. Her dark-brown hair was slightly sprinkled with gray and her eyes were compassionate. Cheri had felt comfortable with her from the start.

Cheri sat up on the examining table, holding the paper sheet against her breasts. "Is there anything wrong with me?"

"Not that I could see during the examination. We'll have the Pap test results to you within a week."

"But... I mean, inside or something. Something that might prevent..." She stopped, embarrassed. How exactly did one go about saying it?

"Something that might prevent you from achieving sexual satisfaction?" Dr. Hanby's manner was brisk, matter-of-fact and very open.

"Yes."

"Why don't you get dressed and come into my office for a few minutes and we can talk."

Once inside the office, Cheri tried to be as specific as possible about her feelings. She couldn't quite meet the doctor's eyes, but she wanted an answer to her problem.

"I've read about all the things I should experience, and the man..." She paused for a second. "The man that I care about, the man I'm involved with, is very understanding." She took a deep breath and looked up. "But most of the time, when he touches me, I don't feel anything. I mean, I feel his touch but I don't feel what I should feel."

"What do you think you should feel?" The doctor's eyes were kind.

"*Something.* Anything. Some kind of enjoyment. Something beyond a fear that things are getting out of hand."

"Ah. So you haven't slept with this man?"

"No, but..."

"But things are getting to the point where you'd like to express yourself sexually."

Cheri nodded her head.

"Can you think of any reason you might be afraid of making love?"

She glanced down again.

"Ms. Bradley?"

The patterned carpet swam in front of her eyes. She tried to keep her voice steady as she began to tell the doctor things she had thought would stay inside her forever.

Afterward, tissue box in hand, she realized it was a relief to have finally told someone.

"Ms. Bradley, you're not abnormal at all. In fact, it would be abnormal if you went through something so traumatic and *didn't* feel—" she paused, searching for a word "—frozen, as you put it."

"But what do I do now?"

Dr. Hanby became all business. "I'm going to give you the name of a therapist and some books you might find helpful. I'm also going to recommend a local support group. Don't look so surprised; your experience is much more common than you think." She tore a sheet off the pad on her desk and began to scribble. "I want you to call me back in a week and tell me how you're doing, all right?"

"Okay."

As she handed Cheri the paper and squeezed her shoulder, Dr. Hanby asked, "Can you tell this man? I think communicating the problem might be the answer."

"No!" The vehemence of her reply stunned Cheri, but she defended her choice. "If he knew...I just wouldn't want him to think that way about me."

The doctor smiled sadly. "A man with such an attitude wouldn't really be worth having around. If he loves you, he'll understand."

Cheri frowned, unsure.

"You'll call me, let me know how you're doing?"

"Yes, I...thank you. I'm sorry I took so much of your time."

Dr. Hanby pushed her glasses up on the bridge of her nose. "If I can help you in any way," she said as she squeezed Cheri's hand gently, "please don't be afraid to call me."

Chapter Four

"You're nothing at all like I expected you to be," Cheri confessed.

Glenda, the therapist Dr. Hanby had recommended, was petite, with curly blond hair and gray eyes. In her early forties, she radiated energy and enthusiasm. But it was her eyes that had made Cheri stay in the office. Clear and direct. Kind eyes. Cheri had the feeling she could tell her anything.

"What did you expect?"

"I don't know... but not you."

"I hope that's a compliment."

Her office was nothing like Cheri had expected, either. Glenda worked out of her home in Santa Monica. Her office was in half of her duplex. The couch and chairs were comfortable, covered with a peach-colored print. Green plants filled every corner of the large room, and muted watercolors of the ocean hung on cream walls.

Glenda didn't sit behind a desk or apart from her, in posture or in attitude. They might have been two women talking in a living room. The atmosphere was that relaxed.

"So how do you feel about coming here today?" Glenda asked.

"Weird. I've never done anything like this. I've never wanted to, before..."

"Before?" the therapist prompted gently.

"Before I met Michael. He's the reason I'm here, I guess."

"Do you want to talk about him?"

Cheri shrugged. "I guess." Suddenly, the courage she'd mustered up deserted her. "Look, what if this doesn't work out? What are you going to do?"

"How about if we just take it a session at a time and see what happens?" When Cheri didn't reply, Glenda said, "You don't ever *have* to be here, Cheri. I'd like to think you want to be. But you can leave at any time."

Slowly, Cheri felt her body relax completely. If she could leave at any time, what was there to be afraid of?

"Scared?" Michael's voice was concerned.

"A little. Not really. I mean, we've practiced the stuff till it's coming out our ears! But I always get nervous." Cheri bit her lip, then looked up at him. "Will you be out there?"

"Through the entire show."

She touched his nose lightly. "I'll sing it all just for you."

"It better not be for anyone else."

She laughed. He reached for her hand, caught it and squeezed it. "A performance without fear doesn't have any fire."

"I know, I know." She sighed in mock exasperation. "I'll be good, I promise."

He kissed her quickly. Backstage, with all the people milling about, there wasn't much privacy.

"The band comes back to the beach house after the show, okay?"

"Okay. Michael?"

"Yeah?"

"If I really blow it out there will you hate me?"

"No! Is that how you see me?"

"I guess not." She caught Rachel's eye as her friend gestured from the dressing-room door. "I've got to go."

"Knock 'em dead." He kissed her again and walked toward the exit.

As Cheri stepped inside the dressing room, Rachel closed the door behind her. "Okay, any last-minute things that need clearing up?" she asked briskly.

"I think we're all set," Ria said. Cheri hadn't missed the sulky looks their lead guitar player had sent in her direction when she'd been standing outside with Michael.

"Is everyone tuned up?" Rachel asked.

Ria nodded.

"We're opening with 'Reckless Love,' so let's really crank it up."

"Is the song list taped to my floor tom?" Though Patti was a terrific drummer, she was notorious for mixing up the song sequence.

"Sure it is, I checked it myself. I should have written it in Day-Glo marker for you." Rachel laughed and Patti stuck out her tongue.

"Cheri, you warmed up?"

"I'm fine."

"You should be," Patti teased. "I saw you out there with Fearless Leader." The women all laughed, but Cheri noticed Ria's expression wasn't amused.

"Rachel?" Cheri plucked at her friend's sleeve. "When we sing 'Desire,' I have trouble getting my opening pitch. I can come in on time, but I can't promise the note."

"Mmm." Rachel scratched her nose.

Patti glanced at her watch. "We're on in fifteen minutes."

Rachel made her decision. "Ria, you give Cheri a cue so she gets the right pitch. Play that higher inversion of the chord like you did the other night so her note will stick out on top." Rachel punched Cheri's arm playfully. "Think you can get it then?"

The banter subsided as each woman retreated into private thoughts before going onstage. Tonight was a night that could decide the direction of the band. After many weeks of intense rehearsal, Michael had decided Tough Cookie was ready to play out at the Starlight, one of the largest clubs in Los Angeles, a place where bands went to be "discovered" once they were good enough. Tough Cookie would be the opening act for Dead Center, also managed by the Stone Agency, and currently one of the hottest bands in L.A. The band would play one set, forty-five minutes, roughly ten songs.

Cheri walked over to the mirror and sat down. Her gaze rested on the single rose from Michael. The bud had barely opened, the delicate pink petals reminded her of the inside of a shell.

She picked up her brush and passed it quickly through her hair. Rachel had talked her into a body wave, and her dark-brown hair curled softly just below her shoulders. She'd decided to dress completely in black for that evening's performance: black leather jeans, a tight black cotton tank top, three-inch high-heeled black boots. Favorite clothes, comfortable clothes. Good-luck clothes, creating an image she was at ease pretending to be.

And Michael. They'd been seeing each other for three months now. It was rare for a day to go by when he didn't call her. They had late dinners together almost every other night, and spent Saturday nights and most Sundays with each other.

He hadn't pressed her for a more physical relation-

ship since their night at his parents' house in Malibu.
Cheri was thankful for his sensitivity to her feelings.
She'd never known a man like Michael. She wanted to
cherish him, to keep the golden moments of their relationship close to her heart. He knew she didn't want to
enter emotional territory she didn't want to experience.

But it would be different with him, she thought, touching the rose gently. *I know it would be. It would have to
be.*

Would it? Her inner doubts came softly, the tiny
voice that so often ate away at her self-confidence.

She pushed the doubt aside, determined to master
her own fate. Her thoughts returned to Michael. The
restraint he placed on his passion made her care for
him even more deeply. And he was capable of great
passion. It had to cost him to hold so much emotion in
check. They couldn't go on this way.

Perhaps tonight, she thought. If things went well, if
their performance made him proud of her, if she could
manage to overcome—

"Ready?" Rachel stood behind her, bass in hand.

"Yes." Cheri stood up and took a deep, calming
breath, then expelled it slowly.

She'd already been on this particular stage several
hours earlier for the sound check. It was large; the pro-
scenium seemed to arch out over the audience. When
she'd stood by her mike before, the tables and chairs
below had been empty, ghostlike. Now she could feel
the crowd. A murmur, a rustle of paper. Small signals
letting her know an audience expected to be enter-
tained.

They waited backstage until they heard the an-
nouncer's voice. "Ladies and Gentlemen, I'm proud to
present Tough Cookie in their first appearance at the
Starlight. Let's give them a big hand."

Cheri closed her eyes briefly as she heard polite applause. *Please let us be good. For Michael.* Then she opened her eyes and walked onstage.

Her first few movements were automatic, motions she'd performed countless times in the past. Cheri adjusted her cordless mike stand—being only five feet four inches was an occupational hazard—and took the mike into her hand. She made a soft *ch* sound and heard it bounce back to her from the opposite end of the room. Satisfied her equipment was working properly, she turned to check on the others.

Rachel and Ria had plugged in their guitars. Patti hit her drums a few times. Cheri heard the first soft chords as both lead and bass guitarists checked the tuning on their instruments, and Michelle struck a few chords on keyboard.

They needed more time. Cheri looked out over the audience and gave them her best smile. Her eyes were becoming adjusted to the bright, hot lights. She saw Michael sitting at a back table, to one side of the stage. He smiled encouragingly and she looked away. *Too nervous.* She knew he'd understand.

"Hi, how's everyone out there tonight?" Her voice sounded rich and full over the microphone.

No response. A typical Los Angeles audience—*I dare you to entertain me.* She kept the smile on her face as she ran the opening lyrics of "Reckless Love" quickly through her head. They'd have to blast this crowd right out of their seats.

She glanced back at Patti, who nodded her head. The drummer caught each member's attention, then raised her drumsticks over her head and clicked them.

One-two-three-four—sticks came down on drums and the beat began. Rachel's driving bass line came in perfectly. Cheri turned toward the audience and raised the cordless mike to her lips.

She loved this song, loved the effect it had on any

audience. Rachel had chosen their opening number well—a song about love gone wrong. Cheri gave it all the power and emotion she could, slipping effortlessly into her stage persona of bad girl: cocky, assured, sensual.

No longer afraid now that the song was underway, she strutted to the front of the stage and looked down at the crowd as if they were there to do her bidding. Each step in time to the beat, she took a deep, controlled breath and let the first note come sailing out, pure and true.

You were trouble from the moment I looked in
    your eyes,
But it took a lot of sorrow to make me realize
I loved you with a reckless love.

She had them. Slowly the noise died down. In its place, the audience began to take shape, a silent animal out beyond the lights. They were with her.

Cheri used the entire front of the stage, moving forward, backing off. Teasing. Promising what she'd never deliver. Her voice catapulted through the club as she crouched down for the low notes, then stood and stretched as if reaching for the high notes, finally throwing back her head when she hit the end of the song, a dazzling climb up the scale in which each note burned with the rage and anger of a frustrated, passionate woman.

They didn't give the audience time to decide what hit them. Rachel had arranged the music so the first number ran into the next. A different song, the tone was humorous and assured, with intricate harmonies by Michelle on keyboard and Ria on lead guitar.

Halfway into the song, Cheri stepped back out of the light as Ria took center stage to begin her solo. She was fast, and to be fast and accurate on lead guitar garnered a band points. She climaxed the solo with a screaming high note, and Cheri deftly approached center stage to finish the song. She strutted, she pranced, she used the stage as if she had been born to it. As the song built in intensity, the vibrations from the drums seemed to go right through her body. Cheri reached for notes effortlessly, plucked them down and sent them hurtling out over the audience like shooting stars.

At the end of the song, when Rachel's bass guitar line built and built, when it seemed that surely Patti was going to break a stick in two, Cheri leaped into the air. When the heels of her boots hit the floor, the music stopped.

There was a moment of silence, then the audience exploded. Cheri pushed her damp hair out of her eyes. "Thank you!" Her voice was husky, breathless. The clapping continued. "Thank you," she said again, then glanced quickly over at Michael. He was clapping harder than anyone, an easy grin on his face. She smiled at him, then turned away to look at Patti.

As soon as she made eye contact with the drummer, the third song began. "Desire." The clapping subsided, and the audience was quiet again, eager for a new song. Cheri glanced at Ria, remembering she was supposed to be cued in.

But Ria had turned away, seemed more interested in the intricate melody she was playing. Cheri waited for her arranged cue, swaying slightly to the softer beat.

It never came.

It was two bars too many before she realized what had happened. She looked at Rachel, sure her friend could see the controlled panic on her face.

Cheri glanced at Ria again. The lead guitarist wouldn't meet her eyes.

Give me my cue.

Nothing.

Then she heard a note come booming out of the bass line and grasped it like a swiftly running ski rope. But the rhythm broke for just a moment and it was painfully obvious to anyone with ears that Rachel had spoon-fed her the note.

... boy who made me see
That love's an emotion too tame for me.
I need desire

Cheri managed to get through the song, then the next and the one after. But she'd lost her audience. Having seen her fail, they were only too happy to dismiss her, to focus attention elsewhere. Her confidence shaken, Cheri knew by their reactions that she was trying too hard to win them back, pushing for what should have been effortless.

Their tenth song, "Love Me," should have been the final moment of the set when they gave the audience everything, pulling out all the stops. A ballad, sweet and slow. A simple song. The hardest type to sing.

There were a few coughs and several chair legs scraped across the floor as Ria began the melody and Rachel picked it up, weaving a musical spell. Someone rustled a paper. Cheri bit the inside of her mouth, tempted to hurl her mike out into the audience. She could feel tears crowding her eyes, wanted nothing more than to get off the stage, go somewhere and die.

She'd let Michael down.

Without conscious volition, she glanced toward his table. His eyes were open, vulnerable, hurting with her. Cheri swallowed quickly, glanced away. She closed her eyes and thought of him as she began to sing.

The song came alive then, as thoughts of Michael made the imagery catch fire. The lyrics and melody were soft, yearning, tender. Different from their earlier hard rock numbers. Whether it was the surprising contrast, or the emotion she managed to convey, Cheri felt the audience begin to settle, like a restless child finally picked up by its mother.

Though many in the audience clapped enthusiastically when the set was over, Cheri couldn't wait to get offstage. She was sure the expression was polite, nothing more. There would be no encore.

Inside the dressing room, she confronted Ria.

"What the hell happened out there?"

Ria busied herself putting her guitar in its case. "What are you talking about?"

"On 'Desire.' There was no way in hell I could have picked up a cue from the mess you were playing!"

Rachel slammed in the door. "Michael wants to see you, Cheri."

Michael. No.

Cheri picked up her jacket and bag and walked quickly out of the dressing room.

"Cheri!"

She kept walking, head down, looking at no one. Outside in the parking lot, she broke into a run.

THE MINUTE CHERI HEARD POUNDING on the door, she knew it was Michael.

She opened the door, imagining how horrible she must look. Crying all the way home, she'd slammed into the house and washed away all her makeup. Then she'd ripped off her stage clothes and tossed them into a corner of her bedroom, replacing them with old gray sweats. Storming into the living room, she'd disconnected the phone with an angry jerk. She didn't want to see or talk to anyone ever again. At least until tomorrow.

"What happened to you?" Michael looked worried.

She threw her hands up in the air and turned away, walking into the living room.

"We stunk. I don't know how much plainer I can put it."

"That's not true. The first two songs were terrific."

"Until—"

"Until you missed a cue." His voice softened. "What happened?"

"I don't know. Ria was supposed to give me a pitch—" Cheri broke off in midsentence. Even to her ears, she sounded dangerously close to whining. She hated herself. "But I should have been able to pick up something, instead of coming in the middle of the first line!"

"Come here."

"Michael!"

He grabbed her wrist and half pulled, half dragged her over to the couch. "Sit down."

She watched as he walked into the kitchen, Buffy trotting at his heels. The little dog had come out of her bedroom at the sound of raised voices.

Sinking back against the couch, she listened as he took something out of the cupboard. In a minute she heard running water. He had to be making coffee.

Her guess was confirmed a few minutes later when he returned, two mugs on a tray.

"The blue one's yours. I put in milk and sugar. Drink it."

She obeyed.

He sat facing her on the couch, watching her. She swallowed the last drop and set the mug down on the coffee table with a sharp click.

"Are you satisfied now?"

She thought she saw the faintest hint of a smile play around his lips.

"Not yet."

She crossed her arms in front of her. "What do you want?" She knew she was behaving badly but was too upset to care.

"I never thought of you as a person who threw in the towel when the going got rough."

"I didn't quit! I finished out the set, I gave them everything—"

"No, you didn't." His tone was firm, but his eyes remained warm.

She looked away from him, staring sightlessly at the far wall.

"Cheri, look at me."

Slowly, she turned her head and met his gaze.

"You let one opening shake you so badly you let your energy down for the rest of the set."

She looked away. Michael was right.

"It's going to get a lot worse the higher up you go," he said quietly.

Cheri didn't reply. What could she say? He had summed up the evening's performance perfectly; he was right to criticize her. She had let everyone down.

He stretched out his long legs in front of him. "I know you can do whatever you set your mind to, Cheri. So you blew a song. Okay, it's not the end of the world."

She turned her head, met his eyes, slowly raised her chin. She had reacted badly onstage, so she'd be damned if she'd make him feel she couldn't take honest criticism.

"I'm sorry, Michael. I was wrong."

His eyes were sharp and clear, and Cheri knew she was seeing Michael her manager, not Michael the man she had a relationship with.

"You've got the talent, Cheri. The band's come a long way in a short amount of time. But if you can't take a little pressure, you'd better get out. Right now."

She closed her eyes against the blur of tears. "Michael, I'm so sorry. It's just... I wanted to be perfect. I wanted to be perfect for you."

He moved slightly toward her and before she could say anything more gathered her up in his arms.

"I felt for you the entire time, Cheri. It's going to be agonizing having you as a client, because every time you perform I feel as if I'm right up there with you."

She leaned back within the circle of his arms and looked up at him, sure he was joking.

"You're still going to represent us?"

"That's what I told everyone else backstage."

"Michael!" She flung herself tight against him, her arms moving up around his neck. Then she hadn't failed him! "I can't believe it!"

"Start believing it now. Everyone else is in Malibu. And asking where you are."

THE PARTY WAS IN FULL SWING by the time they arrived. Rachel disengaged herself from Dead Center's drummer the minute she saw Cheri walk in the door.

"What took you so long?"

"She had to walk Buffy." Michael winked at Rachel over Cheri's head, but she caught the look that passed between them.

Rachel grabbed Cheri's arm. "Get over here and see the food that's been laid out. Shrimp, caviar, something chocolate..."

Their plates piled high, they retreated to the redwood deck.

"What happened, Cheri?"

"I felt like such an ass after what happened during 'Desire.' I just wanted to run away."

Rachel frowned. "I don't understand what Ria was trying to do. I asked her about it after you left and she said she must have misunderstood what I said. What was so confusing?"

"Do you think she did it on purpose?" Cheri spread some pâté on a cracker and took a bite. Now that she wasn't upset, she realized she'd been so upset about tonight's performance she hadn't eaten all day. She was starved.

"I don't know. I'd like to give her the benefit of the doubt. She's a damn good player. But something tells me—"

"I knew there'd be trouble about my seeing Michael."

"Stop it, Cheri. The two of you aren't guilty. She's the one who has to grow up and act like a professional."

Cheri lowered her voice. "I thought I'd blown everything."

"Not the way you sang 'Reckless Love.'"

"Michael was right. He told me I let my energy down for the whole set—over one song."

Rachel nodded, then swallowed some wine. "You did. The same thing that makes you a good singer—the sensitivity—also makes it hard to snap back after a failure while performing. But you've got to learn."

"He said the pressure only gets worse."

"Worse than *this*?" Rachel eyed her half-full plate, then patted her flat stomach. "I think I can handle it."

CHERI STAYED after the party was over and helped Michael straighten the messy living room. He made a fresh pot of coffee and together they finished the rest of the chocolate cheesecake.

"I'm stuffed." Cheri pushed the plate away from her.

"Feeling better?"

"Yeah. Michael?"

"What?"

"I'm sorry I was such an ass."

"Hey, you're only twenty-six. I have a six-year jump on you."

"Are you going to teach me all you know?" she teased.

The expression in his dark eyes was unsettling. "I think I'd better drive you home."

She was surprised to discover she didn't want to go. How much longer could Michael wait for her? The wine she'd consumed gave her courage. "Do you want me to stay?" She watched his eyes darken even further, his facial muscles grow taut.

"Don't play, Cheri."

She didn't look away. "I'm not playing." She took a deep breath. "I'm ready."

She watched him as he got slowly up out of the chair and came around to her side of the kitchen table. Taking her hand, he drew her to her feet, then put his arm around her. Silently, they headed down the darkened hallway.

When they reached the bedroom, Michael switched on a light. He took her into his arms and gently kissed her forehead.

"I'm going to lock up the house. I'll be right back."

What now? Cheri stared at the room, at the queen-sized bed on the far wall, at teakwood shelves filled with books, at small stone sculptures on the recessed window-sill. The room faced the ocean. She approached the window.

Floodlights illuminated the ocean as it swept up and down the smooth white sand. She stared at the shore for what seemed like a long time, trying to keep her fears at bay.

It's not your fault. Didn't Glenda tell you? He'll understand.

How easy to understand mentally. How horribly hard emotionally.

The lights went out below her; the stretch of beach

was plunged into darkness. Michael would be with her very soon.

He came back into the room so softly she barely heard him. Walking up behind her, he placed large warm hands on her shoulders.

"There's a bathroom right through the door." He seemed to be trying to put her at ease.

Cheri bit her lip. "Could I—take a quick shower?" She looked down at the jeans and sweater she'd changed into before leaving her house with Michael. "Performing is like working out."

"Sure." He placed a finger under her chin and raised her lips to his. It was a persuasive kiss, meant to entice rather than arouse.

Cheri broke the kiss before it deepened and stepped away. "I'll be right back."

The bathroom door closed behind her, she stripped off her clothes and turned on the shower. Glancing at her reflection in the wall mirror, she studied herself. Small, slender. Firm, high breasts, slim hips.

Unbidden, a picture of Michael's muscular chest and powerful thighs formed in her mind. *What if she couldn't...?* She stepped into the shower, letting the hot water cascade over her tense body. Afterward, a large bath sheet wrapped around her, she blew her hair dry and gently set the dryer down.

Opening the door, she turned off the overhead light and entered the bedroom.

Moonlight bathed the room in soft, silver light. Michael was already in bed, a sheet drawn up to his waist. Before she panicked and fled, Cheri walked over to the side of the bed.

He lifted his arm, pulling the sheet back so she could slide in beside him as she dropped her towel. She was shaking slightly as he wrapped his arms around her, easing her closer.

"Honey? Are you cold?"

"A little." There was nothing between their naked bodies, and she could feel all of him, hard and hot and smooth. She touched his face quickly, wanting reassurance. *Michael. This is Michael.*

He kissed her palm, then got up out of bed and moved to the windows, shutting them. She watched the way his body moved, the play of muscles over his back, in his sculpted legs. And then he was beside her again. There would be no more delays.

He kissed her, and she willed herself to melt in his arms, but her body didn't respond. Her arms and legs felt stiff and alien. Cheri shuddered as one of his thighs threaded between her legs. It felt rough and hairy against the smoothness of her skin.

She opened her mouth against his, encouraging deeper, more intimate kisses. It took all her courage not to push him away, simply to twine her arms around his neck and attempt to hold him close.

She cared for him—why couldn't she make love to him? He broke the kiss and his lips began to move tenderly over her neck, down her shoulder, to one of her breasts.

As his warm mouth closed over the tip of her breast she caught fire within, the sensation incredibly pleasurable. She moved her hands up to his thick hair, held him while he brought her pure sensation. Then, as she knew it would, waves of guilt followed, seemed to consume her.

Cheri fought her feelings, all alone in the dark. *It's Michael.* She urged him to her other breast, concentrating on how good he made her feel, how cherished. He took time with her, but it seemed to Cheri the longer they were together, the more tense her body became. She willed herself to try to relax, slid her hands over the curve of his shoulders, down to the hard muscles of his buttocks.

She stiffened for just an instant when his hand moved slowly between her legs, and for a second thought of telling him she couldn't continue. Then he touched her, gently searching for the center of her passion. He found it quickly and began to caress her with sweet, slow strokes, causing her legs to tremble and slowly draw apart.

She wanted it over with. Smoothing her hands over his back, she grasped his hips and urged him against her.

His shoulders seemed to block out the moonlight for just a moment. Cheri closed her eyes, swallowed, tried to slow the rapid beating of her heart.

Something—the way his shoulder touched her cheek—triggered a memory deep within.

She couldn't breathe. She felt his body pressing her against the mattress, suffocating her. Within seconds, she changed from a soft and willing partner to a fighting, twisting wildcat. Balling her hands into fists, she beat against his chest until he reared up, quickly unpinning her.

Her deep, agonized breathing sounded harsh in the silent room. She scrambled for the edge of the bed, sat down, put her head between her knees.

Cheri pressed her hands against her eyes as if she could erase the entire moment. But it was impossible. She knew Michael was watching her, knew he was wondering what the hell was the matter with her.

She couldn't look at him.

Her breath still came in short, jerky spasms, and she realized tears were running down her cheeks. When she finally spoke, her voice sounded thin, as if it were coming from far away.

"It's not you, Michael. I just can't. It's not you. *I want to love you, I do*." The words were choked and garbled, painful sounds, as they made their way past the incredible tightness in her chest.

He gathered her into his arms as she began to sob.

Chapter Five

"Were you raped?"

She nodded.

"Why didn't you tell me before?"

Her voice was nasal, clogged from all the crying. "I was scared."

"Of what?"

"Scared...that you wouldn't...that you would think..."

"Think badly of you?"

She nodded. She touched his chest gently, to reassure herself he was still here, with her.

"When did it happen?"

"A long time ago."

"How old were you?"

She didn't have the energy to make up any more lies. "Thirteen."

He was quiet for a long time. When he finally spoke, his voice was tight. "The same year your parents died."

Oh, God, why had she told him that? She remained silent.

"Oh, baby, I'm so sorry."

She stared straight ahead, wondering how she could ever tell him the rest of it now.

"I wish you could wrap up all your pain into a ball and hand it to me. I wish I could carry it for you."

She turned her face into his chest and closed her eyes. Two tears squeezed out. Her voice was a hoarse whisper.

"Oh, Michael, I'm so sorry."

HE TUCKED HER into the big bed, made her a cup of warm milk, stayed with her until she fell asleep. He left the bedside lamp on as she asked him to, and lay down beside her, outside the covers, and watched the gentle rise and fall of her breasts.

I love her. He hadn't felt this way since Nancy, hadn't thought the feelings were inside him anymore. Yet the moment he'd first seen Cheri onstage, everything had fallen into place. As easily as when he'd been a boy.

Everything made sense now. Her shyness. Her fear of physical involvement. At first he'd thought maybe an old boyfriend, a former marriage. He had been content to wait, to see what would happen next. She was such a paradox—such fire onstage, such sweetness and shyness when they were alone.

She had said she wanted to love him, had choked out the words as she'd sat on the side of the bed, her face buried in her hands. But how could he fight something as invisible, as intangible as the dark fears chasing Cheri?

She stirred in her sleep, rolled over and buried her face in the pillow. He leaned across and adjusted the covers, making sure her shoulders were underneath the sheet and light summer blanket.

Michael glanced at the luminous dial of the bedside clock. Six twenty-two in the morning. Maybe Gina would forgive him.

He went into the kitchen and made himself a cup of coffee before he placed the call to San Francisco.

"Hello?"

Michael smiled as he heard his sister's voice. He

could picture her groping for the receiver, pushing her thick, dark hair out of her eyes.

"Hi, Gina."

"Michael?" She sounded groggy, and he knew he had wakened her. A slight thread of fear colored her voice. "Is it Daddy?"

"No, everything's fine. It's me."

"What's wrong?" There was no trace of irritation in her voice, only concern.

"Remember I told you about Cheri?"

"The girl in the band?"

"Yeah. Well, I've been seeing her, and—"

"Wait, let me get a cigarette." He could see her reaching for her purse, getting out the silver lighter he had given her last Christmas. The family hated Gina's smoking, but Michael knew she would quit only when she was ready.

"Okay. Go on."

"I've been seeing her, and last night I brought her back and..." He stopped. How could he tell her?

"Michael? What happened?"

"She told me tonight she was raped when she was thirteen."

Silence.

"Gina?"

"Oh, my God."

"The thing is—I don't know what to do."

"Do you love her?"

There wasn't a second's hesitation. "Yes."

"You'll have to go awful slow."

"Gina, I didn't pressure her at all. She asked me if she could spend the night."

"And then couldn't go through with it. Poor thing."

"I guess I'm calling because I want to know what you would want if you'd been raped and your boyfriend had just found out about it."

"That's a heavy question. Just a minute." Michael heard her talking rapidly to someone in the background.

"Okay, back to the problem. Ben was just wondering who I was talking to at six-thirty in the damn morning." Michael had to smile at his sister's letter-perfect imitation of her husband's annoyance.

"What do you think?"

"I think—Michael, do you remember Beth, that girl I brought home from Stanford on spring break?"

"I think so. Little and blond."

"That's the one. She was raped on a date, by this guy her girl friend set her up with. A date rape, you know? She couldn't talk about it for years, she was afraid no one would believe her."

"Go on."

"She was friends with Gary for over a year before they got married."

"Yeah?"

"She told me the first few times they made love, it was awful. She had to tell him what happened before she got into bed with him, or she couldn't have gone through with it."

He felt his chest tighten. *Why hadn't Cheri confided in him?* But had he ever really let her? Had he pushed her into what happened tonight?

"Michael, are you listening to me?"

"Yeah, yeah." He rubbed his hand over his eyes. "Go on."

"Have you told her you love her?"

"Yeah. No. I told her I care about her."

"No. Have you told her you *love* her? Just the way she is."

"No." He thought of Cheri's choked confession and something twisted in his stomach. *Why had it been like that?*

"I don't know, Michael. Take it slow, reassure her.

Don't make any moves on her until she's ready. Try to get her to talk about it if you can."

"Thanks, Gina."

"Maybe you could call one of those hot lines? Or a therapist or something?"

"Yeah. I don't know."

Her voice softened. "Listen, are you coming home for Dad's birthday?"

"I'm not sure."

"Bring Cheri. I'd like to meet her."

"Okay. Maybe."

"You sound tired."

"I am. Thanks, Gina."

"No problem."

"How's my nephew?"

"Too fat. The pediatrician says I have to start putting water in his bottle."

Michael laughed. It felt good. "I'll see you in a couple of months. Give my best to Ben."

"I will. I love you, Michael. Don't give up."

"Love you, too."

He hung up the phone and started slowly back into the bedroom.

CHERI WOKE UP slowly. It was so bright, so noisy. As consciousness returned, she recognized the crash of ocean waves and the calls of seabirds.

Michael lay beside her on top of the blanket, in a pair of faded jeans, his arm over his eyes. He looked tired in his sleep, the dark stubble along his chin making him seem old and worn.

I failed him again. She averted her gaze from his and stared at the ceiling, at the shifting light. Why had she even thought she was near to being ready? What would she say to him when he woke up? Would he still want to see him, apart from managing the band?

You're not very good for him. He needs someone who can really love him—and express that love physically. And you can't. Even with all her sessions with Glenda, she still had so much work left to do on herself. Was it fair to drag Michael into the deepest parts of her life?

She tried to ease herself out of bed without waking him, but the moment she moved he lifted his arm and opened his eyes.

"Hi."

She dropped her eyes to the bedspread. How could he even still want to talk to her?

"How are you feeling?" Michael, decent to the end.

"Okay." *Don't burden him with any more of your problems.*

"Do you want some breakfast?"

She shook her head, her only thought to get away from him as soon as possible. Even looking at him was a reminder of what she hadn't been able to go through with last night. And she knew, deep inside, if she couldn't be intimate with a man like Michael, then maybe it would never happen for her. Why had she pushed things last night? How could she have possibly thought she was ready?

"Will you sit with me while I have some?" He was studying her face.

"Okay." *You thought you were ready—but your emotions weren't.*

He made waffles, with plenty of sweet butter and warmed syrup. Halfway through the meal, Cheri joined him. He watched her as she ate. Nervous, she cut her food into tiny bites and chewed slowly.

She looked awful and she knew it. Her eyes were still red and swollen, with faint shadows underneath.

Cheri studied Michael as he ate, storing up visual memories for the time she wouldn't be with him. The thought depressed her. She had hoped for so much last night. It had turned out to be a nightmare.

She was in the middle of taking a shower when a horrible thought struck.

"Michael!" She jumped out of the shower and reached for a towel.

"What?" She could hear his voice through the door.

"I'm supposed to be at work today!"

"What time?"

"We open at noon on Sunday."

"It's already past one."

She called the bookstore. Patrick answered, his voice curt. One of the other clerks had called in sick and there were only two people in the entire store besides him. His temper was boiling.

"I'll get there as fast as I can," she promised, hanging up the phone and toweling her hair dry.

They drove to Hollywood in silence, the freeway almost deserted. Cheri was preoccupied with her own thoughts; Michael seemed to be concentrating on his driving.

When he pulled up into the alley behind the bookstore, her fingers were already closed around the door handle.

"Can I pick you up after work?" he asked.

"I don't think so." She could barely look at him, her shame over last night so intense it almost made her shake.

"When can I see you again?"

Oh, Michael. Don't be nice to me. Not now. "I'll call you." She knew the words to be a lie the moment she said them.

And then she opened the car door, got out and ran down the street. She didn't look back. Only when she was safely around the corner and inside the store did she feel secure.

HE DROVE BACK to his house slowly, taking no pleasure in the day. She'd looked like a hunted animal as she raced around the corner of the bookstore. Looking for cover.

Once inside his house, he sat out on the back patio and tried to think of what to do. It was ironic; all the power he had in the music industry, and he couldn't figure out what in God's name to do.

Have you told her you love her? Gina's words came back to him as he gazed at the cloudless blue sky. Could he give her that? Would it be enough? Would she be able to talk to him about it? Would she want to?

He'd never faced anything like this in his entire life, and it was frightening to find out he wasn't sure he was up to it. The anger, the feeling of helplessness—he wanted to help Cheri, yet could barely help himself.

Call her tonight. Tell her you love her.

He closed his eyes and leaned back in the chair, tilting his face up toward the sun.

"BE SURE TO BE ON TIME tomorrow." Patrick seemed to enjoy her unhappiness as he watched her clock out that evening.

"I will. I'm sorry about today." Cheri just wanted to get away.

"I'll talk to you tomorrow."

She left the store, taking the long way home. Cheri hugged the buildings as she skirted crowds, her feet moving rapidly over the bronze- and coral-colored terrazzo stars embedded in the Walk of Fame. It was dusk, and she felt as though she were suspended between light and dark as she moved through the warm air. Before long, the soft blue sky would be transformed into a fiery sunset because of L.A.'s never-ending smog. Strange that there should be such ugliness and pollution behind such beauty.

She could feel her mouth twist into a semblance of a smile. Exactly the way she felt—ugliness behind a facade. Filling her mind and heart was the feeling that Michael had continually given of himself and she had let him down. Professionally. And personally. That hurt the most. She quickened her pace, trying physically to outrun the pain.

She stopped briefly in front of Mann's Chinese Theater and looked up at the facade of an ornate pagoda flanked by wings. It was hard to believe this had once been the site of the movie industry's most glamorous premieres. Now, with crowds of people and bits of litter along the sidewalk, it looked more like Times Square.

"Cheri!"

She turned and, despite her depression, had to smile. No one dressed quite like Lauri. Tonight, the teenager had on a tight denim mini and white boots. The pink tank top had a lace trim, and bright plastic beads hung down between small breasts. Her blond hair flowed halfway down her back and flew out behind her as she ran toward Cheri.

She had all the innate sensuality of a cat. There was something so fluid, so graceful in the way she moved. Cheri held out her arms and the girl ran into them.

"I can't believe it! What are you doing here?" Lauri asked breathlessly.

"Nothing much," Cheri admitted. "Walking home from work." She wrinkled her nose. "Not too exciting."

"I *miss* you. Why don't you come back and work at the center?" Lauri asked.

"I don't have the time. Things are starting to happen with the band. We have representation, and we're starting to play out a lot."

"That's great! Okay, I forgive you for that." She held out her left hand shyly, and Cheri saw the thin gold band.

"Lauri! Is he a nice guy?"

"Bob? The best! I wanted to talk to you for so long. I wanted to tell you—Cheri, I never would have got this far if it hadn't been for you. I can still remember the first time you talked to me—I wanted to be just like you."

No, you don't. Cheri forced a smile, then put her hand lightly on Lauri's arm. "I'm happy for you. Look, I've got to run, but let me give you my number. I live on Fuller, just up from the Boulevard. You'll have to come by some evening and we can sit and talk." She took out a pen and a small pad.

"Okay, I'd like that." Lauri gave her a quick affectionate kiss on the cheek, took her phone number and sauntered off, eliciting admiring male glances as she half walked, half danced down the street.

Cheri watched her disappear into the throngs of tourists, a riot of colorful clothing and varied languages. *Whatever I did for you, I wish I could do it for myself.*

She continued walking, anxious to reach the safety of her room and shut herself off from the last twenty-four-hour period. But she took the long way home, dreading seeing Rachel and having to pretend everything was all right. It was too raw, too new to share right now.

Twenty minutes later, as she unlocked the door, Buffy rushed to greet her, pink tongue flying. Cheri knelt to greet her dog and received a wet kiss.

"How'd it go?" Rachel called from the kitchen.

"Okay." *Awful.*

"More fodder for the *Enquirer*?"

"They'd love it. Come on, Buff, I'm taking you for a walk."

They went to a nearby, well-lit park. She threw the hard rubber ball until her arm ached, until Buffy trotted up and collapsed at her feet, a satisfied doggy grin on her face.

The house was empty when she returned. Rachel had left a note on the bulletin board in the kitchen. *Gone to the movies with Patti.*

Cheri went into her bedroom and lay down, staring at the ceiling. This was her refuge, with its brass bed, red-and-white patchwork quilt, white eyelet dust ruffle. A small collection of pictures hung on one wall, mostly of Cheri with her grandmother. There was a larger picture of her grandmother's house in San Francisco and several smaller photos of various animals. The room was quite small; the only other piece of furniture it contained was an oak dresser with a small music box on top. Another legacy from her grandmother.

Yet even the cheery, homey atmosphere failed to soothe her as it usually did. All she could think of was Michael.

What did he think of her now? Was he regretting their relationship? He could certainly have his pick of any number of women with normal responses. Cheri cringed as she remembered her choked confession of love. He'd be perfectly justified in running as fast and as far as possible.

The phone rang, interrupting her thoughts. She got up, leaving the machine on. Rachel's voice came on with a message to a tune on her guitar. Then a beep—and Michael's voice.

"Cheri, are you there?"

She didn't pick up.

"I was just calling . . . to see how you're doing. I'd like to take you out to lunch tomorrow." He paused. "Cheri, I . . . give me a call when you can."

He hung up and she erased the message, then went back to her bedroom and climbed into bed.

"WE'RE GOING to have to let you go."

Cheri stared at Patrick in amazement.

"You've been late too many times. I know you don't really care about this job—"

"That's not true!"

"—because all that's on your mind is that band. I can't have people like you on the floor when there are people who want to make a career of it."

Like who? she wanted to ask. But Cheri remained silent. A few minutes later, she found herself outside in the brilliant June sunshine. She walked slowly toward home, not aware of the colorful sights around her: mimes, a man singing folk tunes in front of the Wax Museum, a little girl in a white ruffled sunsuit touching one of the stars in the sidewalk.

The house was cool and quiet as she let herself in. She heard Buffy jump to the floor from her bed, then clicking into the living room, wagging her feathery tail.

"Hi, baby." She knelt down and stroked the smooth head. "You'll have to get used to eating cheap food again."

Buffy whined.

Cheri rummaged through a stack of newspapers at the back door and pulled out a Sunday *Times*. Turning to the classified ads, she began to scan the tiny black-and-white print. After the third column, she gave up and lay down on the floor.

She had enough in her savings account to support herself for three months. Maybe Rachel could give her the number of the temp service she worked for. Cheri hated to type, but it was better than nothing.

She must have dozed for a while, lying in the sun on the rug. A sharp knock on the door brought her wide awake.

"Who is it?" She pushed her hair out of her eyes, feeling hot and sticky.

"Michael."

She got up slowly, wondering what she would say to him. Her fingers trembled as she slid back the bolt. He seemed nervous as he walked inside. He still hadn't shaved and was dressed in jeans and a red T-shirt with the logo of one of the bands he managed on the front. Several copies of *The Music Connection* were in his hands.

He handed one to her. "The reviews are good."

She opened the paper automatically, turning to the review column. A large picture of Tough Cookie in action graced the top of the article. She scarcely recognized herself in the foreground of the picture.

Cheri scanned it, but the words didn't make any sense. She stared out the window at the bright green of the hibiscus hedge by the front door. She had waited so long for this moment. Why didn't she feel anything?

"I stopped by the bookstore. The manager told me you didn't work there anymore."

"I was fired this morning."

After a short silence, Michael spoke. "Was it because of Sunday?"

Cheri sighed. "It was because of a lot of things. Patrick doesn't like people who have other interests on the side. He likes people who walk the Pickfair company line." She pushed her hands into the pockets of her blue cotton pants.

He hesitated over the next question. "Do you need any money?"

"No!" The word exploded out of her mouth with more force than necessary.

"Take it easy." He smiled, but it didn't reach the worried expression in his eyes. "What good is a singer to a manager if she's so worried about finances she can't work?"

"I'm sorry." When Michael didn't answer and the

silence became uncomfortable, Cheri blurted out, "Do you want something to drink? It's pretty hot outside."

"What do you have?"

"I've got some orange juice."

"Fine."

She was glad to get away from him, glad to occupy her mind and hands with the more mundane chores of living.

He was absorbed with the paper when she returned and didn't lift his head when she set the glasses down on the coffee table.

"They really liked you," Michael said.

Cheri sat down on the couch with him, but farther away than she would have the day before. She picked up a copy of the paper and turned to the article.

Michael started to read aloud. "'Bradley's vocals were excellent, she demonstrated a wide range of abilities, and her delivery was extremely intense. She is strictly a rocker, and provided the central presence and heart. She knew what the songs were about and never let the lyrics slip by her.'"

"Wow." Her spirits began to lift.

Michael continued. "'Tough Cookie could have given a little more thought to staging and what they wanted to communicate with their moves, since they tended to ramble a bit.'"

"I can live with that. What did they say about Rachel?"

His dark eyes flitted quickly over the paper, and she felt her stomach tighten. She loved to look at his face.

"Here it is. 'Greene's bass was strong and provided the soul of the band's music. Her arrangements were imaginative, each with its own character and enough musical devices to bring it out. Particularly outstanding were the opening number, "Reckless Love," a tour de force by Bradley, and "Desire." Though Tough

Cookie's lead singer had trouble with the opening, she landed on her feet. She's a tough cookie and this band definitely has nine lives.'" He closed the paper and turned toward her on the couch. "Cheri, I'm very proud of you."

"Thanks."

An awkward moment of silence followed. Cheri picked up her juice and sipped it. Michael caught her eye and she smiled. She hated being this uncomfortable with him.

They started to talk almost at the same moment.

"Cheri—"

"Michael—"

He laughed, and it seemed to Cheri he was self-conscious as well. Reaching for her hand, he moved across the couch until their legs were barely touching. She held herself stiffly, slightly apart from him.

"Cheri, we have to talk. About Saturday night—"

"No! Listen, Michael, I'm sorry about the whole mess. It wasn't your fault. You have nothing to feel guilty about."

"Who said anything about feeling guilty?"

She wrenched away. "I think it's time we talked. Since we both know I'm incapable—"

"Stop it!"

"—incapable of functioning like a normal human being."

"Where do you come up with these phrases?"

"Don't make fun of me!"

"Oh, honey, don't do this to yourself." He took her hand again and then his arms were around her, holding her gently. "I love you. What happened to you doesn't affect my feelings."

She was staring at him, her eyes hurting with the effort of holding back tears. "Oh, God. Michael, you don't have to do this."

"What are you talking about?"

She started to touch him, then twisted her fingers together and pushed them into her lap. "I mean, just because of Saturday night. I'll live. You don't have to tell me you love me."

"I'm not...I *love* you, damn it! Why can't you believe me?" He started to speak, then stopped.

Cheri shook her head, wanting to get him out of the room before she broke down completely. "No. It wouldn't be fair to you."

"Let me be the judge of what's fair."

She got up off the couch and walked over to the picture window. She couldn't look at his face and say what she had to. "Can we stay friends?"

"Cheri!" The way he said her name, a tone that mingled tenderness with despair, tore at her heart. She heard him get up off the couch and she turned, holding up her hands to ward him off.

"I don't want to see you anymore."

"Honey—"

"I mean it, Michael."

She watched as he seemed to grow smaller, his shoulders slumping, the fire going out of his eyes.

He made one last attempt. "This can't be the way you really feel. Last night, when you..."

She couldn't bear it. Covering her face with her hands, Cheri stood very still. She felt as if she were made of delicate glass, about to shatter into a million pieces of pure pain.

There was a moment of silence; then she dropped her hands. Looking away from his face, she forced the words out. Words she had to say.

"Michael, please just go."

"I'm taking you out," Rachel called later that evening through the closed bedroom door. "You're not going to sit around mooning over him. No wonder he looked so awful."

After a moment, the door opened slightly and Cheri stuck her head out. "When did you see him?" she asked, her voice husky from crying.

"I was at World Newsstand when he saw me and honked. He gave me a copy of the paper and told me the reviews were good."

Cheri didn't reply.

"He looked like someone had just punched him in the stomach."

She remained silent.

"Don't you care at all?"

"I care very much. Too much."

Rachel turned away in exasperation.

"You can't sleep the rest of your life away. Why don't we go to the Italian deli and pick up some sandwiches?"

Cheri shrugged her shoulders. "Fine."

The deli was within walking distance. Fifteen minutes later, they'd given their order and were seated at a small table with a red-and-white plastic tablecloth. Plastic grapevines and clusters of purple fruit festooned the ceiling. The sandwiches were simple, filling. And cheap.

Rachel didn't waste any time returning to the subject on her mind. "Michael called while you were in your room."

"What did he say?" Cheri felt as if her heart were lodged in her throat.

"He's leaving for New York Tuesday night."

Though she had sent him away, Cheri felt a peculiar emptiness settle over her.

"He needs someone to house-sit for him. He has this old dog—"

"Charlie."

"Yeah. Anyway, I told him we'd do it."

"Rachel!"

"What's the difference? He won't be there."

What could she say? How could she tell Rachel she didn't want to see his house, didn't want to remember anything about him?

"He lives in Marina del Rey. And this is the best. Guess what his house is equipped with."

"What?"

"Come on, guess."

"Mirrored ceilings?" Cheri couldn't stay depressed for long in Rachel's company.

"No, dirty girl. A hot tub."

Strange, how all the time they'd been dating he'd never taken her to his house. Michael had always picked her up in Hollywood.

Cheri didn't want to remember. Pushing away her sandwich, she looked Rachel straight in the eye. "Even though I won't be seeing him anymore, he's still going to manage the band."

"Fine. That'll work out just swell." Rachel's sarcasm wasn't lost on Cheri. "But I'm not going to say anything to Ria about this—she'd be all over him."

They walked back in silence. Even late on a Monday night, the boulevard was crowded with cars and pedestrians. Tourists.

"I'll pick you up when I get home from work and we can head out. Michael takes off tomorrow evening. The dog has to be watched pretty closely. He's on medication."

"What about Buffy?" But even as Cheri asked, she knew Rachel would have an answer.

"Bring her along. She'll be good company for the old guy."

Chapter Six

They drove out the following evening, their suitcases packed. Buffy had run around the house all morning. The minute she'd seen Cheri take out her small suitcase she'd known a trip was in store.

Now the little dog rode in the backseat of Rachel's orange Volkswagen, her head hanging out the window, ears blowing in the ocean breeze.

"Take a right on Washington. Here." Cheri directed Rachel from the directions Michael had given over the phone. As Rachel turned the corner tightly, Cheri leaned back and closed her eyes. She'd never have associated a man like Michael with the Marina. The area maintained a reputation for being the center of the swinging singles life in Los Angeles. The Marina City Towers, round skyscrapers near the harbor, attracted singles of both sexes eager to experience everything Southern California had to offer.

But Michael lived in a house. As the orange VW turned another corner, Cheri realized they were on his street.

His house wasn't what she'd expected. A one-story stucco structure, it could have been mistaken for the house they rented in Hollywood. But it was bigger and in better condition. The walls were cream, the Spanish tiles on the roof a dark red. The front yard was enclosed by a low stucco wall. Fuchsia and bougainvillea trailed over the carport, and clumps of begonias lined the stone walkway to the front porch. Several empty Arrowhead water bottles stood underneath a bush by the mailbox.

Buffy jumped out as soon as the car stopped and began to sniff around.

"Buffy!" Cheri snapped her fingers. "Oh, no. Not the front lawn."

Vivid floral color blazed everywhere: velvet purple and white pansies in the two window boxes, a few rosebushes along the driveway. Their salmon, yellow and pink petals were full blown, and some were scattered along the cement.

Rachel unlocked the front door as Cheri retrieved their suitcases. She froze as she heard her friend start to speak.

"I thought you'd left already. Sorry for just barging in."

"It's no problem. I'm glad you're here early."

Michael.

Cheri was aware of each move she made as she carried their suitcases inside his house. Feeling self-conscious in red terry shorts and tank top with only rubber thongs on her feet, she took her hair out of its hasty ponytail and let it fall over her shoulders.

Michael looked at her briefly as she walked inside, then continued talking to Rachel.

He seemed a different man. Wearing charcoal-gray, pin-striped pants with a matching vest, and a white cotton shirt, he looked more the businessman than Cheri had ever seen him. His dark hair was combed neatly back, but it was long enough so it didn't stay completely in place.

"Could you both come outside a moment?"

Cheri followed Michael and Rachel into the backyard, Buffy trotting obediently at her heels. The area showed the care of a loving hand. Someone had built a latticed shelter over the first section of the patio, and with the high stucco walls, it afforded complete privacy. In the corner of the cemented area was a small redwood deck complete with hot tub.

Cheri only half listened as Michael explained how to operate it, she was so hungry to see him. As he talked to both of them, she noticed he was careful not to glance in her direction. But she couldn't stop staring at him.

When he finished, he turned and headed farther back into the yard, past a redwood fence. When he returned, a grizzled, brindle-and-white bulldog trotted along beside him. His gait was rolling, his massive pink tongue lolled out of his mouth.

Cheri forgot her discomfort as she knelt down on the cool cement, her fingers laced through Buffy's rolled leather collar. "Michael, he's darling."

Charlie approached her cautiously, his brown eyes drawn by Buffy, who was straining against Cheri's grip so hard her two front feet were in the air.

"Let her go." Michael was watching the two animals with an amused expression.

Buffy shot over to the bulldog, and the two of them stood completely still, sniffing and making introductions. Then Cheri smiled as Buffy began to lick the old wrinkled face.

"I knew they'd get along fine," Rachel said, and then addressed Michael. "Anything else we need to know?"

"I've left a list. The main thing I'm worried about is that Charlie gets his pills. He takes them in a little butter. If anything goes wrong, the vet is only a mile away and his number is on the refrigerator."

The two women followed Michael through the rooms,

but Cheri barely saw the house, she was so intent on studying Michael. Before he went away.

"Most of it simply involves taking in the mail and making sure a light is on at night. Charlie has his dog door. I'm sure Buffy will figure it out." Michael glanced at his watch, and once again Cheri had the distinct feeling he was avoiding her eyes. "I've got to go."

When he came back into the living room, he carried a suitcase and a leather briefcase, and wore a suit jacket. Taking a light-gray trench coat out of the hall closet, he draped it over one arm.

"Have a good time." He seemed hesitant.

"We will," Rachel said quickly. Cheri was silent, just watching him. He seemed tired. Older. The lines around his eyes and mouth were more pronounced.

"Walk me out to the car?" He directed the question to Cheri. Rachel suddenly became extremely interested in the shelf of albums in the living room.

"Sure."

It was almost dark. She could see the outline of the Marina City Towers against the setting sun. Its windows were beginning to light up against the deepening summer sky.

Michael opened the trunk of his Ferrari and threw in his suitcase and briefcase. Slamming the lid shut, he walked around to where she stood by the driver's side.

"Thank you for doing this, Cheri."

"What are friends for?" She could have bitten her tongue off as she saw the quick flash of pain on his face. Why was she doing this to him?

Involuntarily, she touched his arm, smoothing her fingers over the material of his suit jacket. She could feel his muscles underneath the soft material. He stood perfectly still. She touched his cheek, then put both her hands on his shoulders and, balancing on her toes, gave him a light kiss.

His arms came around her, gently, his coat against her hip, his fingers locked loosely at the small of her back. Resting his forehead against hers, he sighed.

"I've missed you so much." The words were husky with repressed emotion.

"I know. Me, too." Though it had only been a matter of hours, she already regretted trying to cast him out of her life.

"Can I call you?"

She nodded.

"Will you be here when I get back?"

"Yes."

He kissed her then, with such sweetness she felt tears trembling in her eyes. "I love you, Cheri."

"I know you do."

He was waiting for her to say something. She cleared her throat. "I love you as much as I've been able to love any man." It sounded awful. She tried again. "If I were able to love anyone, it would be you."

He seemed pleased. Some of the tension left his face. "I'll be back in a week. Take it easy."

"Be careful in New York." She stepped back as he climbed into the car and started the engine. Cheri watched until the car disappeared into the night.

"That was a long good-bye," Rachel remarked as Cheri came up the front steps.

"Rachel, if you loved someone but didn't think you were particularly good for him, what would you do?"

"I think—if I were you—I'd let Michael make up his own mind."

THE WEEK PASSED SWIFTLY at Michael's house. Life went on as usual for Cheri—rehearsals, songwriting, feeding Buffy, giving Charlie his medication. And twice a week to her therapist.

"So you tried to put some distance into your relationship and it didn't quite work." Glenda's gray eyes twinkled as she poured Cheri a cup of tea. "He sounds persistent, your Michael."

"He is." Cheri concentrated on scooping just the right amount of sugar into her spoon.

"Do you know what it is that frightens you about him?"

She set her cup down, her throat suddenly tight. She nodded.

"Can you talk about it?" Glenda's eyes were kind.

"I know...I know he won't want..." She stopped. Taking a deep breath, she started again. "He doesn't do anything halfway. He'll want a committed relationship, and I don't know if I can give him that."

"What do you mean, committed? What does that word mean to you, Cheri?"

"Sexual. And *that* was a disaster. I can't believe he still wants to see me."

"Maybe he gets other things from you."

"Like what?" Cheri was quick to challenge Glenda.

"I don't think most people enter into relationships just for sex. I think there are deeper reasons. What do you think you give Michael?"

She couldn't meet Glenda's eyes. "Nothing."

"You tried to give to him sexually and you couldn't respond. You were very vulnerable, Cheri, and he still cared for you. You tried to push him away and he gave you some time, but came right back into your life. He tells you he loves you, and I know you care for him. How do you feel about him?"

The words were physically building up in her chest. Cheri could feel a pressure behind her throat, as if it were all waiting to come out. Forcing herself, she let down the walls. Just a little.

"I *love* him. I'd love nothing more than to be able to have...a full relationship. But I've *lied* to him! How will he ever trust me when he finds out about all the lies? I told him my parents were dead! I told him I was raped! I lied about where I met Rachel, where I went to school. Everything I've told him is lies." Her body was trembling, her hands balled into tight fists.

"Could you tell him the truth?"

She put her head in her hands, hating the hot tears that were squeezing out between her lashes. "Not now! Not right away! I've never had anything like this, and...I don't want to do anything that would take him away from me again. I just want a little more time."

As she started to cry, she felt Glenda put her hand on her shoulder and squeeze gently.

THE WEEK NEARED ITS END. Buffy gave Charlie a new lease on life. The old bulldog huffed and wheezed around the yard, trying to keep up with the younger dog's antics. Cheri occasionally penned Charlie up in Michael's study so he wouldn't overexert himself. Rachel was amused.

"That's all we need. Michael comes home and finds the old guy's dropped dead."

It was a time of reflection for Cheri. She loved living in Michael's house. She found his presence everywhere, in every room, from the tiniest porcelain picture frame to the soft leather couch in his study.

The study was her favorite room. Cool and dark, with gleaming wooden file cabinets and a massive walnut desk, it was both businesslike and comfortable at the same time. Charlie had his private nest underneath the desk. He was invincible, surrounded on three sides, and when Buffy ran in and pulled at his ear to make him go outside to play, he simply growled and dug his squat little body into the plush rug.

Rachel spent most of her time in the large, airy living room listening to albums. But Cheri stayed in the study.

She liked to lie back on the cool leather couch and study the portrait of Michael's family on the far wall. An older brother with the same dark, laughing eyes as Michael. A younger sister with long brown hair and stunning cheekbones. His mother seemed quiet and elegant, his father an imposing figure. And Michael. His face looked younger, more vulnerable than Cheri knew it.

I wonder what they're like. And Cheri, always fascinated by other people's families, gave them elaborate imaginary personalities. She knew Michael's father had managed the agency until his second heart attack, but she wondered what his brother did. Michael had told her his sister lived in San Francisco, and was married to someone named Ben. She had a baby named Robbie. Cheri imagined Michael's mother as the nurturing force behind the entire family, giving them a perfect home life, where all could return at the end of the day and refresh their spirits.

She had also seen the picture in his bedroom, in the tiny sterling frame. It was a radiant photo, compelling a person to study it, then to smile. Michael stood on a patio, barbecue fork in hand. He was wearing a Hawaiian shirt in shades of blue and green. His free arm was wrapped around possibly the most beautiful woman Cheri had ever seen. Nancy Rush. Rachel had identified her face the first night Cheri had picked up the photo and studied it. She remembered countless covers—*Harper's Bazaar, Glamour, Vogue*. Lightly tanned, the girl in the photo had the familiar silver-blond hair and violet eyes. Her mouth, her nose, her smile: perfection. Together they looked like exactly what they had been—two people crazily in love.

But Cheri couldn't feel any jealousy toward the woman. It was so hard to believe she'd died. All she could think of was Michael rushing to the hospital, Michael being told he had lost the woman he'd loved. He had never discussed her, never made any reference to most of his life.

She had asked. But he seemed curiously quiet about his family. And Nancy.

A movement in the doorway caught her eye and she glanced over.

"Are you going to stay inside on our last afternoon here?" Rachel appeared in the doorway in a blue bikini, suntan lotion in her hand.

Cheri scrambled up off the couch. "Give me just a minute."

She joined Rachel outside, Charlie snorting at her heels. Two-thirds of the backyard was lush and verdant. Thick green grass and countless plants enclosed by the stucco wall gave them the privacy to sunbathe.

Rachel had spread two huge beach towels on the grass and mixed up a pitcher of sangría. "I know it's the sign of a diseased mind to start drinking before four in the afternoon, but it's too perfect a day to spoil. Give me your glass."

Cheri laughed as she spread suntan lotion over her pale arms. It was a perfect June day, hot and sunny, with the gentlest of ocean breezes.

"We have to start going back to aerobic dance class," she said, studying her stomach and thighs critically.

"Spare me! All that jumping around you do onstage keeps you pretty fit."

"But my legs, up here—"

"Cheri, take it easy on yourself. But yes, I'd love it if you'd drag me to class with you."

Cheri closed her eyes. Charlie and Buffy had retired underneath a small orange tree at the far side of the yard and were engaged in digging a hole to lie down in. Cheri had given up on them, she would repair the damage before Michael returned tomorrow.

The two women lay in the sun for a long time. The heat was soothing, and Cheri felt like a lizard on a rock. Her body relaxed, her mind wandered.

She missed Michael. Often, during the day, she wondered what he was doing in New York. He had called every night to check on any messages he might have. Cheri smiled. It took all of five minutes, yet they had talked far into quite a few nights. She'd hate to see his phone bill.

The wine loosened her mind, and her thoughts wandered to the night after the party in Malibu. For the first time since that night she allowed herself to picture the bedroom in her mind's eye and to visualize Michael's body. In the light of day, safe in the warm sun, physical intimacy didn't seem so frightening.

She took another sip of sangría and lay back down on her stomach. If there was any man she'd want to make love with, it was Michael. Cheri buried her face in her arms as she remembered deep, slow kisses, the slight scratch of his beard on her chin.

She felt hedonistic and free, covered with plumeria-scented oil, her stomach filled with fruit-sweetened wine. A slight breeze washed over her body, lifting a strand of hair off her neck. Sounds seemed muted and far away. Cars drove by. A door slammed in the distance.

She felt Rachel sit up abruptly. "Welcome home."

Cheri opened one eye, then lifted her head. Michael was walking toward them, his white shirt unbuttoned, the slacks of his suit looking out of place against his bare chest. He looked tired but happy. Charlie tore out of the hole he'd been lying in and raced around his master's legs, yapping excitedly.

Cheri sat up quickly, hugging her knees to her chest. "I thought you weren't coming back until tomorrow!"

He grinned. "I wasn't supposed to, but..." His gaze remained steadily on her. "I found myself missing someone so much I finished my business sooner than I expected." He took in the scene before him—beach towels, the half-empty pitcher of sangría, the bottles of tanning oil. "Can I join you?"

Cheri wanted to meet him halfway. "I'd like that."

He disappeared into the house and she rolled over and looked up at the sky. When Michael came back out, he was wearing a brief black bathing suit. Laying his towel next to Cheri's, he sat down and touched a strand of her hair.

"I'm going to get more sangría," Rachel announced. "This calls for a celebration." She picked up the pitcher and headed for the kitchen.

Cheri turned her head so she could see him.

"I missed you." His voice was soft. Intimate.

"I missed you, too." She reached out and took his hand. "You look tired." She wanted to comfort him, give to him, make his life as happy as he had made hers. "Why don't you lie down?"

He stretched out beside her, on his stomach. Observing him quickly, while he wasn't watching, she took in the muscled perfection of his masculine body. He looked like a living Michelangelo marble statue.

"You work out, don't you?"

He turned his head so his cheek rested on his forearm. A stray lock of dark hair tumbled over his forehead. "Why do you ask?" He was teasing her, clearly enjoying the moment.

"Egotist." She switched position and settled on her side so she could face him. "It's just the way your muscles look, they're so clearly defined."

"You should try it."

She could feel her face express her dismay before

she could conceal it, and heard Michael give a whoop of laughter. "I'm not complaining! I meant for the sense of satisfaction."

He shaded his eyes with his hand. "What kind of suntan stuff do you have over there?"

"There's a lotion and an oil."

"Give me the oil."

Cheri enjoyed watching him as he covered his arms and legs with suntan oil.

"I smell like a tropical garden," he muttered as he attempted to reach his back.

She thought of Glenda's words. *Try touching in a non-sexual situation.*

"Let me." She was surprised to find she wanted to touch him. What could be safer than the backyard in broad daylight? She held the oil in her palm for just a second to warm it, but it was already warm from the sun, then began to spread it over his back with slow, deep strokes.

He leaned into her massage, a deep sigh of pure pleasure escaping his lips. "Heaven."

Cheri dug her fingers gently into his flesh, feeling the tightness in his neck and shoulders. "You're awfully tense."

"Mmm."

"Lie down. I'll give your shoulders a massage."

He complied and she straddled his back, sitting on the base of his spine as she reached for his shoulders, stretching them to ease the tight knots of tension out of his muscles.

Rachel reappeared, set down two glasses of sangría, then winked at Cheri and strolled back inside the house.

Finished with Michael's shoulders and neck, Cheri worked her way down his back, releasing tension and loving the feel of his hot skin underneath her fingers.

"Don't stop."

She massaged his legs, then his feet, gently pulling each toe, then digging her fingers into each strong arch.

Michael groaned softly. "Where did you learn to do this?"

"Rachel and I took a class in Santa Monica."

Then his arms, right down to his fingertips. Each hand was gently administered to, and as she worked each finger, Cheri remembered how much comfort they had brought her, whether touching her cheek or her shoulder.

I can go this far without being afraid. The realization made a slow, soft joy well up inside her.

She lay down on her towel beside him and wasn't surprised when he reached out and pulled her against his body.

"You have no reason to be afraid." His breath was soft against her temple. "I couldn't ravish anyone in this state."

She laughed and he gave her a quick hug. "Hungry?"

"A little," she admitted.

"I took out three steaks before I came outside. Do you feel like barbecuing?"

The picture of Nancy in his bedroom formed in her mind with startling clarity. "Sounds great."

The evening turned out relaxed and lazy. The three of them grilled steaks and vegetables outdoors, and Cheri threw together a salad. They finished up the meal with generous helpings of chocolate-chip ice cream.

"I'm going to be sick," Rachel groaned from the depths of a hammock.

Michael laughed.

Rachel swung herself out of the hammock, a hand on her stomach in mock agony. "I'm going to head out. Cheri, are you coming?"

Before she could make a decision, Michael answered. "I'll drive you home later." His eyes were questioning.

Cheri wanted to prolong the magic of the day. "I'd like that. Rachel, can you take Buffy home with you?"

"Yeah, but Charlie may die of a broken heart."

Once Rachel left, Cheri did the dishes while Michael unpacked. As she rinsed the last of the suds from a glass and turned off the water, she could hear Michael's slightly off-key humming from the bedroom.

It would be like this if we were married. The thought came from deep inside, almost frightening her. It was followed immediately by another. *But that can never happen. He deserves so much more than I can give.* She gripped the sink tightly, her knuckles white.

But she could have one night with him, could pretend they were going to be together forever. She wiped her hands on a dish towel and hung it up to dry, then joined him in the bedroom.

"Do you want some wine? There's a little bit left in the bottle."

He studied her face, then curved his fingers around her jaw, cupping her face.

"What do you want, Cheri?"

"I want..." She swallowed, hoping her voice wouldn't tremble. "I want to start all over with you. I want to spend the night and see if I can do any better."

His face darkened. "This isn't some endurance marathon you're talking about. I don't want to put pressure on you."

"No, Michael. I want to do this. I don't want to think about anything. I just want to be with you."

He leaned forward, sliding his fingers around the back of her neck and brushing her lips with his thumb. "It's the nicest homecoming a man could ask for."

But he didn't kiss her. He seemed restrained, in

check. They stood in silence until Cheri snuggled up against him. He put his arms around her, but she sensed he wasn't there with her.

Something had to be done. "I'd like to use the hot tub."

He grinned. "Did you and Rachel use it at all?"

"Every night. It leaves me feeling like I want to melt into the mattress."

"It's my own way of relaxing at the end of the day." He held her against him, but loosely, so she wasn't pressed close. "I designed the deck."

"It's gorgeous." She backed away from him and he dropped his arms. "Are you coming?"

"Just let me get my suit on."

She took a deep breath. "Who said anything about a suit?" Without waiting for an answer, she peeled her cotton sweater over her head.

Cheri heard his sharp intake of breath, knew he had a full view of her naked breasts. Before she lost her nerve, she quickly stepped out of her jeans, then started for the back door.

She left the patio in darkness, didn't turn on the outside light as she rolled back the top of the hot tub and stepped into the steaming water. Michael came out a moment later, wearing his suit. Draping two towels over one of the deck chairs, he approached the tub.

Cheri sank lower in the water, suddenly thankful for its protection. Ducking her head underneath, she surfaced, pushing long dark strands of hair out of her face.

"Come on in." She reached for his hand.

He had a curious expression on his face, something she couldn't define. But he climbed onto the top level of the redwood deck, then lowered himself into the water.

The night was perfectly still. The darkness made the yard their own private world.

He didn't come near her. They sat on opposite sides of the tub, facing each other. The moonlight silvered the surface of the water, giving the scene an unworldly glow.

"Bubbles?" she asked, wishing he would make a move, make the decision for her. At his nod she pressed the button on the side of the tub and felt the water begin to swirl gently up from the bottom. It tickled its way around her naked body.

Michael remained where he was.

"More bubbles?" Before he could reply, she touched the second button and the water came to life, churning furiously, splashing out the top, making the deck gleam darkly wet in the moonlight. The sharp smell of chlorine steamed up for just a second, and Cheri shifted until her breasts were above the churning water. She looked up at Michael. His eyes were expressionless; he held himself away from her. Cheri sank back into the roiling water, content to let it buffet her shoulders and neck.

She bumped her leg into his and he pulled away.

What was wrong with him? Was it something she was doing? She'd thought about this moment the entire time he'd been away. Why did things have to suddenly go wrong?

"Michael?"

He couldn't hear her soft expulsion of breath over the bubbling water.

She pressed both buttons and the water slowly stilled. Silence filled the black velvet night.

"Michael?" Suddenly she sensed what was wrong. She eased her way over to his side, their legs bumping awkwardly. Sliding her wet body against his, she put her arms around his neck, began to wrap one of her legs around his waist, the water buoying her gently against him.

"Cheri, I can't—"

"I don't want you to control yourself. I want you to make love to me." She could feel his intense arousal through his suit and, with instinct born out of wanting to please him, she reached down, gently freeing him from the confines of the tight black material. His soft groan sounded loud in the silence.

"Please." She wasn't begging, simply reassuring.

And then his carefully maintained control slipped. With one fluid motion, he brought his lips down over hers, pressed his hands against the small of her back, brought her as close as possible to his body. She opened her mouth under his, wanting to go quickly, wanting to test herself.

His lips were like soft fire against her temple, her cheek, her nose, then back to her mouth again. She pressed her breasts against the hard muscled wall of his chest, gripped his shoulders tightly with her hands, moved her other leg up and locked her ankles behind his back. She could feel the water around her hips and thighs, but the rest of her body felt just as hot.

He eased her out of the tub, just enough so they were both lying on the deck. Stretching his arm and leaning toward the deck chair, he managed to pull down both towels.

He settled back against her gently, as if afraid she might break. Nestling her head against his shoulder, he turned her face to his with persuasive fingers and kissed her gently.

"Do you want this, babe?" His voice shook.

"Yes."

"I don't want to hurt you."

"Michael, I love you. I want to make you happy."

"But I don't want—"

"Stop talking," she whispered as she lowered her mouth over his.

As the kiss deepened, he rolled her completely on

top of him, and she stretched out full length. His arousal was strong, taut and full, pressed hotly against her
belly. She rubbed herself against him and heard him
make an anguished sound, deep in his throat. It pleased
her.

He made love to her slowly, hands moving with infi-
nite care over her breasts and hips as his mouth
touched her everywhere. She didn't feel any shame;
she concentrated on moving, shifting to give him ac-
cess to any part of her he desired.

Lacing his fingers together at the small of her back,
he pulled gently and she lowered her body until he
could reach her breasts with his lips. He kissed the
swollen tips, pulling them into his mouth, teasing them
with his teeth. Cheri recognized short, sharp breathless
cries as her own, and she bit her lip in case someone
might hear them. He kept one hand firmly on her back,
fingers spread, holding her close to him when she
might have pulled away from too much sensation.

She felt his other hand move slowly down her rib
cage, his fingers exploring every inch of her skin. Over
her stomach, down farther, moving with unerring accu-
racy. He stroked her gently all the while his lips made
love to her breasts.

Cheri panicked for just an instant, felt her body start
to tighten as if to push him away, but he moved his
other hand from her back and threaded it through her
hair, brought her face down to his and kissed her,
crooning very softly.

"Oh, Cheri, no. You're so beautiful." He kissed her
again, stroking her between her thighs. "You're beautiful there, I love you and I want to touch you."

She could feel her fears dissolving, could feel the
tension leaving her. He continued to stroke her, slowly
building an erotic fire between her thighs.

"I don't want to hurt you," he whispered against her

hair, close to her ear. "I want to make love to you."
She was grasping his shoulders so tightly she was sure
she must be hurting him. The hardness of his muscles
offered her the only reality in a world of rapidly shifting
sensation. Cheri had never felt this way before, like
molten glass being formed to a man's hands.

"I won't do anything unless it feels good to you." He
kissed her again, teasing her lips apart and matching the
rhythm of his caresses with playful movements of his
tongue.

Cheri felt intoxicated by his love, by his passion, by
his caring.

"Michael, give me more," she whispered.

"Tell me what you want, I'll give you anything you
want. I love you, Cheri, and that makes this beautiful."

She lost herself in his words as he slowly brought her
toward deepest passion. He continued to talk to her,
softly, reassuringly, seeming to realize she needed to
know it was him. And how much he cared.

Wanting to please him, she reached down and took
him in her hand. Her fingers closed around his powerful arousal and she marveled at the smooth hot texture
of his skin.

"Michael." She was so full of feeling she could
barely say the words.

"Show me. Let me love you."

She let go of him, leaned forward on top of his strong
chest. Kissing his neck, she whispered, "I want you
inside me. But..."

"Tell me. Cheri, you can tell me anything."

"I'm scared. It looks too...like I can't..."

He took his hands away from her body, then pushed
her hair back off her face with his fingers. "Whatever
happens, I'll love you. I won't be mad." He smiled,
and she could see from the slight trembling of his

mouth what an effort his control was costing him. "Only as much as you want. Nothing more."

She blinked back tears of fear. "Help me."

He lay back on the deck, placing his hands lightly on her hips. "I won't move. You're in control."

She hesitated. *I want this more than anything in the world. But if I fail again...* Cheri leaned down and kissed Michael, lifting her hips slightly at the same time. She reached down and grasped him gently, intimately, holding him away from the hard flatness of his stomach.

She had to look at his face. Glancing up, she met his eyes and never broke contact as she slowly began to join their bodies in a pure act of love.

Cheri felt a moment of pain and she winced. "Talk to me, Michael," she whispered. She needed to know he was with her, more than physically.

"You're so sweet, Cheri. Everything you've done has felt so good, so right. I love you so—" He broke off abruptly as she moved, taking more of him inside her.

There wasn't any pain. The realization stunned her. Cheri moved again, and tears of happiness and relief sprang into her eyes. Leaning down, she whispered, "Michael, help me. Make love to me."

He moved then, slowly, carefully, sliding deeper and deeper with each stroke. And then he was within her and she felt an emotional completeness she'd never experienced before.

This is the way it can be. The realization came upon her as if her soul were shattering. To be this close to someone was an incredible luxury, something she'd never experienced. Only the hatred, the fear...

She slid down onto his body, wrapped her arms around his neck and held him tightly, tears running down her face. He kept his arms around her as she cried. Then she was kissing him wildly, on his lips, his eyelids, behind his ear and down his neck. She wanted to memorize his body. He was hers.

"Cheri." His whisper was barely a groan and she didn't listen, only moved her lips back to his and gave to him, completely without reserve.

"I can't—" He groaned, and she watched in fascination as his head tilted back, the tendons in his neck tightening as his hips moved, thrusting up. And then she felt him pulse within her and she knew she had satisfied him. It gave her the deepest possible joy.

After a moment of silence, he spoke. "Cheri, I couldn't—"

She put her finger over his lips. "I love you, Michael. You made it wonderful for me."

HE CARRIED HER TO BED, then brought her a cool washcloth and held it between her legs, easing the slight soreness.

To Cheri, everything had changed. Michael was her lover, had guided her through their first lovemaking as if she'd been a virgin. The tenderness, the care he had shown her, all melted together to form a warm happy glow that suffused her body.

He locked up the house and came back to her, sliding into bed in the darkened room. She went willingly into his arms, rested her head against his shoulder, listened to his heart. And for the first time she felt they belonged together, as if what had happened between them had forged a link that could never be broken.

"Michael?" Her voice was barely a whisper.

"Hmm?" He was playing with a strand of her hair.

"Did you like it?" She wanted to hear him say it all over again.

He slid down beside her in bed so their noses were touching lightly, reached behind her and gave her a gentle spank. "Did I like it? What do you think?"

"I think I love making love with you."

He laughed then, and pulled the covers tightly around them.

"Are you okay?" he asked softly.

She leaned upon one elbow, smoothed a few strands of hair away from his forehead. She would never tire of touching him. "Are you asking me if I hit the big time?"

"That's not—"

"It was all wonderful for me." She snuggled closer. "It wasn't so much what I felt as what I *didn't* feel."

"What do you mean?"

"No fear. No pain. Just you."

"C'mere." He turned her in his arms so her back was pressed against his chest. "I'm glad."

She moved his hand so it covered her breast, over her heart. *How I love you.*

Smiling, Cheri drifted off to sleep.

Chapter Seven

Cheri didn't go back to her house in Hollywood after that night. Later, they laughed over the date, trying to remember just when she formally moved into Michael's house. But it was a gradual process, and neither remembered.

First her clothes. Buffy followed, and Charlie was delighted with the return of his favorite playmate. Then a few tapes, some albums. Her headphones, her music books, her red-and-white quilt. The brass bed.

The summer days were long and lazy. Michael insisted he wanted her to rest, so she spent her days sunning, playing with the dogs, working in the garden. Nights were filled with rehearsals. And Michael. She enjoyed fixing meals for him, and almost every evening found them in the hot tub talking over their day.

But the biggest step, emotionally, was moving into his bedroom. As a lover, Michael was tender and demanding, thoughtful and passionate. Though Cheri was acutely conscious of not responding fully, she enjoyed their lovemaking, enjoyed the feel of his rough, warm masculine body next to hers while they slept.

They did all the things couples do. Watched old movies late at night, listened to music, washed the cars, shopped for groceries. But for Cheri it was a totally new experience, and she regarded each day as a gift. She delighted in finding out new things about Michael. He didn't like okra; he loved her fried chicken. He waxed his collection of cars, worked on them with a passion. Cheri couldn't have told a Mustang from a Ferrari, but she helped him, standing next to him on the cement driveway and holding the hose, or running to the garage for another sponge.

He didn't care for televised sports, but both of them watched all the rock concerts on cable and afterward talked about what made a particular performance stand out. He loved to hear her sing in the morning before he left for the office.

And he looked after her in countless ways.

Cheri came to understand herself better, came to realize she didn't have to be such a perfectionist. If the dishes waited until morning, it didn't matter. If the kitchen floor looked like a big dog print, at least they were healthy and happy.

It was an important time for her artistically, as well. Free from financial tyranny, happy in her emotional life, songs poured out of her at an amazing rate. She wrote down sheets of lyrics as they flooded her mind and passed an incredible amount of material on to Rachel. There were times when she worked eighteen to twenty hours at a stretch on her music, and Michael simply encouraged her.

Early in July, Michael decided Tough Cookie was ready to move into the studio and record a professional demo tape.

The studio he picked was one of the best in Los Angeles. When Cheri heard she was going to work in the same building that had housed the Rolling Stones, Fleetwood Mac and Joni Mitchell, she was thrilled. She prepared for the big event, attended singing lessons, worked over various arrangements, polished lyrics.

At her insistence, Michael drove her to the studio

early the first evening, despite the fact that vocals were always the last track to be added.

Cheri was headed into the women's room, her canvas bag in hand, when the sound of a familiar voice stopped her.

"She's really something! But I guess I can't be too upset. She's sleeping us all straight to the top." Ria.

"Shut up! You don't know anything about their relationship." Patti. Loyal to the end.

"What I can't understand is what a man like that could see in a cold little—"

Cheri pushed the door aside and entered the suddenly quiet bathroom.

"Hi, Patti. Ria." Miraculously, her voice didn't shake.

"How's Michael doing?" Patti asked, her face red.

"He's a little tired. But he's as excited as I am." She looked at the other woman. "How are you, Ria?"

"Fine." Ria's reply was mumbled, almost inaudible. She looked shrunken and pathetic in the fluorescent light.

"I meant to tell you..." Cheri dug through her bag and unearthed her hairbrush. "I really like that new lick you were playing during the chorus of 'Reckless Love.'"

Ria's small features seemed to soften and she looked slightly ashamed. "Yeah? Well, I was kinda messing around with it before rehearsal and everyone else liked it." She picked up her small backpack and hurried outside.

Patti stared as Cheri arranged her hair, put the brush back in her bag. She opened her mouth to say something, but Cheri spoke first.

"Yes, I heard her before I opened the door."

Patti was clearly amazed. "I wouldn't have let it go by like that."

"You would have if you knew we started recording tonight."

But Cheri was glad Ria would be recording her part separately from the vocals.

As she walked into the engineer's booth, she stood quietly watching one of the men mixing down a tape from a previous band. Cheri counted twenty-four VU meters, each needle inside flitting to a different part of the music.

"Roll off the treble on the bass drum. You're pegging the meters." The engineer's voice was businesslike as he addressed the second engineer. The young woman obeyed.

Patti came up next to Cheri. "It's all Greek to me," she whispered. Cheri smiled. Before they were finished with the demo, she hoped they'd know what they were doing.

Once the previous band's equipment was cleared away, Patti unloaded her drums and set up in the small isolation booth prepared for her. Cheri watched an engineer arrange mikes and stands: one on bass, one on snare, and two overheads. It seemed like a long time before a voice sounded over the main speakers.

"Patti, pick up your sticks and put on your headphones."

Patti complied. Cheri watched as she ran through several rolls and some stock drumbeats.

"Jim, move the bass drum mike a little closer." Again, the anonymous voice. Patti continued to take direction.

"Hit your cymbals one at a time."

"Can you tighten that high-hat?"

"Go ahead and play the introduction to 'Reckless Love' so we can get a level check."

Cheri felt a light touch on her arm and turned to see Michael standing in the doorway to the engineer's booth. He motioned her to come outside.

They walked down the carpeted hallway.

"Now do you see why I wanted you to stay home and rest?"

"But I've never seen any of this before! Do they have to go through the same thing with each of us?"

He nodded. "First drums, then bass guitar, then guitar, keyboards, and finally, vocals. I may have Ria stay after you're done so she can take a few passes at the solo."

"Why can't she do it her first time through?"

"We want to have Ria play rhythm guitar for the whole song, even underneath her solo. It isn't the same as playing live."

"If they're only on Patti now, what time will I go on?"

Michael glanced at his watch. "It's around five. We'll probably go until midnight. I want you to do all the harmonies and double your lead vocal, so I'd like to have you start by ten."

"I don't know all the parts." She started to panic.

He pulled her gently against his side. "Honey, they can punch you in a line at a time."

Time passed quickly, and before Cheri knew it, she was inside the vocal booth adjusting her headphones.

"Sing the first verse while we play the tracks through your headphones." She couldn't see the engineer through the bright light's reflection on the glass.

Cheri winced as her voice overpowered the instrumental tracks. She stopped, halfway through the verse. "Can you turn me down a little?" She pointed to her headphones.

"Sure. Let's try it again."

After a while, Cheri became used to the feel of the lightweight headphones and the sound of her own voice layered on different tracks.

"We're ready for the lead vocals, Cheri. Let's start with 'Reckless Love.'"

She closed her eyes and lost herself in the melody. She sang it three times and the engineer picked the best two to keep. "Doubling" he called it.

She finished the song by midnight.

"Cheri, can you hang out while we do a rough mix of the vocals? We need to patch up a few lines."

"Sure." She took off her headphones.

"Come on in and listen."

She sat with them in the engineer's booth, Michael by her side. After listening to the completed track, they went through it piece by piece and had her sing where the phrasing didn't quite match.

"Okay, we're through with you."

She walked out into the hall while Michael talked with the engineers. After a moment, he stuck his head out the door.

"Could you go get Ria? We need her for the solo."

She found her asleep in the musicians' lounge. Shaking Ria's shoulder gently, Cheri woke her up.

"Ria, they need you now."

She sat up, rubbing her eyes. "Thanks, Cheri." She stared at her a moment, her green eyes slightly bloodshot. "Cheri?"

"Yeah?"

"I . . . I'm really sorry. About Michael, I mean."

"Hey, forget it. Now go out there and burn it up."

Ria smiled, suddenly looking much more attractive. "All right!"

THEY WERE BACK in the studio a few nights later.

"I feel like an old pro at this," Rachel said as she plugged her bass into input number seven.

"We need you in number twelve this time, Rachel." The engineer seemed amused.

"I *felt* like an old pro." She grimaced. Everyone laughed.

Cheri was glad Michael had suggested one of her newer songs, "More than Destiny," for the demo. Later in the evening, as she stepped into the vocal booth, she wondered if he'd suspected she'd written it for him. He wasn't with them tonight. He'd had to go see a new band playing out in the valley.

When they reached lead vocals, she knew she'd never sounded better.

"Let's try a take all the way through." Their engineer's voice was endlessly patient.

As she began to sing, the images in her mind brought color and feeling to her vocals. Cheri remembered so many things about Michael: the utter concentration on his face when he watched a band perform, the laughter in his dark eyes as he teased her about her cooking, the passion etched into his features as he made love to her and gave her everything.

The emotion she brought to the lyrics was powerful and true as she finished the second verse.

Ria's guitar caught the last note of the verse and continued the melody. Eight bars later, Cheri heard the final chords signaling the key change. She closed her eyes and breathed in, Michael's image clear in her mind. Then she started to sing, and her heart felt as if it were melting, flowing up out of her mouth and into song.

You've seen me through the deepest, longest night.
My darkness clears; I'm headed toward the light.
Your love gave me much more than destiny.

The last note faded sweetly, then she opened her eyes and grinned. The engineer's voice was excited as he called down to her over the speakers.

"That's a keeper!"

DURING THE DAYS THAT FOLLOWED their demo tape, Cheri felt a curious letdown, a diminishing of energy. She talked with Michael about her feelings, and he assured her she was quite normal and right on schedule. He found most artists felt depressed after finishing a demanding project.

Early one evening, as she was watering the begonias and roses in the front yard, Cheri realized what she was feeling had to do with more than the tape.

It wasn't hard for her to recognize the first, tentative stirrings of depression. She slept a little longer, didn't take as much time with her appearance. She stopped writing and waited impatiently for Michael to come home each night. He was her lifeline to the real world. It seemed her day truly began the moment he walked in the door and she asked him how his day had been.

Noticing she'd been watering the same plant for the last three minutes, Cheri pulled the hose away and began to sprinkle the lawn. What was the matter with her?

If she was honest with herself, it all came down to one question: *What did Michael see in her*? She could understand their professional relationship. Since they'd recorded the demo, Michael had sent it out to the major labels and had assured her it was only a matter of time. The band practiced faithfully three times a week for four or five hours, and Cheri managed to drag herself out of her black mood long enough to give rehearsals her care and concentration. They were improving, she was sure of it. Michael had made suggestions about their image, what they wanted to project onstage. Tough Cookie had opted for the "bad girl" look, all black clothing and lots of cocky energy.

But the personal level of her life confused Cheri most. Life went on much as it had since February. Spring had faded into summer. Cheri and Michael lived together companionably, yet she felt she was walking on eggs.

She had come to respect Michael and his work. Cheri had never seen anyone who could so effortlessly connect the right group with the right label, the right studio, the right producer. He knew everyone in the music industry, had superb instincts as to who would work well with whom. A curious mixture of high-powered business energy and sensitivity, Michael was never too busy to take a phone call, talk over a problem, reassure a frightened musician, try to find a workable solution.

She was amazed by everything he did. In the face of such assured professionalism, Cheri felt totally inadequate. No matter how many times she talked to Glenda, she couldn't seem to shake these feelings. On top of everything else, he'd allowed her to move in, and found joy and satisfaction in making love with her. He seemed content. And Cheri found herself waiting to see how long it would last.

She had to do something to take her mind off her fears. That afternoon, in a flurry of activity, she pushed herself into finishing the gardening, making lasagna, and straightening up the living room.

Two hours later, when she glanced at the clock, she knew Michael would be home within the hour. What to do till then? She knew he was worried about her not working on new material, so she got out one of her tapes and slipped it into the cassette player. A melody filled the air, almost complete. She'd been working on it with little success.

Songs came in different ways. Sometimes a lyric, sometimes a bit of melody. Whatever way it approached her, Cheri had enough experience to know she had to catch it on paper before it eluded her. She listened to the beginning of the melody several times before more began to take shape. Getting out her staff paper, she began to transpose notes in her head to the sheet before her.

She was so engrossed she barely heard Michael come in the door. When he touched her shoulder and kissed the back of her neck, she jumped.

"Michael!"

He looked tired. Taking off his jacket, he sat down on the couch next to her and stretched out his legs.

Cheri jumped up and turned off the tape, then came back to the couch. "Hard day?"

He had shut his eyes, but now he opened one. "You could have left the tape on. I like the melody."

"It's okay; I have most of it down. Now I just need some words."

"They'll come." He reached behind and ran his fingers through his hair, then down to the back of his neck. "It's good to see you working again."

"It feels good. I made lasagna for you."

He smiled. "It smells good." He was awkwardly trying to massage the back of his neck.

"Let me. Sit down there." Motioning him to the floor, she scooted over to the side of the couch until she was sitting above him, his shoulders resting against her thighs. Running her palms through his thick hair, she eased his head back into her lap. "Just relax."

As gently as she could, she began to knead his neck and shoulders. The muscles were bound tightly, hard knots of tension. He sighed, and she could feel the tension beginning to leave his body. She worked his muscles loose, one by one, loving the feel of his warm skin underneath her fingers, loving this small amount of comfort she could bring him.

Several minutes later, when he seemed totally relaxed, Cheri moved to get up, only to realize he'd fallen asleep. Smiling, she smoothed the dark hair away from the planes of his face and studied the man she loved.

If she had to sum up Michael in one sentence, Cheri would have said: Here is a man who cares passionately. Michael persevered, made his own opportunities, took chances, made decisions. He tried to do the best for his people. Funny how, until tonight, she'd never thought how exhausting that could be.

She felt totally confident being managed by him. But not loving him. Cheri touched his cheek gently, ran her fingernail lightly over the slight stubble on his jawline.

She'd never realized it was possible to love someone so much it hurt. She loved Michael with an intensity that was frightening to her. The pleasure he gave her made her that much more vulnerable to the pain.

He moved slightly, turned his head so his cheek rested against her knee. Her leg was starting to fall asleep, but Cheri didn't move.

As the light in the living room slowly faded to a deeper blue, she sat in silence with Michael.

THEY ATE DINNER LATE. The lasagna was slightly burned, but Michael scraped away the darker part and declared it was the best he'd ever had. They drank a lot of wine and laughed, then gave the leftovers to the dogs.

Much later, in their queen-sized bed, Cheri watched Michael as he read over a contract. Totally unaware of her scrutiny, he was obviously immersed in some legal detail. Cheri stretched against the cool percale sheet and was content simply to observe him.

Twenty minutes later, he put the document back into his briefcase and took off his reading glasses. Settling back into the pillows, he glanced over at her and raised his arm.

Wanting to please him, she slid to his side willingly,

snuggled against his body, put her cheek against his chest.

They rested for several seconds in silence, content to be close. Michael reached out and turned off the light and the bedroom was plunged into darkness.

His voice sounded disembodied when he finally spoke. "Cheri, what's wrong?"

Without thinking, she replied, "Nothing."

He sighed, then turned toward her. "Tell me."

She touched his face, reassuring herself it was Michael beside her. "I just don't have any energy."

He kissed her gently, smoothed her hair in a gesture meant to comfort. "You seem depressed."

She could almost hear Glenda's voice. *Trust him.*

She nodded. "Yes."

"Are you worried about the demo?" He was going to let her tell him in her own way after all.

It hadn't been on her mind. She contemplated using it as an excuse but couldn't do it. "No."

"Is it something I can help you with?"

She shook her head. "I think it's something I have to do myself."

"Does it involve me?" His voice sounded strange.

She swallowed at the sudden tightening of her throat, felt her chin tremble. "Yes." It was barely a whisper.

His arm loosened slightly and he raised himself up on his elbow. "Are you unhappy living here?"

"No!" The sound was anguished as it exploded from her throat. How could she make Michael realize living with him had been the happiest time of her life?

"Can you tell me about it?"

The perfect opening. Even in the dark, she was afraid to see disgust in his eyes. But she had to try.

She took his hand, played absently with the strong fingers, the muscled arm. "It's just...sometimes...I feel so inadequate."

GIVE YOUR HEART TO HARLEQUIN®

FREE!

Mail this heart today!

AND WE'LL GIVE YOU 4 FREE BOOKS, AND A FREE MYSTERY GIFT!

SEE INSIDE!

✺ IT'S A ✺

HARLEQUIN HONEYMOON
A SWEETHEART
OF A FREE OFFER!

FOUR NEW "HARLEQUIN AMERICAN ROMANCES" ™.— FREE!

Take a "Harlequin Honeymoon" with four exciting romances—yours FREE from Harlequin Reader Service. Each of these hot-off-the-presses novels brings you all the passion and tenderness of today's greatest love stories… your free passports to bright new worlds of love and foreign adventure!

But wait…there's <u>even more</u> to this great offer!

SPECIAL EXTRAS—FREE!

You'll get our free monthly newsletter, packed with news on your favorite writers, upcoming books, and more. Four times a year, you'll receive our members' magazine, Harlequin Romance Digest! <u>Best of all,</u> you'll <u>periodically receive our special-edition "Harlequin Bestsellers," yours to preview for ten days without charge</u>!

MONEY-SAVING HOME DELIVERY!

Join Harlequin Reader Service and enjoy the <u>convenience</u> of previewing four new books every month, delivered right to your home. Each book is yours for only $2.25— <u>25¢ less per book</u> than what you pay in stores! Great savings plus total convenience add up to a sweetheart of a deal for y<u>ou</u>!

START YOUR HARLEQUIN HONEYMOON TODAY— JUST COMPLETE, DETACH & MAIL YOUR FREE OFFER CARD!

HARLEQUIN READER SERVICE "NO-RISK" GUARANTEE
- There's no obligation to buy—and the free books and gifts remain yours to keep.
- You pay the lowest price possible and receive books before they appear in stores.
- You may end your subscription anytime—just write and let us know.

HARLEQUIN READER SERVICE
⊷§ FREE OFFER CARD ?⊶

**PLACE HEART
STICKER HERE**

**4 FREE
BOOKS**

**PLUS AN
EXTRA BONUS
"MYSTERY GIFT"!**

**FREE
HOME
DELIVERY**

☐ YES! Please send me my four
HARLEQUIN AMERICAN ROMANCES books, <u>free</u>, along with
my <u>free</u> Mystery Gift! Then send me four new
HARLEQUIN AMERICAN ROMANCES books every month, as
they come off the presses, and bill me at just $2.25 per book (25¢
less than retail), with no extra charges for shipping and handling.
If I am not completely satisfied, I may return a shipment and
cancel at any time. <u>The free books and Mystery Gift remain mine
to keep!</u>   154 CIA NA3P

FIRST NAME_____ LAST NAME_____
                              (PLEASE PRINT)

ADDRESS_____ APT._____

CITY_____

PROV./STATE_____ POSTAL CODE/ZIP_____

"Offer limited to one per household and not valid for present subscribers.
Prices subject to change."

PRINTED IN U.S.A

Limited Time Offer!

Make sure you get this great FREE OFFER— act today!

BUSINESS REPLY CARD

First Class   Permit No. 70   Tempe, AZ

Postage will be paid by addressee

Harlequin Reader Service®
2504 W. Southern Avenue
Tempe, Arizona 85282

NO POSTAGE
NECESSARY
IF MAILED
IN THE
UNITED STATES

"You shouldn't."

She felt a sudden flash of anger. *How would you know, Michael?* But she tamped it down as quickly as it had flared.

He kissed her again, teasing her mouth open slightly, touching her tongue with his. "There's nothing inadequate about you."

"But I feel you should have more. A woman who..." She couldn't finish the sentence. Cheri closed her eyes and the rest of her words came out in a rush. "Someone who can respond, who can feel, who doesn't freeze up every time you—"

"Is that how you really feel?" He sounded quietly amazed.

"Yes. I feel like—Michael, you deserve more than I can ever give you."

"Do you love me?" His voice was very quiet.

"So much." Her arms crept up around his neck and she kissed him softly. "But sometimes I think—"

"Cheri." Michael lay back down among the sheets, gently pulling her with him so their bodies stayed in close contact. "When I touch you, it isn't as if I'm touching just anybody. The feeling has to be there, and what I feel for you—" He broke off for a second, then began to caress her back. "It makes it special." His hand moved again, slowly, up her rib cage. When his long fingers closed around her breast, Cheri closed her eyes against the sensation.

Michael's breath was warm as it tickled her ear. "I know you're still scared. I know there are times you don't feel things as much as you'd like to. But I don't love you any less." His thumb gently rubbed the tip of her breast. He kissed her, then whispered, "The reason I become aroused is because I'm touching *you.* You're so much more to me than a sexual object."

"Michael." Cheri felt herself dangerously close to

breaking. "You can't tell me a physical relationship isn't important."

"It's very important," he whispered as his hand glided down the smooth skin of her stomach to rest gently, intimately, between her thighs. "But it isn't everything. And it isn't the only reason I love you."

She put her hand over his. "Why do you love me?" She gave him her soul with the question, and trembled in anticipation.

He moved then, shifted both his hands until he held her by the waist. Easing her gently on top of him, he threaded his fingers through her hair and held her face in his palms.

"I don't know if I can put it into words. But I'll try. I think what I first fell in love with was something my professional instincts recognized. When I saw you onstage that first night—Cheri, I see a lot of bands, and ninety percent just can't cut it. There has to be something special to make an act come to my attention. To make me *want* to represent them. There was so much honest emotion packed into the way you sang! I felt as if I'd been hit by a brick." He laughed then, and she could feel his body shake slightly underneath hers.

After a moment, Michael continued. "When I met you, you were genuine. When I first took you out to dinner and we talked, I found myself hoping it was the real you."

Cheri could feel herself growing cold. *Real? Genuine? Oh, Michael.*

"I meet so many people in the business who just aren't all there. You were a nice change." His fingers moved lazily down her back to cup her bottom and pull her closer. "After you told me what happened to you—"

"Michael—" *Tell him now.*

"Wait a minute. After you told me, I admired you

even more. To have gone through it and not become bitter. I can never know what that was like for you, Cheri. I've had some tough times in business, but I've never had my physical body violated, my soul." He pulled her tighter against him with one hand, continued to caress her hair with the other. "I fell in love with you because I'd never met anyone like you. Because when I hear you sing, it makes me so happy I can barely breathe. Because I look forward to coming home and having you here, sharing the day with you. Because you remind me of a little kid when you get enthusiastic about a song or a person or an idea."

She was crying now, had buried her head against his shoulder.

"I don't care if we never make love again. I just love you. And nothing's ever going to change my feelings for you."

CHERI LAY AWAKE a long time afterward, listening to the steady sound of his breathing, watching the rise and fall of his chest. Michael was a sound sleeper and rarely moved around in bed once he found a comfortable position. Cheri knew she had wakened him several times as she restlessly tossed and turned, but he never seemed to mind.

I don't care if we never make love again. I just love you. And nothing's ever going to change my feelings for you. But what if she told him the truth? Would he still love her, still believe in her? She'd come so close to telling him tonight. But something still held her back. She didn't know what.

Michael muttered in his sleep and she turned her attention back to his sleeping form. One arm was thrown up above his head, the other rested outside the sheet by his side. The moonlight filtered in through the window above the bed, turning the white sheets silver.

Cheri burrowed back into the warmth of the covers, but turned her head on the pillow so she could still see him. *Someday, Michael, I'm going to surprise you and you'll know, even though I may not show it physically, I always want you emotionally.*

For a moment the darkness in the bedroom seemed almost threatening, and Cheri reached over and put her hand on Michael's shoulder. The warmth of his skin, the feel of his muscle, relaxed her and she closed her eyes, and tried to sleep.

She was almost asleep when the sound of the sheet's rustling captured her attention. She opened her eyes, leaned up on her elbow slightly, then watched, amazed, as Michael's hand moved slowly downward toward his thighs. It was a purely instinctual movement, totally unconscious. As she watched him, she realized he was intensely aroused.

A strange sensation washed over her as she watched this purely masculine display of sexuality. His hand touched lightly, once, twice, then he sighed and shifted position so he lay on his side. His hand moved up, above his head, then he settled his body deeper into the mattress.

Intrigued, she moved closer, then lifted the sheet and began to study his body. Hard and virile, it was as if each muscle lay waiting. Expectant. His breathing was a soft, intimate sound in the silent bedroom.

Hesitating only slightly, Cheri moved her hand until she touched his stomach. Her fingers almost recoiled, but she forced herself until her palm lay against his flat stomach. Satiny skin covered powerful flesh. Willing herself to go on, she slid her hand to the potent proof of his masculinity. She was surprised to find that touching him excited her.

He sighed and she almost took her hand away. Then he moved in his sleep, bringing his body closer to her touch. She pushed him gently with her free hand. With the willingness of a small child, he rolled over onto his back.

Pulling away the sheet, she ran her fingers lightly over his chest, up to his face. She touched his cheek, but he crinkled his eyes tightly shut and turned his face away from her. Leaning back on her haunches, Cheri hesitated.

She wanted to make love to him. To give him back some of the pleasure he'd given her. Easing the covers completely away from the length of his body, she bunched them at the foot of the bed. Then, placing a hand on either side of his chest, she slowly climbed on top of him, trying not to waken him.

It was impossible. Cheri watched as his eyes fluttered open, a sleepy, dazed look in them. Before he could fully comprehend what was happening, she shifted her hips and slowly lowered herself over his aroused body, making them one.

That woke Michael up in a hurry. He grasped her hips and groaned, then put his arm around her neck, drew her head down and began to kiss her. In his half-awake state, he was more demanding than usual. It was what Cheri wanted: more than anything else, she wanted to please him as any other woman would.

The kiss deepened as he began to move inside her. Then instinct seemed to take over and Cheri felt both of them become caught up in a brief, intense storm of passion. Grasping his shoulders, she accepted his thrusts with her own, gave him as much as he usually gave her. They moved together with a tense, erotic rhythm, each totally absorbed with the other.

Then it changed. Michael slowly shifted the rhythm. Moving more slowly, he was in control now, seemed determined she receive as much sensation as possible. When she felt she could bear no more, he stopped and simply urged her down so their bodies touched their whole length.

"What a nice surprise," he whispered as his lips touched her eyes, cheeks, temples, then moved back to her mouth. It was a slow, unhurried, sweet kiss. It melted her, made her feel so close to him.

They lay quietly, though Cheri's legs trembled. It was an unbelievable feeling, holding this much masculine sexual power inside her body. He moved slightly inside her and she breathed in sharply, then he playfully tugged at a strand of her hair to bring her face closer to his.

"What do you want?" he whispered.

She wished she could pretend she hadn't heard his softly whispered question. All her old doubts began to flow through her body, freezing her.

"Honey, it's Michael. I want you to feel good." His lips moved to her ear, down her neck. "What do you want me to do?"

She didn't answer. Couldn't.

"Please trust me." His whisper was a poignant plea.

Slowly, very slowly, she reached up and took his hand in hers. With only the slightest hesitation, she moved their twined fingers down the length of their bodies, then shifted her hips so there was a small space where they joined. Directing him, she placed his hand on her most sensitive part.

He brushed the hair away from her flushed face with his other hand, his fingers tender. "Show me. Show me how."

Cheri felt a single tear begin to slide down her cheek. He traced it with a gentle finger, then sighed. "Oh, baby, don't cry."

"I just wish—I wish it would just *happen*." She swallowed, so ashamed. *Ugly. Freak.*

"We have all the time in the world. Tell me what you want. Show me."

She did. As he stroked her, he whispered loving words, the sound of his voice relaxing her.

And then things changed. Sensation began to pile upon sensation. *Too fast.* Cheri tried to pull away, scared, but Michael held her close to his caresses, refusing to let her move.

"Michael—" Her voice was tight. Afraid.

"Oh, baby, it'll be good. I promise."

And it was.

Incredible sensation shimmered through her body, waves of pure color and heat catching her up and pressing her closer to him. She heard Michael groan but the sound seemed muted, far away. It was as if every cell in her body had become incredibly sensitized.

Cheri fell forward onto the hard muscles of his chest, curled her body against his and put her cheek against the hollow of his neck. He stroked her back gently, pressing her body closer to his.

Several minutes passed before either of them spoke. Cheri raised her head slowly and put her lips to his ear.

"Michael?"

"Hmm?" He sounded pleased with himself.

"Thank you."

He turned his head toward her, a smile on his lips. "It was no hardship."

"I never knew..."

"I know."

It was a night of long, slow loving, and Cheri felt every part of her body, even her soul, had been touched by love. She responded without conscious volition, startled at how easy it had become.

Later, wrapped in each other's arms, after much kissing and caressing, they talked.

"Are you all right?"

"Uh-huh." She burrowed deeper against his chest.

"Did I hurt you?"

She shook her head. But when his hand slipped between her thighs, she winced.

"What's wrong?"

She reached down and took his hand in her own. "Just tender, I guess."

"I'm sorry."

"I'm not." She smiled up at him, his face clearly visible in the early-morning light. "Michael, I wrote and sang all those songs about love and I never knew what it was really like."

He kissed her forehead. "I'd give you more if I could."

She began to laugh, then stopped, her body still too tender for any more movement.

"Darling Michael," she said, cupping his face in her hands and looking deep into his dark eyes, her heart set free at last. "I don't think I could survive it if you did."

Chapter Eight

"Why don't you come down to the office and meet me for lunch?" Michael's voice was soft, intimate, for her ears alone.

"What's in it for me?" she teased. Cheri loved the new easiness between them.

"You'll never know unless you get your butt down here." She could almost picture him grinning over the phone.

"Oh, yeah?" She paused for a split second, then capitulated. "What time?"

"I won't be out of my meeting until one. Why don't you come by then?"

"Sounds good."

Driving east on the Santa Monica freeway, Cheri wondered at how much she'd grown in the last two weeks. Since loving Michael, she'd made an about-face and begun to rebuild her emotional life. So much had come bubbling out of her. And he'd accepted it all, without reservations. She had told him about Glenda, about her twice-weekly sessions. She'd thought about going to a support group, and Cheri felt that might be her next step. She had even let him know how feelings of inadequacy had haunted her most of her life.

And Michael had been wonderful. He had listened patiently, soothed her, told her how much he loved her.

He had shown her as well. That evening two weeks earlier had released a great outpouring of feeling in both of them. A day rarely went by when they didn't make love. *Making up for lost time,* she thought with a smile as she exited and drove north toward Beverly Hills.

Carole, Michael's secretary, greeted her with a smile. A tall redhead, Carole looked as if she'd walked off the pages of *Vogue.* But behind the dazzling smile, the deep-green eyes, was a quick, analytical mind, and a loyalty to her boss that spanned seven years.

"Michael should be out shortly," Carole said. "Would you like some coffee, Cheri?"

She shook her head. These days she flew so high she didn't need caffeine.

Michael's office was soothing, done in blues and grays. His windows looked out over tree-lined streets, where people strolled and shopped, browsed and kept lunch dates. Cheri walked to the window and looked out at the people. For the first time in her life, she felt a connection to them, knew what it was to be in love. To be happy.

She studied the scene outside until she heard a familiar voice call her name.

"Cheri! What are you doing here?" Rachel.

"I'm having lunch with Michael."

"He told me to meet him here at one. There's something he wants to tell us." Rachel settled herself down on a sleek gray sofa. "You look good. What's it like, living with the big M?"

Cheri laughed. She missed Rachel. Even though they talked on the phone almost every other day and saw each other at aerobics classes and rehearsals, it wasn't the same.

"I'm sure I could make *millions* from the *Enquirer*," she replied, enjoying their old joke.

"That good, huh?" Rachel drawled. Cheri felt herself turning a furious shade of red and her friend let out a hoot. "*That* good?"

Carole looked over at them and Cheri glanced away. "Rachel!"

Her friend grinned. "You look bright-eyed and bushy-tailed. Just keep that same little glow when we play at Paradise."

Before Cheri could reply, Michael opened the door. "Come in."

Once they were inside his office, he swept Cheri up in his arms and gave her an affectionate kiss. She knew he would only do this in front of a close friend like Rachel. Michael kept their business relationship serious.

"Sit down." He waved them both into the black leather chairs that flanked his desk. "I have good news."

"What?" Rachel sat at the edge of her seat.

"I've convinced one of the A & R men from Blue Lightning Records to come out to Paradise this weekend and see you perform."

Rachel simply stared at him, for once at a loss for words. Cheri felt her stomach begin to tighten. This was it. Everything Tough Cookie had worked for over the past six years was to be bound up in one emotion-packed evening.

Blue Lightning Records was one of the most innovative, creative labels in Los Angeles. They had produced many acts Cheri admired. And once a band was signed on, they rarely walked away. Blue Lightning delivered what they promised.

"I had lunch with Ted the other day," Michael continued, and Cheri knew he had to be referring to the A & R man. "He was impressed with the vocals on the demo, and he liked what he heard of the original material." Michael smiled. "He flipped when I told him you had more originals. In fact," he said as he leaned forward and placed his elbows on the desk in front of him, "I'm pretty sure it's just a matter of seeing if you can deliver onstage."

"Oh, we will," Rachel breathed, her hands clenched into excited fists. "We will."

"I have no doubts. I just wanted you to know so you can be at your best."

Cheri opened her mouth to speak, but Michael held up his hand. He gave her a look of apology. "The last thing I wanted to discuss with both of you is that I've arranged for several other A & R men to be there, so it isn't all riding on what Ted thinks. But I remember—" he looked toward Rachel "—when we discussed goals, you told me you loved the way Blue Lightning put records together. I thought you all had a right to know. Patti and Michelle couldn't make it today, so I'm trusting the two of you to get in touch with them. Ria is running late."

Rachel excused herself soon after, and as the door closed behind her, Cheri stood up, ran around the desk and threw herself into Michael's arms.

"Thank you! Thank you! Thank you!" Now she could truly make him proud of her.

"Hey." He held her tightly, stroking her hair. "You did the work. All I did was make a few phone calls."

THE BAND WENT ON before Cheri had a chance to get too nervous. The crowd at Paradise was enormous, the lights blinding. She was aware of a few catcalls and groans of disappointment as they stepped onstage, but she remained calm, almost haughty, as she lowered her mike stand and checked her equipment. Once she heard the opening beats of "Reckless Love," she faced the audience with bravado and let the first note soar out over their heads.

The pace was relentless. They barely finished one song before Patti started the next. Halfway through, Cheri was pushing soaking-wet hair out of her face, but her voice was still clear and true, emotion-packed and strong. She sang for Michael; her feelings came out of every hurt she'd ever experienced. There was no holding back, no playing safe anymore. She was a woman of intense emotion; she knew it showed in her phrasing, the way she reached for notes, the lyrics she'd chosen to write.

At Michael's suggestion, they saved "More Than Destiny" for last. As Ria began to play the opening melody, Cheri felt sudden tension twist her stomach. They had a tough audience. She was sure she'd won their respect, but how would they react to a song about love? Their other songs, like "Reckless Love" and "Desire," dealt with love gone wrong, a popular theme in women's rock 'n' roll songs. How would they react to a song celebrating the sweeter sides of that emotion?

Before she had time to think, she was singing the opening lines.

I was destined for sorrow,
Heartache all I ever knew....

Cheri continued to sing, giving her performance every ounce of courage and power she had. The emotion came freely, with greater intensity than she'd had in the studio. She knew about love now.

As they moved into the chorus, she still couldn't tell how it was affecting the audience. Total silence met each note as it left her throat and shimmered out over the silent, black animal beyond the footlights.

Suddenly she wished she hadn't decided to sing the last verse a cappella. It was risky to sing without the backup of the band. But there was nothing to be done.

'Cause, Baby, when you take me in your arms

Each note was pitched perfectly, remarkable because she had to rely on her own ear and not on the instruments.

There isn't any way I'll come to harm.
You raise a passion deep inside of me.

She thought of Michael and a soft, secret smile played over her face. Her emotions gave her strength.

You've seen me through the deepest, longest
    night.

A rich feeling of tenderness came over her, and for a moment she felt she wanted to gather up the entire audience in her arms.

My darkness clears; I'm headed toward the light.

Still, total silence. But now she was unafraid.

Your love gave me much more than destiny.

The last note rang rich and true over the silent audience. Slowly, she let it fade away.
Total silence.
For just a moment she felt she couldn't breathe. Then a voice out of the crowd called out, "All right!"
She smiled as one voice was joined by two, then a few more, until a deafening cacophony of clapping and

whistling filled the air. Staring out over the audience, she willed her thought to find him.

Thank you, Michael. We did it.

HE MET HER BACKSTAGE in the dressing room with bottles of champagne and roses for each band member.

"Ted wants to meet with me tomorrow."

"Wa-hoo!" Rachel tossed a cup of champagne at Patti and she screamed. Cheri laughed at the sight of Patti's hair, all wet and spiky. Excitement bubbled over and enveloped them all.

As the noise became too loud to talk over, Michael put his mouth next to her ear. "I've got to stay through Bad Boys' performance. Do you mind waiting? Or do you want to go home with Rachel?"

Before Cheri could decide, Rachel touched her shoulder. "Party at my house tonight. I expect to see both of you there—don't you dare refuse! All right?" Not giving them a chance to reply, she shouldered her leather bag, picked up her bass case, and walked out the dressing-room door.

Cheri looked up at Michael. "I guess I stay."

He kissed her quickly, then hurried out toward the stage.

"WHERE'S YOUR CAR?" Cheri asked as they made their way through the crowded parking lot. Bad Boys had put on quite a show. It was much later in the evening than she'd expected.

"Right over there."

Her eyes widened as she saw a sleek black limousine with tinted windows. Before she had time to think, a chauffeur opened one of the rear doors and Michael helped her inside.

Once the car began to move, he locked the doors and pushed a button. A panel of thick tinted glass came down and sealed them away from the driver in front.

It was an experience in luxury. Deep leather seats, a built-in bar, tinted windows, soft carpeting. They were snugly cocooned in their own private world. Cheri ran her hand over the leather seat, let her booted feet sink into the deep carpet. She touched the bar tentatively. She'd never seen anything like this in her entire life.

"This is gorgeous."

"I'm glad you like it." Reaching over to the bar, Michael swiftly uncorked a bottle of Dom Perignon with ease. He filled two crystal goblets and handed one to her.

"To you, Cheri. For all the hard work behind the dream come true."

She felt her eyes begin to fill. He was too good to her. "Oh, Michael!" In an attempt to ward off tears, she tried to joke. "I could get used to this."

"I hope you do."

They drank in silence, the smooth motion of the limousine almost hypnotizing. When Cheri finished her first glass, Michael poured her another.

"I'll get drunk." She smiled at him, wrinkling her nose as bubbles stung her face.

"We have plenty of time before we get to Rachel's. I told the driver to take the long way."

"How long is long?" She took another sip of the French champagne, then laughed as the bubbles tickled her nose.

He glanced at his watch. "We'll be in here for close to an hour."

When he poured her a third glass, Cheri smiled up at him. "Why do I get the impression you're going to seduce me?"

He laughed. "You have good instincts."

She felt her heart begin to beat slightly faster "Here? Won't someone see us?"

He was gentle now, teasing her. "Ms. Bradley! Don't tell me you've never made love in a limousine!"

She hesitated, then glanced in the direction of their driver, behind a wall of tinted glass.

"The great thing about limos," Michael continued, "is that we can see out but no one can see in. At least that's the way this model works."

"Are you sure?" She could feel her inhibitions lessening as she sipped her fourth glass of champagne. Suddenly she wanted to be wild and daring with Michael, wanted to do all the things she'd missed out on.

"Would I lie to you?"

"Oh, I don't know." She looked up at him from under her lashes. Flirting. Teasing. Delighting in her feminine power.

"Yes?" He kissed her softly, then touched her chin gently with his fingers.

"Yes." She wound her free hand around the back of his neck and leaned toward him until her breasts touched his chest.

"Yes." He barely breathed the word as his mouth came down over hers.

"WHERE WERE YOU? The party's almost over." Rachel came racing to the door as she saw them walk in, her blond hair flying behind her.

"Business, as usual." Michael gave Rachel a quick hug and followed her into the kitchen.

Cheri, right behind him, was convinced everyone knew what had really held them up. Their bodies were scented with sensuality, her lips were tender, she'd barely managed to squeeze herself back into her black leather jeans. Though she'd brushed her hair and touched up her makeup, she was certain everyone could see the fluid softness of her body.

But she soon forgot her embarrassment back in her old familiar kitchen as Rachel led her toward a table piled high with food.

"Patti made the quiche; Ria made brownies. I put together the fruit salad and a regular salad and there's red or white wine."

"No wine, just food," she said, remembering the champagne.

She ate while Rachel talked excitedly about the evening, about the A & R man, about the possibility of signing with Blue Lightning Records, about how the concert had gone.

When she was finished, Cheri put her paper plate in the garbage and wandered into the living room with Rachel. She spotted Michael in a corner, deep in conversation with an excited Ria. The sight didn't bother her at all.

Patti joined the group in the corner, began to talk to Ria. Cheri watched Michael glance up, then slowly search the room until his eyes came to rest on her. He smiled, a slow, intimate expression for her alone. Above the noise of the stereo and people talking, he mouthed the words, "I love you."

"Me, too," she replied, then slowly began to thread through the crowd until she stood by his side.

THREE DAYS LATER Cheri was out back hosing the patio, the stereo blasting, when Michael burst through the back door. She was so surprised she almost turned the hose on him.

"Michael, what are you doing home so early—" She stopped talking as he grabbed her in a bear hug and lifted her completely off the ground. She dropped the hose and it went wild, snaking around the cement and spraying them both.

"Michael!" Her hair was soaked and she pounded

playfully on his chest. He set her down and they stared at each other as water sprayed all around.

"I'm wondering exactly how I go about congratulating you. Ted decided to sign the band."

"Ted—" Suddenly she realized exactly what Michael was talking about. "Blue Lightning?" As his grin widened, her voice grew higher and more excited. *"Blue Lightning!"*

"You've got yourself a recording contract, Cheri." He wrapped his arms around her and pulled her close against his wet shirtfront. "I'm so proud of you."

She couldn't stay still. "When do we start? How soon do we go back to the studio? When can we—"

"Whoa!" He threw back his head and laughed, then began to take off his jacket. It was soaked. Next, he peeled off his shirt. "I'm going to go inside and change before I die of pneumonia; then we'll talk about this like two sensible adults." But he was grinning.

Cheri grabbed his arm. "I don't *want* to be sensible, I want to talk right now!" She ran over and turned off the water, then trotted back to Michael. Her feet made little squish-squish noises on the wet cement.

Michael sat down in one of the deck chairs. "You'll be going into the studio within a month, after the lawyer and I look over the contract they gave us." He frowned. "Did you ever see about getting a lawyer?"

"We can just use the same one you do."

"Uh-uh. That's not good business."

"Michael, I trust you."

"I know you do, darling. But I'll give you the name of another good attorney."

"How long will it take to get everything settled?"

"Not long. Ted agreed to get the contract to me as soon as possible so I can look it over. I'm not going to do anything to jeopardize the deal, I'm simply going to make sure you get what's rightfully yours."

Cheri thought of all the times she'd overheard Michael in one-sided business discussions over the phone. She didn't envy the person on the receiving end. Michael drove a tough bargain.

"You're shaking." He stood up and put his arm over her shoulder. "Let's go inside."

Though Michael insisted he should take her out to celebrate, Cheri fixed dinner at home. She knew Michael ate out too often in his line of work. A night at home gave him an opportunity to relax.

Later that night in bed, she couldn't stop talking about the recording contract.

"I'm going to have to gag you if I expect to get any sleep tonight," Michael grumbled. But it was clear he wasn't mad, simply amused.

Cheri jumped out of bed and brought back a note pad and pencil. "I'll have to start thinking about which songs we should use on the album."

"The company decides that."

She felt her heart plop into her stomach. "You mean I don't get any say?"

"We'll see. I may be able to put something into the contract.

"Thank you, Michael." She flung down the pencil and pad and launched herself at him, throwing her arms around his neck. "You're so good to me."

He laughed softly as he reached up and turned off the light.

CHERI COULDN'T SLEEP that night; she was too keyed up. As she listened to Michael's breathing, she restlessly pleated the bedspread between her fingers, watched the patterns of moonlight on the fabric.

She thought about turning on her night-light and reading, but found she was content simply to lie still and think. As simply as a scale, a thought flitted into her mind.

When did I stop fearing the dark? Back at the house she'd shared with Rachel, she'd always slept with the light on in the bathroom, with her clock radio playing softly. Buffy, who now preferred sleeping outside in the doghouse with Charlie, had previously been a warm and comforting lump at the foot of her bed.

To keep away the monsters, she thought, then was startled to find quick, painful tears fill her eyes. The pain was always there; it never went completely away. Sometimes she felt as if there was so much inside her head she didn't dare close her eyes.

She looked back at Michael's still, relaxed form underneath the sheets and reassured herself. *This must be what it's like to be married.* Cheri had never thought of marriage as something she wanted. But with Michael, everything had turned out differently.

You can't have him. The thought came softly, slyly, out of her subconscious.

If he asked me— But she knew her answer would be no. Michael was too special.

Restless now, she got out of bed and quietly padded into the living room, turning on the light. As she studied the room, she thought about how many happy times she'd spent there with Michael. When she'd first moved in, they'd gone on a rampage of decorating and renovating. She'd loved walking along Melrose Avenue with him, picking out the perfect oak chest, or an intricate pair of candlesticks. The soft blue of the walls looked like the sky on a sunny day, the small print that covered the sofa and draped the windows gave the room a country cottage look.

She sat down at the baby grand piano in the far corner and turned on a small overhead light. Playing a few notes tentatively, she began to work out a melody that had come into her head earlier that evening.

It was a slow, painstaking process. A few notes played, a few notated on the staff paper. She wished she had more technical expertise, but Cheri usually relied on Rachel for the knowledge she lacked. Deep inside, it made her feel ignorant. She wished she'd had time to enjoy school instead of simply racing through it on her way to nowhere.

Forget it. She closed her eyes tightly for a moment, then put the pencil down. Useless. Getting up, she went into the kitchen and poured herself a glass of apple juice.

And then it happened. Quickly, cleanly. Simply. The tune began as she took her first sip, then she set her glass down and raced to the piano. As she played quickly, the scratching of her pencil was the only other sound in the quiet room.

She wasn't aware of the time, as the room slowly began to lighten, sunrise colors bathing the pale walls. Cheri had just finished her arrangement when she looked up and saw Michael leaning in the doorway.

"Am I disturbing you?" he said.

"No." She wanted to share the discovery with him. Patting the piano bench, she motioned him over. "Michael, it came so quickly I couldn't believe it. It rarely happens this way for me."

"I bet it will more often with practice."

She blinked her eyes, squeezed the hand he gave her. What a good man. Always thinking the best.

"Can I hear it?"

She nodded, raised her hands over the keys, and slowly began to play. Delicate sounds filled the room, harmonies deepening, drawing away. Then the melody. Simple, something people would remember and whistle as they listened. A happy song, full of hope and wonder.

When she finished, she glanced up at him, everything in her universe contained in his face. He was smiling.

"Beautiful." He kissed her. "I'll see what I can do on the contract. That should be on the album."

As he walked into the kitchen, he called over his shoulder. "Do you want some coffee?"

"I'd love some. Michael," she called as she ran into the bedroom and began to pull on her sweat pants and T-shirt, "I'm going to the bakery to get some croissants. Do you want a chocolate one?"

"Okay. Wait a minute and I'll go with you."

She jogged into the kitchen, her heart feeling so light she thought she might explode with happiness. "No, I'm doing this for you. Just relax and start on your coffee." She ran out the front door, grabbing the Ferrari keys as she went.

As she started up the car, it seemed her entire world was lit by pale golden light, cleansing everything, making it whole. Another day with Michael. She could have a little more time with him, after all. She backed out of the driveway carefully.

By the time she arrived at the bakery, she was singing.

Two DAYS LATER Michael called her at home.

"Just a minute, let me turn down the stereo. I can't hear you." Once she'd done this, Cheri picked up the phone. "What were you saying?"

"I said I figured out how we're going to celebrate. I want you to be standing outside the door tonight at six, with bags packed for both of us."

"Where are we going?"

"It's a surprise. I've made all the arrangements, so don't call the airport."

"What about the dogs?"

"Rachel's agreed to house-sit. She'll be there at five-thirty. Give her your house key."

"Michael, this is ridiculous! Can't you at least give me a hint?"

He laughed. "Pack casual stuff. Make sure we both have our bathing suits."

She wanted to tease, to keep him on the phone. "Alaska?"

"Don't guess again!" He hung up.

Cheri practically burst with unanswered questions the rest of the day. Knowing Michael's penchant for outdoor activity, she included suntan oil, insect repellent and comfortable walking shoes for both of them.

Checking her watch, she drove to the local market and bought a jumbo bag of dog chow and some treats for Rachel. Back in the kitchen, she crammed everything into the refrigerator, along with a note fastened to the door. *Yes, Rachel, the chocolate chocolate-chip is all for you.*

At five-twenty, she saw the familiar orange VW turn into the driveway and she burst out the door.

"Rachel!"

"Hey, Cheri." Rachel extricated herself from behind the wheel and ran right into Cheri's hug. "I guess we're going to be stars after all." She laughed and adjusted her sun visor. "Blue Lightning, can you believe it?"

Rachel took her arm as both women headed toward the front door. "Before Michael gets here, fill me in on who, what, where—all I heard from him was that they signed us."

By the time Michael turned in the driveway and honked, Cheri had filled her friend in. As they loaded the suitcases into the trunk, Rachel called out, "Just bring her back in one piece, Mr. Stone, or you and I are *both* going to be out a lot of money!"

He laughed, then slammed the door and started up the engine.

Chapter Nine

"Can I ask where we're going yet?" Cheri got up from the plastic chair as Michael came back from the ticket counter where he'd picked up their tickets and checked their bags.

"Wait until you get to the gate." He was clearly enjoying the suspense as he took her arm and helped her through the crowd. "We want Gate 6B."

Cheri glanced at each gate's destination as they walked, and was relieved when they passed a sign that read "San Francisco." She'd follow Michael to the ends of the earth—but not there.

Now that she was sure where they *weren't* going, she couldn't wait for the last few steps. She broke free and ran ahead, then stood perfectly still, her mouth open, as she tried to register their destination.

Flight 800 to Honolulu, Hawaii.

She couldn't find any words.

He grinned. "One of my favorite spots. I can't wait to show it to you."

Once they were aboard and in their first-class seats, Cheri turned toward him. "Michael, what if anyone needs to reach you?"

"Carole has my itinerary, and I don't anticipate anything major happening. I thought we needed time together, alone."

After takeoff, an attractive flight attendant with blond hair opened a bottle of champagne.

"To a successful trip," Michael said as they touched glasses. Before they drank, he kissed her.

When he refilled her glass, Cheri leaned over and put her lips to his ear. "Michael?"

"What?"

She bit her lip to keep from laughing. "I think I want to apply for a membership in the mile-high club."

It took a moment for her comment to sink in, but when it did, Michael laughed so hard he spilled champagne all over his suit.

THEY SPENT THE NIGHT on the big island, then the next morning took off in a nine-seat twin-engine Cessna headed for Maui. Cheri had never flown in such a small plane, but she kept her fears to herself. And with Michael by her side, she wasn't really frightened.

They landed at Wailuku Airport, then picked up their rented car and drove almost four hours to the town of Hana, on the east side of Maui. The roads were primitive, rutted and narrow. By the time they reached Waianapanapa State Park, Cheri felt as if every bone in her body had been jolted out of place.

A slender Hawaiian woman wearing a brightly printed muumuu showed them to their cabin, and once they were inside and unpacked, Michael suggested she rest while he checked with his office.

But Cheri was too excited. Hawaii! She lay down for all of two minutes, then she was out on the front porch, looking up toward tropical trees and other foliage. The air was rich with moisture and the scent of growing plants, a far cry from the exhaust and pollution of Los Angeles.

She sat down on the front step, strangely exhilarated. She hadn't been sitting for a minute when a skinny, feral cat came silently out of the bushes. Cheri sat perfectly still, watching. As if by some silent signal, several other cats began to drift toward their cabin. Some sat in the sun and blinked their eyes, some lay down.

"I'll feed you tonight, after dinner," she promised. As she got up and dusted off the seat of her pants, two of the animals darted off into the bushes, but the first cat simply looked up and blinked.

Michael came back within half an hour and suggested they take a walk to the beach. They changed quickly, into shorts and T-shirts, then set off on the well-marked trail, the ocean in sight.

The black sand beach had intricate lava formations. The water looked too turbulent for swimming. Michael took her hand and they walked along the lava cliffs. Cheri could barely hear her own voice above the booming of the waves.

"How did you find out about this place?"

"My family used to camp here. Dad liked to get away from everything about three times a year, and this was one of his favorite spots." Michael shaded his eyes with his hand and looked out to sea. "He hated what happened to Honolulu. I don't think he's spent much time there, except on the way to somewhere else."

"You went camping with your family?" Cheri felt the familiar twinge, the sense of wishing her life had been different, come stealing over her again.

"Yeah. I loved it. Doug and I used to terrorize Gina, but she was a good sport about it. Then—" his mouth twisted with an amused expression "—we finally grew up and let her come along with us on our expeditions."

"Where did you used to go?" Cheri was fascinated at the thought of Michael as a little boy.

"I'm taking you there. To the tide pools. I'll bet you've never seen anything like it."

He was right. Incredible miniatures of ocean ecology,

the tide pools were teeming with life. Michael squatted down and pointed out each type of sea life to Cheri. Her favorite were the hermit crabs.

"They're so cute!" She leaned over, putting a steadying hand on Michael's shoulder, and watched a tiny crab scuttle along.

They explored the beach, walking silently, and Cheri felt the tension leaving her body. It was impossible to feel anxious in a place filled with such natural beauty—the black lava formations, the booming waves, the varied shades of blue in the ocean beyond.

"Can we swim?" She hugged her arms around her as she stared out at the waves.

"Not here. It's too rough. We'll go to Hana beach in the morning." He took her hand and swung it lightly between them. "This is the rough lava beach—aa. Tomorrow, at Hana beach, I'll show you the pahoehoe— the smooth lava."

They returned to their cabin late that afternoon, and Cheri fixed a light dinner from the food their landlady had stocked in the refrigerator. She didn't mind skipping fancy restaurants. Being with Michael was the reason for this trip. It made her happy they were camping together—just like a family.

She was careful to save some food for the cats outside, then sat on the porch and watched them as they ate.

"You are a hopeless soft touch." Michael's voice was gently caressing, teasing.

She turned her head toward him. "I just feel sorry for them."

He sat down next to her. "I'm sure they police the area and get enough to eat." He draped his arm around her and she leaned against his chest, enjoying the closeness.

He bent his head and kissed her on the side of the

neck. "It's too dark to go hiking, we can't go swimming on a full stomach...."

She smiled. "The possibilities are limited, I agree."

He moved his lips to the sensitive skin underneath her ear. "While you were fixing dinner I made up the bed."

"Are we sleeping in the bunk beds?" She loved to tease him. "Do you want the top or the bottom bunk?"

"I took the twin beds and pushed them together," he said, then kissed her cheek.

"I thought we could watch the sunset—" She shrieked as he stood and lifted her over his shoulder.

"Since subtle seduction doesn't seem to be working," he said, sounding as if he was trying very hard not to laugh, "I guess I'll have to use brute force."

She pummeled his back playfully. "Put me down, you bully!"

He did, once they reached the bedroom, and divested her of all her clothing in record time. They made love slowly, neither having a thing to do except be with each other, give each other pleasure.

Afterward, in the dark, curled up against Michael, Cheri felt at peace for the first time in as long as she could remember.

"Are you sorry?" Michael asked, lightly stroking her shoulder.

"For what?"

"Do you wish we'd gone somewhere less primitive?"

She shook her head. "No. I like having you all to myself."

He kissed her on the forehead. "I love being with you." He laughed softly. "I didn't want to share, either."

She fell asleep that night, her arms and legs entwined

in his, and dreamed of a young boy who raced through the tropical jungle and called it his own.

"WHY IS THE OCEAN SO LOUD?" she asked Michael over breakfast. Simple fare, hard-boiled eggs and fruit.

"There are natural arches in the lava that create blowholes. When the waves come rushing up, they go underneath into the caves and explode through the holes. Did you have trouble sleeping?"

"No. I feel terrific."

"Good." He pushed his empty plate away. "I'll do the dishes and then we'll get going. Be sure to bring the sunscreen lotion."

Hana turned out to be a charming town. Cheri especially liked the white mission church surrounded by palm trees. They stopped at the Hasegawa General Store for picnic supplies. It was a funny little store, shelves bulging with everything imaginable. The aisles were very narrow, and as Cheri explored them she had the feeling she had to hold her breath for fear of toppling something over.

Hana beach was much calmer than the beach by their cabin. The water felt silty against her skin, but Michael reassured her, explaining it was only volcanic ash. They swam and sunbathed, then ate their picnic lunch and relaxed. Cheri felt the complete primitive, running around in her bathing suit in their own little stretch of the world.

They carefully cleaned up all their picnic utensils, then Michael tucked the bag underneath his arm and held out his hand to help her up.

"Want to see a special place?"

She nodded.

They walked toward a pier, then took a trail to the right. Following the trail, Cheri almost bumped into Michael as he stopped. He didn't say anything, simply

pointed. She looked down and saw a small marker,
then bent slightly to read it. The marker simply said
Hana was the birthplace of King Kamehameha's favorite wife, Kahumanu.

"I knew you'd like it." Michael clearly saw the pleasure in her face.

She was deeply moved by this tiny monument, far
away on an island, commemorating a special, loving relationship.

"There's more." He took her hand.

They reached a secluded cove surrounded by huge
smooth stones. The water was a brilliant shade of turquoise, and lush vegetation surrounded it on all sides.

Cheri couldn't speak, could only stare at such natural
beauty. She followed Michael to the edge of the water,
then watched as he waded in.

"It's only waist-deep. And totally secluded. Come
in, you'll like it."

She followed him, the water closing around her legs
as warm as if it were from a bathtub. They walked
through the water until they came to a smooth flat
rock. Michael gave her a hand up, and they both
stretched out and lay in the sun.

It was a few minutes before either of them spoke.

"You know what I like about this place?" Michael's
breath tickled her ear. His shoulder was warm underneath her chin.

"What?"

"No phones. Privacy."

"Mmm."

"And you." He twined his fingers in her wet hair
and turned her face to his.

Michael's lips were warm from the sun. He teased
her mouth open and gently explored, taking time with
her, matching her response to his.

She broke the kiss, leaning up on one elbow to look

down at him. With one finger, she traced his jaw, his nose, the firm cheekbones, his forehead.

"I love you." There was so much more she wanted to say. For the first time in her life, those three words seemed inadequate. But she didn't know how to put her feelings into words.

He smiled, traced the line of her cheek with his finger. "I like to hear you say it." With the gentlest of touches, he slid the strap of her bikini down, then eased one of the cups of fabric from her breast. Raising his head slightly, he kissed the tip.

She felt glorious sensation shimmer through her. Somehow, loving Michael seemed more beautiful in the sunlight. The warmth on her back, the deep green smell, the gentle movement of the water beneath them. She curled one of her hands in his thick hair and brought him closer until his mouth closed over her nipple.

And then she was lost to him, didn't protest as he began to make love to her. Cheri didn't think of anything but the man beside her, his lips, tongue and hands molding her until she was quivering with emotion, until she reached up, wound her arms around his neck and begged him to possess her.

He took her quickly, pressing her thighs apart, cupping her buttocks with his hands, kissing her neck and telling her how much he loved her, how she pleased him. He thrust quickly, deeply, and she closed her eyes against the bright sun and gave herself over to the sensations building inside her body. Wanting to please him, she dug her toes into the smooth stone, arched herself against him, ran her hands feverishly over his back and down to his hips, pulled him into her.

Her release came quickly and she cried out, a sharp, high sound. Seconds later, she felt his teeth gently bite her neck as he thrust one last time, then his entire body stopped moving except where she felt him pulsing inside her. Cradling him in her arms, she closed her eyes and lost herself in sweet relaxation.

Whether it was a few minutes or thirty, she couldn't be sure. A short time later, she opened her eyes. Michael had moved to her side, had placed the bottom of her bikini by her legs. Cheri glanced toward the entrance of the cove. No one.

She started to put her suit on, but Michael stopped her. "Let's swim first."

They didn't really swim; the cove was much too shallow. Instead, they ducked each other, splashed and laughed in the sunshine. Clambering back up on the rock, they lay on its smooth surface until they dried off.

"I need more sunscreen." She pressed her finger against the skin of her arm and was dismayed to find it left a white mark.

Michael jumped off the rock and waded back to the other side of the cove, then brought her bag back.

She started to put on her suit, gently pulling her bikini bottom over her legs. When she reached for her top, Michael put a hand on her arm.

"Leave it off. For me."

She could feel herself flush. "Michael..."

"What?"

"I just wish..." With a sickening sense of reality, she knew all her worst feelings were consuming her again. The doubts. The fears. It was so easy to lose herself in the heat of a perfect moment. If only she could keep that feeling with her throughout her life.

"What?" His voice was concerned, his expression intense. "Cheri, you can tell me."

"You're sick of it, I'm sure." She began to rub sunscreen over her arms. "I still feel as if I'm not good enough for you."

"Why?"

"Oh..." She glanced down at herself, then back at him. "Everything. My personality, my body, all of it."

"What do you think is wrong?"

"Oh, just—well, my body is too thin, I hate the way it looks. And my breasts, they're too small." Daring to look at him, she continued: "Sometimes, after we make love, I wonder how you get any pleasure out of my body at all."

"But you're beautiful." As she shook her head and looked away, he touched her neck softly. "You've given me nothing but pleasure from the moment I met you."

She met his gaze, wanting to believe him. Her eyes brimmed. "Do you mean that?"

He gathered her into his arms. "I'll never lie to you, Cheri. About anything."

No, he wouldn't. She was sure he could feel the slight stiffening of her body. For Cheri, the loveliness of the afternoon was overshadowed.

THEY WALKED BACK to their car in silence, except for one instant Cheri would remember forever.

As she made her way through the underbrush, over the narrow trail, she must have made a wrong turn, because Michael put his hand on her arm, restraining her.

"You can't go that way." Pointing to the ground, he showed her why. A stone, completely ordinary except for the green leaf wrapped around it.

"What's that?"

"Whenever you see a ti leaf wrapped around a stone, it means you can't go there. The Hawaiians have areas of the islands that are sacred to them. They feel it's better if these places aren't disturbed."

"I can understand that." Suddenly she wanted Michael to understand, if only part of it. "I think everyone has little parts that shouldn't be touched, don't you?"

Before he could reply, she turned away from the stone and continued down the trail.

THEY LIVED IN THEIR BATHING SUITS for the rest of the week. Occasionally they drove into Hana for supplies, but most of the time they chose to remain alone, with each other. It was a lazy, relaxing time, with nothing they had to do and everything they wanted to.

Nighttime was magical. Cheri grew to love the sound of the waves booming through the lava rocks, the wind through the palm trees, the scent of the ocean in the verdant air. It was cool, with a constant breeze.

They talked, ate, laughed and made love. The cats grew fat as Cheri gave them more and more food.

One evening, after dinner, as Cheri was about to take off her bathing suit and shower to remove the sand, Michael's voice stopped her.

"Look at that sunset. Cheri, come outside and let's take a walk."

Not bothering to put on shoes, she pulled on a rose-colored cotton gauze dress and joined him on the porch. They walked back to the black sand beach. The water looked like silver mist as it licked up the shore and shot into the air. Cheri's skirt was midcalf-length, so she held it up with both hands as she walked along, enjoying the feel of the water over her feet.

The sun was setting over the island, and far out across the ocean she could see the first faint stars of evening.

"Can you see that star over there, Michael?" Cheri pointed to a faintly twinkling star in the summer sky.

"Yeah."

"You have to make a wish on it." She danced ahead of him on the sand, her feet barely touching the ground.

"You first."

She stopped, stood perfectly still and squeezed her eyes shut. *I want us to always be as happy as we are at this moment. I don't want anything to come between us.* She opened her eyes.

"Your turn."

He was looking at her oddly, something in his expression she couldn't quite define.

"Your turn, Michael." She teased a little, suddenly afraid.

He caught her hand, turned her toward him. One side of her skirt dropped into the surf, clung wetly to her legs.

"It's something you can give me." His voice was quiet. Serious.

"Michael?"

"Something I've wanted for a long time."

Cheri knew what he was going to ask her a split second before he did. She almost put up her hands, as if to ward off the moment physically.

"I want to marry you."

She stared at him, knowing her face had gone quite pale, her eyes were dark with shock.

"Michael, I can't—"

"Yes, you can. I don't want anything to come between us."

The words of her wish came back to her.

She looked out over the ocean, over waves as violent as the feelings churning inside her. *How can I ever explain how I feel?* Michael stood perfectly still, the ocean breeze whipping his hair.

She turned back toward him, pushed a strand of hair out of her face. "I love you, Michael." *That's why I can't.*

"I love you, too."

Tell him now. Tell him why you're scared.

She pushed the thought out of her consciousness, concentrated on the man standing in front of her, looking down at her with vulnerable eyes.

"I'm an old-fashioned man, Cheri. I guess I want commitment."

Why was it so hard to take this final step? Would it always be this way, would she always feel as if some invisible wall held her away from him?

His expression slowly changed. His eyes first. They lost their dark glow, seemed to die a little. Then he looked away.

Cheri felt something burst within her, cleansing part of her pain. *I can't do this to him.* Sliding her arms up around his neck, she pressed her cheek against his bare chest, where she could hear his heart pounding furiously.

"Yes," she whispered. Everything else could wait.

LYING IN HIS ARMS that night, Cheri whispered a question she needed an answer to.

"Michael, tell me about Nancy."

He was silent for so long she thought he wasn't going to answer. Then he began to speak, slowly.

"I met her at a company party. She was..." He paused, then moved both arms behind his head. "She was the most beautiful woman I'd ever met. I wanted to get to know her very badly. The next day I sent a dozen yellow roses to her agency with a note asking her to go out with me."

Cheri waited. Listened. She had to know.

"We dated quietly for about six months. There were times when we had to be apart—she'd go on location for a magazine, I'd go on location to check a touring group. But when we were together, we were happy."

He sighed, lost in private memories. For a moment Cheri considered asking him to stop. It was none of her business, really.

"She'd had a rough family life. Pretty abusive. She ran away from home as soon as she could and began to model. But she never got over the feeling of not being good enough. And her career reinforced the idea she was only as good as the next job." He closed his eyes, pain etched into his features.

"It was amazing to me. At one point she was voted one of the ten most beautiful women in the world. Two nights later I had to break into her apartment because she'd taken an overdose of pills. She told me later she didn't want to live anymore."

Cheri closed her eyes.

Michael's voice cracked slightly. "The second time she tried it, I insisted she get help. She checked herself into a hospital for a few weeks. I went to see her every night after work. No one ever found out." He opened his eyes and they were blank, expressionless. "I had to pay off a few people to make sure it never hit the papers."

Cheri stared at the ceiling of the cabin. What had Rachel told her? *Something internal.* She knew what Michael was going to say before he said it.

"She checked herself out right before Christmas. I asked her to come home with me over the holidays. I wanted to marry her. To protect her." He sighed, and his whole body tensed. "She killed herself two days before she was supposed to come home with me."

Cheri felt tears running down her cheeks, into her ears. *Michael.*

"I always felt I failed her. I couldn't look at another woman for years. There didn't seem to be any feeling left inside me. I buried myself in work because there was nothing else." He reached out a hand across the sheet. "Until you."

"Michael, I'm so sorry." She moved toward him, wrapped her arms around his shoulders and held him tightly. He didn't move for a long time, but she continued to hold him, felt his body slowly relax.

After Michael fell asleep, Cheri got out of bed and walked over to the window. But looking out over the ocean failed to soothe her. The waves crashed in the distance, their whisper hypnotic. But not calming. Not tonight.

You can't go on this way with Michael. No matter how scared you are. He gave her so much, and she felt she gave him nothing. Obviously he thought she was much stronger than she was. As much as it might hurt, she had to tell him the truth. No matter what the cost. If he still wanted to marry her afterward, she would know he really loved her.

A sharp knocking on the door brought her out of her thoughts.

"Mr. Stone?" She recognized the voice. The woman who ran the campground.

Cheri ran into the bedroom and woke Michael. Grabbing a pair of shorts, he jumped out of bed and pulled them on hurriedly as he ran to the door.

"What's wrong?"

The woman's face twisted with anxiety. "Something bad has happened. Your secretary called."

Michael sprinted off toward the main cabin and its phone, the woman jogging quickly after him.

Without waiting for him to come back, Cheri began to pack their suitcases.

THEY LEFT MAUI the same day. As they drove to the airport in the early morning, Michael explained what had happened.

"'Bad Boys' lead singer got busted in Dallas—cocaine."

Their flight back to Los Angeles was quiet and tense. "What will happen to him, Michael?"

"I don't know." He leaned back in his seat and closed his eyes. "I'm sorry about the way our vacation ended."

She covered his hand with hers. "Don't be." She kissed him lightly on the cheek. "It was the happiest time of my life."

MICHAEL DROPPED HER OFF at the house and drove straight to the office even though he hadn't slept on the flight back. Rachel, with a surprised look on her face, let Cheri in.

"I thought you weren't coming back until next Monday."

"So did I. Bad Boys' lead singer got busted."

Rachel grimaced. "So that's it. What a jerk!"

Cheri nodded wearily. "I think I'm going to turn in as soon as I get out of these clothes." She carried her suitcase into the bedroom and began to peel off her T-shirt and jeans.

"You look beat." Rachel followed her into the bedroom. "Can I do anything for you?"

"No...I'm fine."

Rachel sat down on the bed. "Did you have a good time?"

Cheri nodded, then felt her chin start to tremble. She put her hand over her mouth.

"Cheri?"

"He asked me to marry him." And she burst into tears.

Chapter Ten

Michael flew to Dallas the same day they returned and didn't come home until two days later. He was exhausted and simply fell into bed. Cheri answered the phone, cooked meals, made sure he ate, kept the dogs out of the house so he could sleep, and made herself useful any way she could.

After a week, their lives were back to an established routine. Michael went to work; Cheri prepared for the studio. This was more than a demo. This was the real thing.

She rehearsed endlessly with the other women in the band, polished the lyrics on all her songs, worked out new harmonies and arrangements, pushed herself further than she ever had before. She wanted to be perfect.

Michael negotiated their contract with the help of their lawyer, and the band won more points than it lost. Michael was so pleased, he took her out to dinner that same evening, to a little seafood restaurant along the coast. But he seemed tired; the lines in his face were more pronounced.

They had finished their main course and were relaxing with after-dinner drinks when she noticed a grin beginning to play around his mouth.

"Michael, what—" Before she could continue, their

table was surrounded by waiters singing "Happy Anniversary to You." A piece of chocolate-mousse cake with a single candle was in one of the waiter's hands.

Cheri covered her face with her hands, embarrassed. Michael simply laughed.

As the entourage walked away, she started to laugh. "I've never been so embarrassed! What—"

"Seven months today from the moment we first went out. Do you remember, the movie and the marshmallows?"

"Yes." She couldn't stop smiling.

"I thought we needed something to remember this night by." His voice was deceptively casual. Michael reached into the pocket of his jacket and extracted a small velvet box.

She held her breath as he pushed it across the table to her.

"Open it up; it's not a bomb."

Cheri picked it up slowly, feeling the soft velvet. She found the catch and opened it. Inside, nestled on more velvet, a sapphire surrounded by small diamonds winked up at her.

"Do you like it?"

Her throat tightened. She couldn't reply.

"It reminded me of the water in Hawaii—in our cove. And your eyes."

"Oh, Michael." She could barely breathe, she was so full of happiness. "I love you so much."

THAT EVENING, as Cheri brushed her teeth, Michael called to her through the bathroom door.

"Would it be okay if we spent the last weekend in October with my parents?"

"Sure." She was curious to meet them now. And confident she could go through just about anything with Michael at her side. She finished brushing her teeth and stuck her head out the door. "When are you going to tell them?"

He came into the hall, his blue terry bathrobe belted loosely around his waist. "We'll wait till you meet them."

"Oh." It felt strange to know she'd be meeting Michael's parents. Would they like her?

"Where do they live?" she asked.

"It's Dad's birthday, so we'll all be out at the house in Carmel."

For a moment, she thought she would never get her breath back. Her knuckles whitened on the doorknob as she gripped it to steady herself. Michael had already turned back toward the bedroom.

"We can leave on a Friday and come back Sunday night," he called over his shoulder.

"Fine." She hoped he couldn't hear how weak her voice sounded.

Lies, lies and more lies. They had finally caught up with her, and now she was trapped. Cheri closed the door of the bathroom and sat down on the edge of the tub.

Tell him.

As quickly as the first thought came to her, another arrived to take its place.

He'll despise you.

Maybe she'd be lucky. Maybe she wouldn't meet anyone from her past. Maybe she could simply spend a pleasant weekend with Michael's family.

As was her habit, she pushed her fears to the back of her mind, opened the bathroom door, and walked down the hall to the bedroom.

"WHY ARE YOU SCARED of this trip, Cheri?"

Cheri stared at one of the delicate watercolors on Glenda's office walls, then took a deep breath to get past the sudden tightness in her chest. But she couldn't respond.

Glenda changed the direction of the discussion with another question. "Have you talked to Michael?"

"No. I...can't."

"What do you think will happen if you tell him the truth?"

She stared at the watercolor, and the edges of the painting began to blur gently.

"He'd leave me," she whispered.

"He didn't leave Nancy."

She was silent.

Glenda continued: "He loved Nancy no matter what happened. He felt very deeply when she died. You tried to push him away once and it didn't work." When she didn't answer, Glenda went on: "Cheri, from what you've told me, he's a man you could count on being there for you emotionally."

She felt almost physically sick as words began to push themselves past the tightness of her chest, her throat. Quickly, before she lost her nerve, she covered her eyes with her hands and leaned forward in her chair.

"Glenda, I never meant for things to go this far! I thought we'd date for a while and then he'd move on. I've *never* thought I was good enough for him, and I thought Michael would find out—see that. But he kept asking me out, then when I moved into his house—I don't know what I was thinking. I just...I just wanted to be normal, to see what it was like to be with a man I cared about. To be close to him."

Her voice was coming out in harsh rasps; her hands trembled, but she kept them pressed against her face. More words exploded out, feelings she'd kept inside for so long.

"I've never been as close to anyone as to Michael.

I've always felt as if I were looking in at other people, like there was this wall and I was on the outside. I just wanted to be on the inside. I never meant for him to want to marry me."

"Tell me why you're afraid to marry him."

She sat up, wiped her eyes, and gripped the arm of the chair. "I don't want to hurt him! He thinks I'm an entirely different person than I really am! I've lied to him about so many things, I can't even remember what I told him! I'm lying every day I stay in his house."

"You're hurting yourself, too."

"I don't care about—"

Glenda grasped her hand tightly. "I wish you could see yourself as you are instead of what you think you are. Cheri, you're so much more than what you believe."

She shook her head.

Glenda spoke quietly. Firmly. "I see you as a woman who didn't let her early life destroy her. Who kept her compassion, who gives everyone a break—except herself. Cheri, you have to be kinder to yourself. It *wasn't* your fault! It *wasn't* something that you made happen—you weren't responsible!"

It was almost a minute before she answered. "I wish I could believe that. I know it in my mind, but not... My feelings are always different."

"Remember we talked about why people get married?"

Cheri nodded.

"You and Michael have that, Cheri. The emotional understanding."

"He does; I don't—"

"You must give him something, Cheri. He's not a stupid man. He wouldn't stick around."

She remained silent. Not believing. Staring at the painting. Not wanting to touch pain so near the surface.

Glenda sighed. "Why don't we think about setting a date? A goal. A time to tell Michael." She waited, her eyes anxious as she studied Cheri.

When Cheri didn't meet her eyes, Glenda said softly, "I know you can trust him. From everything you've told me, I don't think he'll leave you. He may have a little trouble at first, but you can bring him here—both of you can see me and talk out your fears."

It was the beginning of the most frightening journey she'd ever take with Michael. What was that saying? The longest journey begins with the first step. Slowly, ever so slowly, Cheri turned her head, met kind gray eyes. Eyes that felt her pain.

"Okay."

THE LAST SUMMER DAYS passed quickly. Cheri circled three dates on the calendar: September seventh, October twenty-seventh and November first. The first was Tough Cookie's beginning date in the studio. The second was Michael's father's birthday. The third was the date she'd set to tell Michael the truth.

She thought of all three of them as challenges, but in a different sense. One was professional, the other two personal. The final date would decide the outcome of her relationship with Michael. And Cheri wasn't sure she was ready for any of them.

The morning of the first day in the studio, she picked a fight with Michael over breakfast, then burst into tears as he walked out the door.

"I'll pick you up at three," Michael said quietly.

How could he be so understanding when she was so nasty? As soon as his car disappeared around the corner, Cheri picked up the phone and called Rachel.

"Cheri? What's wrong?"

"I can't stand it! I'm not strong enough! I can't do it,

Rachel. I'll make Michael sorry for the day he ever thought we had any talent.''

"I'm coming over. Stay right there." Rachel hung up.

Thirty minutes later, when Rachel walked inside the house, she came straight to Cheri and hugged her. "Come on. It can't be so bad. Did you guys have a fight or something?"

"Oh, nothing that easy! Michael never lets anything *get* to him. He's like a machine! I can't live with someone like that, I can't work...." Cheri knew she was being totally unfair and dishonest, but something was driving her.

"Hey, kiddo, I know. I went through it two nights ago with Patti. We both got drunk and decided we never *really* intended to get this far in the business." Rachel sat Cheri down at the oak table in the dining room and pulled up a chair beside her. "I just thank God you didn't have this little anxiety attack in the studio." Glancing around the kitchen, she asked, "Can I make myself some breakfast? You got me out of bed."

"I'm sorry, I'm sorry. Yes, go help yourself." Cheri lowered her head into her arms.

"Hey." Cheri felt Rachel touch the top of her head. "The tapes you gave me are terrific. Steve's a hot producer. Michael's matched everyone up perfectly." When Cheri didn't respond, Rachel continued: "It's only tape. If we're that bad, they just have to erase us."

Cheri laughed and felt some of the tension leave her chest.

"Hell, Cheri, what's the worst thing that can happen? Steve takes Michael aside and says, 'I thought you said these girls had talent! I hear better sounds every week when the guy comes to collect my garbage!'"

Cheri laughed again.

"So we blow our deal with Blue Lightning. We're back to the club circuit, and we never go anywhere. Is it so bad?"

Talking about it this way made Cheri see her fears were ridiculous. She touched Rachel's arm. "Thank you. For making me see what a fool I was."

"Everyone does it. You don't have exclusive rights." As Rachel cracked eggs into a bowl and beat them with a wire whisk, Cheri stared at the phone. She should call. She wasn't being fair to Michael.

Picking up the receiver, she thought for a moment, then got out the phone book. After she dialed, she covered her ear with her free hand as Rachel emptied the eggs into a sizzling frying pan.

"Beverly Hills Flowers? I'd like a dozen white roses. With lots of greenery." She paused, listening to the florist. "That'd be great! Could you send it to the Stone Management Company? To Mr. Michael Stone?" She waited while the young man on the other end of the line took down this information, then said, "Could you enclose a card? It's a long message, but I'll pay extra if necessary."

Rachel smiled as she dished the eggs onto two plates and popped several slices of bread into the toaster.

"Just put 'Another example of the six-year jump you have on me. I wish this morning had never happened. I'll drive to the studio with Rachel—'" Cheri eyed her friend, who nodded, her mouth full "'—and I'm taking you out after. I love you very much.'" She shot a glance at Rachel, then lowered her voice. "'From your sweet pea.'"

Rachel started to laugh as Cheri hung up the phone. "Don't you say a word to anyone," Cheri said, then reached for her plate and joined her friend at breakfast.

THEY LAY OUT IN THE SUN for the rest of the morning, listening to tapes, talking, not doing much of anything. Rachel had brought her bass guitar and a change of clothes with her, so she wouldn't have to return to the house in Hollywood before they drove to the studio.

"Want some?" Rachel extended a spoonful of chocolate chocolate-chip ice cream toward Cheri's mouth.

"Can't. Worst thing in the world before I sing is any milk product." She closed her eyes and let the hot sun soothe her body. "You guitar players have all the luck!"

Rachel snorted inelegantly. "You think so. Well, keep in mind that I can't even take a quick shower tonight or I'll ruin the calluses on my fingertips. I had to bathe this morning."

Cheri giggled. "We'll smell like garbage as well as sound like it." Then she shrieked as Rachel threw an ice cube on her bare back.

AT QUARTER TO FIVE that evening, both of them stood in front of the recording studio.

"This is it, kiddo," Rachel said gently. "There are no excuses now."

Cheri touched her friend's arm gently. "Rachel." She stopped, then blurted the rest out. "I could never have come this far without you."

Rachel squinted against the still-bright evening sunshine. "Hey, Cheri." She cleared her throat. "We couldn't miss. With your voice and my brains..."

Cheri smiled.

"Your voice and my dedication..."

Cheri frowned.

"Your voice and my terrific bass playing, your voice and my Fearless Leader personality—"

Cheri punched Rachel's arm playfully. "I should never have complimented you. Fathead!"

Rachel smiled smugly. "It's only a record, right?"

"No, I didn't mean about the band. I meant—you know."

"Yeah, I know." Rachel awkwardly patted Cheri's shoulder. Her eyes were suspiciously bright.

They walked through the steel-and-glass front door.

"Take it again, Cheri."

She moistened her lips and listened carefully as the melody played, then came in precisely on cue. But her voice sounded flat and lifeless to her ears. Eight bars into the song, she stopped.

"Let's try another one. I think 'Desire' can be saved for later." Steve Browning looked more like a college student than the excellent producer he was. Dressed in jeans and a T-shirt, with an unruly mop of red hair, he was a casual and unhurried type of man. And sensitive. "Cheri, I'd like to talk to you for a second."

She closed her eyes and slipped off the headphones. *Oh, no.*

Outside the vocal booth, Steve put his arm around her shoulders. "You're pushing too hard. We don't have to do the entire album in one evening." His voice was warm, the tone reassuring. Once again, Cheri marveled at how well Michael managed to match personalities. Steve was the perfect producer for Tough Cookie.

"Why don't you try 'Dream Lover'?" Steve had picked several of the new songs from the second tape Michael had sent during contract negotiations. "Everything's done but the vocals."

She nodded and slowly returned to the booth. Before she slipped on her headphones, Steve's voice pierced through her consciousness once more. "Rachel told me to tell you—remember the garbage men."

She smiled and started to relax.

This time, her vocals were better. Cheri blocked out

the studio, her desire for perfection—even Michael—
and just concentrated on the emotions she'd felt when
she wrote the song.

> Baby, I could love you
> If you'd open up and see
> How the pedestal you put me on
> Is only hurting me.

Her vocals had power; the melody seemed to flow
through her body, out of her blood, as she swayed
slightly to the beat. She could feel the emotion, almost
felt like crying, and Cheri knew she was all right again.
It was only when she felt the song as intensely as when
she'd created it that she sensed her voice was expressing true emotion.

> Someday things I hid inside
> Will shatter, set me free.
> You'll see all my heart
> And love what's really me.

She sang the last verse again, knowing the final ver-
sion would be a fade-out. Opening her eyes, she saw
Steve give her the thumbs-up signal. She smiled.

"Take a break. Michael's here to see you."

She slipped off her headphones and stepped out of
the booth. Michael stood up as she entered the musicians' lounge, and Cheri went straight into his arms and
kissed his cheek gently.

"I'm sorry about this morning."

He smiled, that same crooked smile that always
made her feel slightly sad. "I'm sorry, too. You were
nervous. How's it going?"

He sat down on a black leather couch, and Cheri sat
next to him. "Steve's marvelous. He's real low-key,

doesn't yell, and he seems to agree with us on how most of the songs should go." As Cheri continued to talk, her tone grew more excited. "He listens to me and thinks a lot of the same songs should go on the album."

Michael put his arm around her shoulders and hugged her. "I thought you'd all get along."

She noticed the tired look in his eyes and touched his face soothingly. "You don't have to stay if you're tired. We can go out another night. Rachel can bring me home."

He stood up and stretched. "I think I may do that." Linking his fingers through hers, he started toward the door. "Walk me to the car, okay?"

Outside, the parking lot was dark, the night moonless and cool. When they reached the Ferrari, Michael leaned against the driver's door and gently pulled Cheri against him.

"I heard your last song. It's new, isn't it?"

"Yes."

"I like it. Steve must, too, if he's having you record it this early into the album."

She nodded.

He kissed her then, tilting her chin toward his face and holding her lightly. Her lips parted, and he moved his arms until they were linked loosely around her waist. When he raised his head, he seemed to be studying her.

"The flowers were very nice."

"I'm glad you liked them."

"I've never had a woman send me flowers before."

"I'm glad I was the first."

He was silent, yet Cheri sensed there was something more he wanted to say. When he finally spoke, his voice sounded soft against the evening air.

"Am I a hard man to talk to?"

She looked up at him, recognized the vulnerability in his dark eyes. How could she have been such a fool? Michael wasn't an insensitive man, and she had laid her soul out on those tapes, the same tapes he had given their producer, Steve. And Michael must have listened to them first. It was part of his job.

She knew she had already spent too long trying to reply. He was looking at her as if he had never seen her before tonight, as if she were a stranger. Quickly, she placed her hand on his cheek.

She couldn't give him anything less than the truth.

"You're not a hard man to talk to, but—there are some things I'm unable to talk to anyone about." As his mouth tightened and his face began to close over whatever emotion he was experiencing, Cheri cried out, "Michael! I've tried harder with you than with anyone I've ever met! I love you so much it—scares me sometimes. I don't know what I'd do if you left me."

He tightened his grip around her waist, put his lips against her hair. "I'm not going to leave. Nothing you tell me can change the way I feel about you."

They remained close, silent again for a short time.

"Do I put you on a pedestal?" His breath tickled against her temple.

"I feel that you do." The words came out slowly, haltingly. "I feel as if I owe you too much. There's nothing you don't do to make my life easier. Then when I feel like yelling or screaming, I feel so guilty, I can't stand it."

"Hey." He pulled slightly away from her, looked down into her eyes. "You're *paying* me for some of those services. I'll be taking a percentage of the money Tough Cookie earns over the next few years."

She started to speak, but he held up his hand. "Just a second. I think you're confusing me as a manager with the man who loves you."

"Michael." Cheri took a deep breath. "I can never live up to what you think I am. If you really knew—"

She stopped, frozen. She had already said too much.

"Knew what?" he prompted gently.

She averted her eyes, studied the pavement at her feet.

"Give me some time, Michael."

He nodded, slowly, then kissed her good-bye and got into the sports car. She watched until the Ferrari was a tiny speck among the evening traffic.

"Good job, all of you," Steve Browning said as they met that evening in the musicians' lounge. "We'll meet again tomorrow at the same time. I'm *very* pleased with the amount of work we got done."

Rachel winked at Cheri, and she smiled.

Outside in the parking lot, the women converged around Rachel's van.

"Let's go to Ma Maison!" Patti suggested, only to be met with laughter.

Rachel made a big show out of searching through her denim pockets. "I think I can just about afford a chili dog at Pink's."

"How about Fellini's?" Cheri suggested. "It really all started there."

They agreed; then each member of the band piled into cars and drove to the restaurant.

When their waitress found out what they were celebrating, she took them straight to the largest front booth. Cheri hung back as everyone else was being seated and whispered into Rachel's ear. "I'm going to call Michael."

"Invite him if he wants to join us."

The public phone was outside, on the street. Melrose Avenue was crowded, and Cheri covered her free ear with her hand after she dialed.

He answered almost immediately. "Cheri?"

"Hi, sweetheart. We finished up about fifteen minutes ago and decided to go to Fellini's for coffee. Do you want to join us?"

He sounded tired. "No, baby. It's a moment for just the band, I think."

Her throat closed. Michael, always thinking of others. "We'd really like to have you here."

"I know." There was a slight pause; then he asked, "How long do you think you'll be?"

"Not more than an hour—maybe you'd better make it an hour and a half. I think Rachel's going to eat."

"I'll wait up."

"Michael..." She pressed her hand against her forehead. "I'm sorry about tonight. I feel like such a—"

"If there are two words I could take out of your vocabulary, they'd be 'I'm sorry.' You don't have any reason to be." When she didn't answer, he continued: "You'll tell me whatever you want to tell me when you're ready."

"I love you, Michael."

"I know you do, baby. Now go have a good time and forget about everything but the band."

It was easier said than done. Though there was much talking and laughing and Rachel kept a steady flow of champagne coming, Cheri found the noise gave her a headache, the champagne hurt her stomach, and far from pushing problems to the back of her mind, they were all she could think about.

But she put on a bright face, laughed at Patti's jokes, ate whatever Rachel put on her plate, participated because she didn't want to spoil anyone else's fun.

It was after two when they broke up. Rachel drove her home and Cheri was content to remain silent as the van skimmed over the dark freeway.

Her friend watched until she was safely inside the house, then drove off down the street.

Cheri took off her shoes. Despite what Michael had

said, she wasn't going to wake him. He had to be at the office early tomorrow—no, *today*, she amended wryly. Padding into the kitchen, she took the pen off the top of the refrigerator and crossed another day off the calendar. Counting quickly, she calculated she had over three more weeks in the studio and almost six weeks until Michael's father's birthday. And Carmel. Her stomach twisted at the thought, but she turned away.

She took off her clothes in the bathroom and pulled on a long white cotton nightgown. Quietly entering the bedroom, she tried not to make any noise. Michael's hair looked black as night against the pale sheets. She slid into bed gently, anxious not to wake him.

"Cheri?" His voice was thick with sleep.

"It's me."

"How was the celebration?"

"Wonderful. I wish you could have come."

He smiled and she scooted across the bed where he enfolded her in his arms.

"You're cold."

"That's because you're nice and warm under the covers."

He laughed and hugged her tighter. "I'll warm you up, then."

She put her arms around his neck and kissed him, then lay back. "I'd like you to."

"Cheri." His tone changed, became serious. "About tonight. I did a lot of thinking when I came home. I didn't see it before, but I feel like I might have rushed you in Hawaii."

She thought quickly about her engagement ring, safe in the top of her dresser drawer. She had insisted on keeping it there, despite Michael's protests. The cool pressure of the metal felt strange on her fingers.

"You feel uncomfortable with the idea of marriage, don't you?"

She couldn't lie. "Yes."

"Is it anything I've done?"

"I think it's just another example of the six-year advantage you have over me."

He took a deep breath. "Okay. Cheri, will you be honest with me?"

"Yes."

"Do you still want to live here with me?"

"Michael..."

"Are you sure you're not scared of telling me because I manage Tough Cookie?"

"No, no, it's nothing like that! I want to live here. I feel like I don't see enough of you even when I *do* live here! You come home and I'm at rehearsal. I sleep in the morning and you get up to go to work."

He kissed her forehead, laced his muscular legs through hers. "I know. The next few weeks are going to be rough because you have to give all your energy to recording."

"And you can't keep staying up all night waiting for me to come home! You looked terrible tonight."

"Maybe." Michael sat up in bed, taking her with him. "Maybe we could set up a long lunch, instead. Maybe once or twice a week I could come home early and we could just sit and talk in the backyard."

"Or I could meet you at the office. Or maybe you could come home and have dinner with me before I go to work."

"Sounds good." He slid beneath the covers again, and his hand moved to cover her breast. "But right now, there's something much more important on my mind."

"Oh, no. Let me guess."

His hand slowly inched down her stomach toward her inner thighs.

"Why, Mr. Stone, you *do* have a way of getting straight to the point."

He laughed, then gently pushed her back against the

pillows. She surrendered with a soft sigh as his body moved to cover hers.

"WHY DIDN'T SOMEONE TELL ME the higher up you went, the more work it involved?" Rachel grumbled as she fixed a broken string on her bass. "Where are the male groupies? The limos? Where's the champagne?"

"You love it and you know it," Patti said. "Like you told me a few weeks ago, we'll all look back and laugh at this someday."

Cheri lay quietly on the black leather couch in the musicians' lounge and listened to the two women banter back and forth.

Tough Cookie's album was two weeks into production, and things were going as smoothly as could be expected.

"Where are the reporters from *Rolling Stone*?" Rachel stood up and struck a sultry pose. "My favorite color is black, and I like my men the way I like my musical arrangements, lean and mean."

Patti howled with laughter.

Cheri smiled, then raised one of her arms and put it over her eyes, trying to shut out the bright light. The past two weeks had been tough. She'd never worked as hard in her life.

You're just tired.

"Hi, Michael." Patti's voice was bright and cheerful.

Cheri sat up with a quick, fluid motion. He had obviously gone home, rested and changed. Looking fresh and relaxed in a pair of jeans and a black T-shirt, he grinned and sat down next to her on the couch.

"I talked to Steve. They don't need you for almost four hours."

She stretched. "I know. I was trying to rest up so I'd be feeling better later on."

He took her hand in his, pretending to examine the small palm. "I asked him if I could take you away."

"That depends on what you have in mind." She liked to tease Michael. It was a skill Cheri had only learned in this relationship, and she delighted in making him laugh.

"Trust me?"

She nodded and stood up.

Once outside, he helped her into the passenger side of the Ferrari, then drove swiftly toward Sunset Boulevard.

"Where are we going?"

"I'll give you a big hint." He tossed a hotel key into her lap.

She could feel her cheeks warming. "Michael!"

He laughed. "I think it's pretty pathetic that for the last few nights you've come home you haven't been able to wake me up."

"I didn't want to. I told you I think it's unfair—"

"So do I."

The sports car moved slowly through evening traffic on Sunset Boulevard. Gigantic billboards vied for space with restaurants and clubs. The entire stretch of Sunset between Laurel and Doheny was alive with cars, people and lights.

Cheri leaned out the window, glad for the fresh cool air on her face. Sometimes, she had a closed-in feeling inside the recording studio that was almost claustrophobic. It was good to be outside again. She only half listened to Michael as he began to speak.

"I thought we could go out and get something to eat, then go back to the suite I reserved at the Château Marmont and rest."

She turned back toward him and flashed a smile. "Sounds terrific."

They were crawling along in traffic. Los Angeles, the

city that made the car a king. Mercedeses, Rollses and
gleaming sports cars jockeyed for positions in the slow-
moving lanes.

Cheri loved to watch people and she did so now, taking in outfits ranging from the expensive to the ridiculous. Torn sweat shirts, minis, jeans and boots, a lone
suit and tie—anything went on the Strip.

And then her attention was caught by a bright-blue
pair of hot pants and a T-shirt top. But it wasn't the
clothing. Something in the way the girl moved, the way
her soft blond hair caught the neon light as she
turned and began to walk toward the Mercedes slowing
ahead...

"Michael, stop the car!" While the Ferrari was still
moving, Cheri opened the door. A car horn blared as
she got out of the sports car in the middle lane of traffic
and darted across the street toward the sidewalk. Michael caught a quick glance of her in his rearview mirror, running toward the sleek black Mercedes.

He double-parked the car as soon as he could turn
off Sunset, then ran down the block until he rounded a
curve and saw her.

Cheri had her arms around the girl's waist and was
physically pulling her away from the car. Two men in
expensive business suits were yelling abusive remarks,
yet Cheri was swearing right back, in language Michael
found it hard to believe she'd ever used.

And the girl. She was kicking and scratching, biting
and punching. She had dropped her white plastic purse
and its contents were spilled all over the sidewalk. Pedestrians were giving both women a wide berth.

As Michael ran up, he could hear the end of the ar-
gument.

"What the hell is it to you what she does? We were
going to pay her—"

"I don't give a damn *how* much money either of you

have! *Get the hell out of here!*" Cheri's eyes were bright, her hair disheveled and spilling over her shoulders. The girl in her arms bit her hand, but Cheri held fast.

"Let me *go*, Cheri! Stay out of this!" As Michael finally saw her up close, he realized the girl couldn't be more than seventeen years old.

"Lauri, no!" Michael watched in amazement as Cheri tightened her hold, then looked at both the businessmen with fire in her blue eyes. *"Get going!"*

He made up his mind in an instant. Walking briskly toward the car, Michael confronted both men. "You heard the lady. Get moving."

"Lady?" One of the men stared at him in disbelief. "Hey, bud, what the hell are you talking about? That's no lady, she's a—" He stepped back as Michael advanced menacingly, then got into the car and slammed the door.

"Stupid little tramp!" His curse echoed as the Mercedes squealed away.

Michael turned and saw Cheri sitting on the sidewalk, the girl curled in her arms, sobbing. Without stopping to think about the sudden suspicion building inside him, he quickly crossed over to both women and knelt down.

"Cheri, what do you want me to do?"

When she looked up at him, her face looked so tired and old, he was shocked. Her voice was scratchy, almost a whisper as she answered.

"Help me, Michael."

CHERI EMERGED from the bedroom of the suite and began to walk toward the soft light in the living room. Michael was sitting on the couch, his hands clasped between his knees.

She sat down next to him and put her hand on his shoulder. "She's asleep. I managed to calm her down and get her to relax." She pushed a wisp of hair out of her eyes with a weary gesture.

Michael sat back on the couch and looked at her as if he were seeing her with new eyes. "What was wrong with her face?" he asked softly.

Cheri bit her lip, then answered him before her nerve failed her. "She scratched it up with her nails. She's high on something." Before Michael could answer, she hurried on. "It's the only way Lauri could ever—" She stopped speaking, and the rest of the sentence hung between them.

After a moment of silence, Michael stood up. "I'm going to make some coffee. Do you want some?"

She nodded, then followed him into the small kitchen. She watched Michael as he measured the grounds and put water in the coffee maker. Then he took out two china cups, his back toward her the entire time.

It was obvious he was going to let her tell him as much or as little as she wanted.

They sat down in the living room again. Cheri was just about to speak when Michael's voice pierced the stillness.

"I called Steve and told him you wouldn't be in for the rest of the evening."

She looked at his face then, and it was her undoing. In spite of his conflicting emotions, his eyes remained warm, his expression understanding. There wasn't any hint of shock or condemnation, none of the disgust she'd been prepared for. Cheri took a deep breath.

"I met Lauri through a program I used to work for. I used to go to a center in Hollywood and work with runaway teenagers."

"You never told me any of this." It was a statement, not an accusation.

"I just..." Cheri set her coffee on one of the end

tables and crossed her arms in front of her. "I wasn't really sure you'd be interested."

"I'm interested in anything that concerns you."

"Lauri had been picked up for prostitution a couple of times before she was referred to us. I worked with her for a long time."

"Why was she soliciting tonight?"

She closed her eyes tightly, was surprised by the hot tears that squeezed past her tightly shut lids. "I guess she's going through a bad time."

"Do you miss working with her?"

"Yes. I do."

"How did you manage to get started working with runaways?"

Cheri took a sip of her coffee. "There was an ad on television late one night, talking about the center. It just...really got to me. And you see these kids on the streets all the time. I used to...stop and try to talk with them. I wanted to *do* something instead of complaining about how awful it was."

"Why did you stop working there?"

"It was a volunteer job, and I had to work more hours at the bookstore, and with the band and all..." Her voice trailed off. She took another sip of coffee. It had cooled. "But I shouldn't have stopped. There aren't that many people who understand why someone would..." She stopped, looked down, then looked straight at Michael. "I understand why someone would feel so bad they might...do all that stuff."

He took her hand then, moved closer on the couch. "Tell me, Cheri. Whatever it is that eats you up inside. I won't go away."

"Michael, I—"

"Cheri?" Lauri stood in the doorway to the living room, rubbing her eyes.

The moment was broken. Michael watched as Cheri

got up off the couch and went to the girl, put her arm around her. He only half heard the gentle murmuring of her voice as she walked Lauri back to the bedroom.

In the morning, when the three of them left the hotel, Laurie gave Cheri a hug and a kiss and promised to phone. The girl looked younger in the early-morning sunlight with her blond hair pulled back in a ponytail.

As he drove back toward Marina del Rey, Michael didn't ask any more questions. Cheri kept her face averted, seemed to be fascinated with everything they passed. When they pulled into the driveway, she jumped out of the car. By the time he came inside, she was in the shower. Michael sat down on the sofa and put his head in his hands.

He wouldn't push her. He would wait until she was ready. He would give her time.

But he played last night's scene on Sunset Boulevard in his head over and over again. There was something that wasn't right. She seemed scared of him again.

He closed his eyes and leaned back against the couch, tried to ease the pounding inside his head. It seemed only minutes later when he heard her voice.

"Michael?"

He opened his eyes and glanced toward the door. She looked small and vulnerable in his blue terry robe, the thick sash belted tightly around her slender waist. There were dark smudges underneath her eyes and a new tension in her face.

He smiled, but he could feel the muscles in his face tremble. *Please trust me, baby.*

She padded across the room and sat down next to him. "I'm sorry about last night. Please don't..."

He put his arm around her shoulder, noticing for the first time how thin she'd become in the past weeks. She was pushing herself too hard. "Please don't what?" He tried to keep his voice light.

Her voice trembled. "Please don't hate me." And then he felt her body against his as she raised her face and put her hands on his shoulders.

"I don't hate you, Cheri. It's just that—" He fell silent. She wouldn't tell him until she was ready. "I'd better get ready for work."

Her lips were soft against his ear. "Make love to me, Michael. Make me feel better. Please." The last word was so soft, he almost thought he'd imagined it.

Several hours passed before he left for the office.

Chapter Eleven

The master tape was finally finished. On their last night of recording, Michael arranged for a large cake in the shape of a musical note and several cases of champagne to be delivered to the studio. The party lasted well into the next morning.

Life settled back into its usual routine, except that Cheri was acutely conscious of the fact that her meeting with Michael's family was less than two weeks away. And Carmel. One place she thought she'd never see again.

She pushed her fears aside and concentrated on making life easy for Michael. The house had never been cleaner, meals never more delicious. Even the dogs seemed more obedient.

All too soon, she was sitting in the kitchen with Rachel early Friday morning while Michael checked the house one last time.

"Come on, Cheri. Let's go."

"Have a good trip, guys." Rachel waved from the doorway, her fingers curled around Buffy's collar. "If you want to stay a few extra days, it's no big deal to me."

"I'll remember that," Michael called as he settled himself behind the wheel and turned on the ignition.

"Lauri may come by on Saturday. If she wants to

stay with you, it's okay." Cheri waved until they turned a corner and the house was out of sight. Everything familiar in her world was slowly slipping away, out of her grasp.

Relax, dumbo, you're only going to his parents' and meeting his family. Her thoughts failed to soothe her.

Once they were on Pacific Coast Highway, Cheri sat back and closed her eyes. She thought of the past weeks with Michael. He was there for her, but . . . she'd caught him looking at her, trying to study her without her knowing. She'd tried not to let him know she'd caught him at it. A slight tension had sprung up between them that hadn't been present before.

At times, she'd catch his face at a vulnerable moment, and it was as if he was yearning for something, wanted something just beyond his grasp. And then the look would leave his eyes and Michael would become Michael again, in control. She knew he was worried about her.

Shaking her head slightly, she opened her eyes and glanced out the windshield at the bright blue sky, the fresh clean air. A rare day for Los Angeles.

"You can sleep if you'd like." Michael kept his eyes on the road as he talked to her. "I know how you hate to get up this early, but I wanted to beat the traffic."

"I'm okay." She curled up in the bucket seat, facing him. She wanted to talk as they always had in the past, wanted to reassure herself everything was the same. "Is there anything about your family I should know?"

"Douglas won't be home this time. He's in England on sabbatical. Gina's driving down from San Francisco tomorrow with Robbie, the baby. Ben can't get away from work."

"I'm confused again."

"Doug's my older brother. Ben is Gina's husband."

"Right. Go on."

"Mom and Dad are pretty harmless."

"How old is your father going to be?"

He thought for a minute. "Sixty-four. He's getting up there."

Cheri tried to figure it out, then gave up and asked. "So how old was he when he married your mother?"

"Twenty-six. It's a pretty funny story. Dad said he never wanted to marry, but when he was stationed in Italy he met my mother. We have pictures in the album. Mom was gorgeous."

The men in the Stone family seem to have a predilection for falling in love with beautiful women, Cheri thought, remembering the picture of Nancy.

"His parents were against the idea from the start, so on his last night in Venice, my mom and dad married. She spoke no English when he brought her to America. Doug was born four years later, and I came along two years after that. Gina was the little latecomer, as my mother calls her. She's twenty-nine."

"What are they like? Your parents, I mean?" Cheri could clearly imagine the picture on the wall of Michael's den, and she smiled as she thought of the imaginary personalities she'd assigned each member of the Stone family.

"Dad's quiet, but nothing escapes him. I used to be scared to death of him as a child, because he demanded the best you were capable of giving. Later I realized how much he loves us. He just doesn't show it easily."

"Your mother?"

"She's terrific. You'll like her. She makes you feel at home right away. She'll probably think you're too thin and try to feed you a lot. We won't be able to sleep in the same room—"

"Michael!"

"But I'll sneak by to see you once in a while." He grinned.

"I wasn't thinking about that at all. I was looking forward to getting a little rest!"

"I know you'd miss me," he teased.

Suddenly, the slight stiffness between them was gone. Cheri was happy; she wanted to hang on to the moment and cherish it. "Tell me about your sister."

He laughed. "Gina's something. She constantly amazes Mom. My mother expected she'd be a wife and mother. She's never gotten over the fact that Gina went out and got a law degree."

"I'd think she'd be very proud."

"Oh, she is. But Mom doesn't know how Gina manages it all. Sometimes I don't think Gina does, either. She has a lot of nervous energy, and she smokes—no one in the family can stand it, so she tries not to in the house."

"Sounds like you all get along very well." For just a minute, she felt a small ripple of something. Longing? Jealousy? She didn't examine it.

"We have our moments." Michael glanced over his shoulder as he smoothly changed lanes and passed a camper. "Dad and Doug had some pretty tense times when Doug told him he didn't want to work at the agency."

"Did all of you work there when you were growing up?"

"All of us. Even Gina gave it a shot. But Doug was one of those people who knew what he wanted to do right from the start."

"And what was that?"

"He was a science nut from the word go. He teaches geology at Stanford and supervises field trips over the summer. This year he's in England."

"Is he married?"

"Yeah. He met Katie while she was taking one of his classes."

"Do they have any children?"

"I don't think they want any."

Cheri digested this news in silence. "So you're the last of the Stones to take the final leap."

"It looks that way." He glanced toward her, his dark eyes twinkling. "My mother despairs over my ever finding a nice girl to take care of me. Don't let it get on your nerves; she means well."

Cheri tried to stay awake, but the droning of the engine and the curves of the highway along the Pacific Ocean began to have a hypnotic effect. She closed her eyes for just a moment.

When her head fell back, she jerked awake.

"Go to sleep." Michael's voice was amused. "You've worked hard the past few weeks."

"If I sleep, will you wake me up before we get to your parents'?" She needed the little bit of time to prepare herself emotionally.

"Sure. Put your seat back."

She used her jacket as a pillow and, with her hand in Michael's, slowly drifted into sleep.

SHE WOKE UP when they passed Santa Barbara and she switched places with Michael, taking over the driving until they reached Big Sur. Then she asked him to drive. So much was coming back in her memories—she'd spent vacations as a child among the tall redwoods, playing not far from the wild coastline. She'd always loved the way the shore dropped off into pounding waves, but this time she kept her eyes on the road, not wanting to remember.

Finally, she sought solace in sleep again. If she could close her eyes, she wouldn't have to remember.

"CHERI. CHERI, WAKE UP. We're almost there." She felt a gentle nudge on her shoulder and slowly sat up, feeling hot, sticky and disoriented.

"Where? Michael..."

"We'll be at my parents' in ten minutes."

She pushed her hair out of her eyes. "I thought you were going to wake me up!"

"You were out like a light."

Digging into her purse, she brought out a comb and began to rearrange her tangled hair. "Michael, I'm a mess!"

"We can pull over for a minute if you'd like."

They did, and she fixed her hair, then put on some lipstick and blush.

As he started up the car, Michael glanced over at her. "Now don't make this a bigger deal than it is. They're going to love you."

But his reassuring tone didn't help stop the racing of her heart, the uneasiness in the pit of her stomach.

They'll know I'm not good enough. The words played through her thoughts like a silent litany as they drove by expanses of twisted cypress trees and immense houses, set back from the winding road.

"Here we are." Michael turned the wheel and the car glided up a circular drive.

Pressing her fingers to her temples, she could feel the beginnings of a headache. But before she had time to think, or become more frightened than she already was, Michael honked the horn in front of a redwood-and-glass house, set far back on the large lot. Within a minute, the front door opened.

A small dark-haired woman came outside. Her deep-brown hair didn't have a trace of gray, and for a moment, Cheri thought Gina must have come home early. But as the woman advanced toward them, Cheri realized she was Michael's mother.

"Michael!" He had to bend slightly to embrace her, and she hugged him with such fierce love that Cheri turned away, embarrassed. The woman stepped away, looked up into her son's face. "You've lost weight."

Michael laughed. "Mom, you look terrific."

Mrs. Stone turned and studied Cheri for what seemed a long time.

"You are Cheri."

She nodded.

"Come here." Michael's mother held out a hand.

Cheri obeyed instinctively and was instantly swept into a reassuring embrace. Quick tears filled her eyes as she stepped back.

"Come in, Cheri. I want you to feel this is your home." Mrs. Stone placed an arm around her shoulders as the three of them headed toward the door. When it closed behind them, it took Cheri a moment to adjust her eyes to the dim light.

"Your father is out by the pool. His arthritis is acting up today, so he's not in the best of moods. You go outside, Michael, and I'll show Cheri to her room."

Michael nodded and started down the hall.

Mrs. Stone led Cheri down the wide hall, finally pausing in front of a door. "I hope you'll be happy in here. There's a sliding door that leads to the backyard and a private bathroom." As they stepped inside, Cheri caught her breath.

Done in pale shades of green and peach, the room was airy and filled with light. The four-poster bed had a hand-knit coverlet, and a crystal vase by the window was filled with salmon-colored roses.

She didn't know what to say. "Thank you. It's...exquisite." She smiled and forced herself to extend her hands. "I'm sure I'll be very happy here."

"You're nervous."

Cheri didn't look away. "Yes," she admitted.

Mrs. Stone took her hand and squeezed it. "I like you already, because I know you've made my Michael very happy."

Cheri looked at her questioningly.

"I know, because he never would have brought you here if you didn't mean the world to him."

She could feel herself beginning to blush.

"Sit down on the bed with me."

The two women sat side by side, and Cheri waited for Mrs. Stone to speak.

"I know what it is to be afraid. When my husband took me to meet his people, I saw the looks in their eyes and wanted to run from the room. It was only Robert holding my hand that prevented me from doing so."

Cheri remembered what Michael had told her in the car. She admired the woman's courage. And wondered why she was telling her such private thoughts.

"They thought I wasn't good enough for their son, but by the time my first child was born, we were on speaking terms." She sighed and looked out the window, and Cheri sensed the memories weren't easy for her. She faced Cheri again, her dark eyes proud. "I told myself I never wanted anyone to come into my home and feel as badly as I felt so long ago."

Cheri interrupted. "Oh, I don't feel that bad—"

"But it's hard to come to a house full of strangers and feel at ease."

"I'll be all right."

"If you need anything, come to me and ask. Michael told me about your parents leaving you so young. I want you to know I'm here." She touched Cheri's hair gently, then got up and walked out of the room, closing the door behind her.

Cheri stared after the woman, her hand moving up to her hair where Mrs. Stone had touched her. She wondered if Michael knew how incredibly lucky he was.

A FEW MINUTES LATER, she heard an impatient knock on the door.

"Cheri, come out and meet my dad. He wants to see you."

Like some prized cow, she thought, and the image brought a slight smile to her face.

"I'll go get our suits so we can have a swim before lunch. But come with me now."

She followed him down the hall, into what looked like a family room, one whole side of it made of glass. It overlooked a large pool in the backyard.

As the sliding glass doors opened and she stepped out onto the flagstone patio, she squinted against the bright light and saw a man in the pool, swimming with easy strokes in their direction.

Robert Stone hauled himself out of the water and pulled on a terry robe. Pushing his wet hair off his forehead, he extended one of his large hands. "Hello, Cheri."

She liked him instantly, understanding his natural reserve with strangers.

"Hi." She extended her hand. He squeezed it gently, then gestured toward one of the tables on the terrace. "We can get acquainted over there." His dark eyes were stern. He looked like Michael; they shared the same facial structure and coloring. And he had that same quality, that of a man used to giving orders and having them obeyed.

She almost said "Yes, sir." Instead, she walked ahead of him quietly, then lowered herself into a chair.

"Michael tells me you sing." He was studying her now, quite candid in his appraisal.

"Yes, I do. With a band." She took a deep breath. "We just finished recording an album last week."

"Who produced it?" He was all interest now, and Cheri caught a glimpse of how he must have been at a younger age—like Michael.

"Steve Browning."

"Good man." He looked at Michael. "Good choice."
The piercing gaze was directed at her again. "Were you
satisfied with the results?"

"Yes, sir, I was."

He roared with laughter, and it was a moment before
she realized exactly what she'd said.

"So Michael's got you scared to death of me, has
he?"

"No, I..." She could feel her face flushing.

"Dad..."

"I'm sorry, Cheri. I wasn't laughing at you."

They were interrupted as Mrs. Stone joined them on
the patio with a tray of glasses.

"Lemonade with mint from the garden. Cheri." She
handed her a glass, distributed the others, then sat
down. Glancing at her husband, she chided gently.
"Robert, you've been scaring our guest."

"I do my best." He smiled, a slow, tentative smile.
Cheri realized it was his attempt at a joke and she
smiled shyly in return.

Michael seemed restless. "I'm going to get the suitcases out of the trunk. Be back in a minute."

After he left, Mrs. Stone smiled sadly. "We try so
hard and you're tied up in knots. Forgive us, please."

"It's me," Cheri began, then stopped as Robert interrupted her.

"Sometimes we forget around here that people have
different ways of getting acquainted. You take your
time, Cheri."

At that moment she understood why Michael's
mother had risked the disapproval of family and friends
and married into a hostile family.

"Thank you." Cheri took a sip of her lemonade and
set it down. She searched for something to say. "You
have a garden?"

Mrs. Stone beamed, and Cheri knew she'd made a

good choice. "A greenhouse. I grow my own vegetables—nothing is as fresh as I like it in the market."

"My grandmother had a garden. I used to love to
help her."

"You can come with me to select the vegetables for
dinner if you'd like."

"I would. Where is it?" She shaded her eyes. All she
could see was flagstone, a pool with a cabana, and a
guest house.

"Beyond the little house. It's not big, but I manage
to grow what we need."

"Even sunflower seeds for the damn bird," her husband grumbled. But he didn't sound angry.

"You don't understand Caruso," Mrs. Stone said
soothingly. "He likes his food fresh, the same way I
do."

Cheri watched them, fascinated by their interplay.
They seemed the oldest, most comfortable of friends.
She wondered if she and Michael would ever grow old
together, be happy. In the gentle sunshine of the backyard, anything seemed possible. She began to relax.

"I found your suit, Cheri. Let's go for a swim."

Michael dropped her suit in her lap, and for a moment Cheri wondered what his parents thought about
his familiarity with her clothing.

"You can change in the cabana." Mr. Stone answered her unspoken question. "The water feels good
on a day like this—it's heated."

Cheri changed quickly, then walked outside. Standing at the edge of the pool, she started as Michael dove
into the water.

He surfaced, looking like a sleek, playful seal. "Jump
in, it's great!"

She hesitated for just a second, then jumped in, feet
first. The water felt heavenly against her tired body.

Swimming to the surface, she pushed her hair out of her eyes just as Michael caught her ankle.

"Hey!"

He pulled her underneath, then wrapped his arms around her and they surfaced together. Cheri glanced nervously toward Michael's parents.

When she glanced back at him, he kissed her.

"Michael!" she whispered.

"What. Them?" He laughed softly. "They don't mind. I know they like you."

"They just met me."

"Yeah, but Dad's taken with you, and he's always the hardest to win over."

They swam until they were exhausted, then pulled themselves up on air mattresses and floated lazily around the pool. Michael playfully tried to sink her a few times, but Cheri finally convinced him to let her float in the sun.

Later in the afternoon, Mrs. Stone called them inside for lunch. She had arranged a large platter of meats and cheeses, along with French rolls and a green salad.

Cheri was famished. She made herself a large sandwich, and Mrs. Stone piled still more on her plate.

"Michael told me how hard you worked on the record. This is your time to relax and feel better."

"Thank you." She accepted a second roll, filled with cheese.

They ate outside by the pool, in the shade of the house. Michael and his father did most of the talking, all about agency business. Mr. Stone seemed pleased with what his son was telling him.

Cheri almost dropped her sandwich as he turned his attention to her. "You look awfully familiar to me, Cheri. Where are your folks from?"

She slowly set her roll down on the patio table as she felt the color leave her face.

"Robert!" Mrs. Stone's voice was soft and clear.

"Cheri's parents are no longer alive," Michael said quietly.

Mr. Stone cleared his throat. "I'm terribly sorry."

She continued to stare down at her plate, the half-eaten sandwich no longer appealing. *Say something. Tell him it's all right.*

She forced herself to look up. "It's all right. I guess I just never get used to it." *That much at least is true.* "Sometimes it's... hard to see a family and remember..." She could feel tears stinging her eyes. Not wanting to disgrace herself, she got up from the table and walked quickly to the sliding door.

Michael rose to go after her, but his mother put out a hand, detaining him.

"She needs a little time to herself," she told him quietly.

STARING AT THE CEILING of her room, Cheri tried to still her furiously racing mind.

It can actually be like this. A family that likes one another, gets along. She rolled over on the bed and buried her face in the pillow to soak up the tears.

No wonder Michael is the way he is.

And no wonder you're the way you are. Her thoughts mocked her.

Did Michael's father know her parents? She could hardly bear to think about it. But what if he did? Then Michael would catch her in her lie.

They're as good as dead to me.

More than anything, Cheri wanted his family to like her, wanted them to take her in and make her one of its members.

You could have it all if you married him. The doubts refused to be stilled.

But I don't want to do anything to hurt him.

She rolled over as she heard a knock at the door.

"Cheri?" Mr. Stone.

"Yes."

He let himself in gingerly, leaving the door open. It was obvious he was uncomfortable.

"I'm sorry I upset your lunch."

"Please." She couldn't bear to see him apologize for the wrong reason. "I'm fine."

"You've been crying." He stated the fact with quiet conviction.

"But not because of..." She trailed off, stared at the wall beyond him. How could she possibly tell him?

"Can I help you with anything?" He asked the question cautiously. Here was a man who understood and respected private emotion.

"I want you to know something." She slid off the bed and walked toward him, wrapping the towel she had around her bathing suit a little tighter. "I wasn't crying because of my parents." She took a deep breath, but continued. "They were horrible people. I was upset because—"

"You don't have to tell me anything, Cheri."

"I was upset because you have a terrific family, and I...was wishing it could have been different for me." She brushed her hand against her eyes, furious with herself for starting to cry again. "Pretty stupid, huh?"

He stared at her for a long moment, and Cheri thought wildly that maybe she'd said the wrong thing. When he spoke, his tone was measured, understanding.

"I think I can empathize with you better than anyone else in the family." He paused, looked up and out the window overlooking the rose garden, then back at her. "I went through some pretty difficult times with my own folks."

"What did you do—" Her voice broke and she swallowed against the tightness in her chest. "What did you do to make yourself feel better?"

He patted the top of her head awkwardly. "There isn't really anything to do. Other than just keep on living. That takes a lot of courage in itself."

His eyes were filled with painful understanding, and Cheri knew with deep certainty she'd found a friend.

"Thank you." She extended her hand and he grasped it firmly.

Chapter Twelve

Michael's sister arrived the next morning. She burst
into the breakfast room with no warning and threw her
arms around her father's neck, causing him to spill his
coffee.

"Hi, Daddy!" She kissed him on the forehead, and
Cheri was amazed to see Robert Stone turn a deep pink
before he smiled his slow smile.

"Michael!" She hugged her brother next. She was a
beautiful woman, with her mother's dark hair and high
cheekbones. As soon as she'd given her brother a hug
and a kiss, she turned to Cheri.

"Hi." Gina's dark eyes were kind, but there was
something in their expression that made Cheri wonder
what Michael had told his sister about her.

"The baby?" Mrs. Stone asked, wiping her hands on
her apron as she came into the breakfast room and
opened her arms for her daughter.

"He's asleep. He was really fussy this morning about
getting up so early, so I laid him down on the living-
room couch."

A loud squalling sounded from down the hall and
Gina ran her fingers through her hair, then looked at
her mother with an imploring expression. "Mom, I
don't know what—"

"Bring him here." Mrs. Stone was all confidence.

As Gina ran down the hall in her heels, Michael turned toward Cheri with an amused expression in his eyes. "Imagine all that energy and passion in the courtroom."

"She must really be something."

"That she is," Mr. Stone replied, and Cheri felt the tiniest pang of jealousy for Michael's sister.

When everyone finished breakfast, Gina suggested they go out by the pool and see how well Robert, Jr. could swim, thanks to his classes at the local YWCA.

"At nine months?" Cheri asked, incredulous.

"He's chugging right along. Children aren't afraid. I don't even think Robbie knows the meaning of the word." Gina took her son from her mother's arms and burped him gently.

"MICHAEL, YOU BE CAREFUL," Gina warned. "If you drown my baby, I'll never speak to you again!"

"Gina, don't talk that way to your brother," Mrs. Stone said without looking up.

Cheri dangled her legs in the pool as she watched Michael gently hold Robbie. The baby kicked his chubby legs and screamed with pleasure.

"He's just darling," Cheri said as Gina sat down next to her and put her legs in the water.

"We like him." She splashed some water on her pale arms. "Michael told me you just cut an album. That must have been pretty exciting."

Cheri nodded. "He made it perfect every step of the way."

"Michael has his methods, I agree." Gina looked up as Robbie started to cry. Michael folded the baby into his strong arms, rocking him gently. The crying stopped.

"He'll make a good dad someday," Gina mused, half to herself.

Michael's children. She could picture them, wiry and dark, with big trusting eyes.

"Hey, Dad, all right!" Gina called out, and Cheri turned her head to see Mr. Stone step outside the sliding glass door in his swim trunks.

"I thought I'd take my grandson for a swim."

Michael walked over to the shallow end of the pool and handed the infant into his grandfather's arms. Humming softly, Robert Stone headed slowly into the middle of the pool. Then, supporting the baby in one large hand, he let him float softly in the water.

Cheri felt her eyes begin to fill, watching the infant look up into the older, wiser face. Glancing at Gina, she saw her eyes were also suspiciously bright.

"I wish I'd brought my camera," Gina muttered.

"I brought mine," Cheri offered. "I'm sure it has some film inside—I'll go get it."

She brought it back in record time, and Gina managed to take several photos before either grandfather or grandson were aware they were being photographed.

LATER THAT EVENING, when the house was filled with the delicious aroma of chocolate cake baking, and Gina and Michael were mock-squabbling over who got to lick the beaters, Mr. Stone stuck his head into the kitchen.

"Cheri, there's something I'd like to show you."

She followed him down the hall to his large den. It was a tasteful room, quite similar to Michael's. Dark wood gleamed softly. The paneled walls showed evidence of his career. Gold and platinum albums hung from the far wall, along with pictures of Mr. Stone with several prominent musical acts.

Cheri was fascinated. "I didn't know you managed her!" She pointed to one of the pictures on the wall, of Mr. Stone and a famous singer. "What was she like?"

"A very sweet woman. A pro from the start. She was singing down in Nashville when I signed her. Before that she hadn't done anything but sing at church every Sunday." He shook his head, his expression fond. "She doesn't record anymore, but she still sends us a fruitcake every Christmas. Her mama's secret recipe, she says."

"You must have loved your job, working with people like her."

"They come along once in a lifetime. If you're lucky." He took out a cassette and slid it into the stereo. When music filled the air, Cheri recognized her voice.

"Michael sent me a copy of your demo tape as soon as he heard it. He'd already decided to work with you, but I told him if he hadn't, to hurry up and catch your act before someone else did. I asked him to continue sending me tapes as you progressed."

She listened to the hard beat of "Reckless Love" until Mr. Stone pushed the fast forward button and the tape skipped ahead. He watched the counter, intent on stopping at the right place. Before he played the tape, he said softly, "This is the song that's going to be your hit."

The notes were pure and sweet, the lyrics full of emotion. Cheri closed her eyes and remembered the early days in the studio, making her first professional demo tape.

The melody filled the air, the arrangement simple and harmonious behind it. Cheri listened to the lyrics as if for the first time. She stayed quiet, comfortable alone in the den with Mr. Stone. For some reason, though she was usually self-conscious when she listened to her voice in front of people, this time it didn't bother her.

As the last note slowly faded, Mr. Stone shut off the tape. "Do you see what I mean?"

And suddenly Cheri knew he was right. "Yes."

"All your power as a singer lies in the emotion you give over to a song. And though the others are as authentically emotional as 'More Than Destiny,' people like a song with a little hope."

She nodded.

"I understand the type of pain you went through to get that quality of emotion," he said quietly.

Cheri remained perfectly still, hardly believing what she'd heard. His eyes were old, wise, a little sad.

"She had that same quality." He tipped his head toward the wall of pictures.

She could barely breathe. "Oh, no."

"Yes." He smiled as he remembered. "The first thing I did after I heard your tape was phone my son and tell him someone like you comes along only once in a man's career."

She couldn't reply, couldn't think. She simply stared, incredulous. Such a gift, coming from this man.

"Michael usually phones me from his office every Thursday night. You know what he likes about working with you?"

She could only shake her head.

"He said you were the most consistently solid performer he'd ever encountered. Not self-destructive."

She couldn't believe what she was hearing.

"Not like that boy in the band—what was their name?"

"Bad Boys."

"Bad Boys. Or Nancy."

So he knew. "I don't know if what you're saying is true."

"You're here, aren't you? You were scared to death to meet us, but you came."

Her legs started to tremble, but she braced herself against the heavy wooden desk.

"You put in all the time to get your band to the point where Michael took notice of it."

She nodded, slowly.

"Whatever else you are, Cheri, you're a survivor. And you have my respect."

"Thank you." Not sure if she could take any more, she got up and left the room.

LYING IN THE BIG FOUR-POSTER BED that night, Cheri relived her first day with Michael's family.

I never knew it could be this way. Images of Michael being hugged by his mother, Robert Stone in the pool with his grandson, the whole family around the dining-room table, talking, laughing, eating.

She shifted nervously underneath the covers, then got up and turned on the bedside lamp to its lowest setting. The strangeness of the room upset her. She wished she knew which bedroom Michael was in. Not because she wanted to sleep with him, simply because she wanted to be close to him.

She'd called Glenda after talking with Mr. Stone, needing to hear her voice, have her reassurance. But the answering machine had been on, and Cheri hadn't wanted to leave a message.

She got out of bed and walked over to the window overlooking the rose garden. Her fingers gripped the sill tightly. Consciously, she relaxed them. She was restless tonight. All her instincts were tangled—her life was out of control, quickly spiraling away from her. She felt she was running after her emotions, desperately trying to catch up, make sense of what her life had become.

The light tap on the door caused her to reach for her robe. "Come in," she called softly as she belted it around her waist.

Michael entered, barefoot and dressed in a pair of

faded cutoffs. He closed the door gently behind him. "Can't sleep?"

"No."

"Neither can I." He grinned. "I miss you."

Cheri sat down on the edge of the bed, and Michael joined her. He picked up her hand and played with her fingers.

"How're you doing?"

"Fine."

"Is it too much? All at once?"

"No. It's not that at all." She didn't want to talk about what she was feeling.

"They like you, Cheri. They really do."

"I'm glad." She felt forced and stiff with him.

"Is something wrong?"

"I'm just not feeling very well." If she feigned sickness, then she wouldn't have to be present for the party tomorrow evening.

"Do you want me to call a doctor?" He was all concern.

"No, I—it's just nerves, I think."

"Why don't you lie down and try to sleep? I'll sit with you for a while."

She was glad he didn't want to make love. With all the emotion pent up inside her, Cheri felt if she let any of it out she'd never be able to stop crying.

He lay down beside her, outside the covers, his body warm and reassuring against hers. She enjoyed the feel of him next to her for several minutes. He touched her cheek gently and she went into his arms, content to feel the hard muscles of his chest underneath her cheek, hear the steady beat of his heart. He smelled of soap and shampoo, clean and fresh.

This was familiar, this was her life now. She kissed his chest and snuggled against him. She didn't want to look back, to think about her life long ago.

"I like the way your parents are with each other."
She wanted to convey what she was feeling.

"I know. They were lucky they found each other."
He kissed her hair, then her temple, then eased his
head back down on the pillow.

"What have you told them about us?" She thought
about the engagement ring he had given her, back in
the top drawer of her dresser, hidden away.

"I told them you wanted to wait until you were very
sure of your feelings before you agreed to marry me.
And Gina doesn't know anything yet."

"Oh."

"They understood. I told them we only met in February."

"Do they know we live together?"

"They've never asked. I don't think they want to
know."

She closed her eyes, wishing with all her heart she
had more to offer Michael. Somehow, just herself
never seemed enough.

"I don't want to do anything to hurt them." Her
voice sounded small in the big bedroom.

"They're a little more resilient than we give them
credit for. Mom especially."

Michael was quiet for such a long time, Cheri
thought he'd fallen asleep.

"Do you still want to marry me?" Her words were
barely a whisper.

"What?" He was all attention now. "Cheri, are you
serious?"

She adjusted her body so they were face to face, on
one pillow. "Will you marry me?"

"Of course I will!" He pulled her toward him and
kissed her, but broke the kiss before it became too intense. Afterward, he got up out of bed and headed for
the door. "I'll be back in a minute."

When he returned, he had something clenched tightly in his hand. Taking her left hand in his, he slid the ring on her finger.

"You carried it all this way?"

He nodded. "I always kept hoping."

He lay down beside her, on top of the covers again, and took her in his arms. "What made you change your mind?"

"I don't know. I guess seeing what your parents have; it made me want the same thing for myself." As Cheri said the words, she felt tears fill her eyes. She bit her lip to keep her emotions under control.

"I'll make you happy, Cheri." His eyes were tender.

"I know you will, baby." She kissed his cheek, then slid her arms around his neck and held him tightly. But even with a ring on her finger and Michael in bed beside her, she had the most uneasy feeling that her silent struggle to keep her life from shattering was swiftly coming to an end.

"SO YOU COULDN'T just manage her, you decided to marry her." Robert Stone's voice was gently teasing as he studied them.

"It looks that way," Michael said.

"When? Where? Have you set a date?" Gina was all breathless excitement.

Cheri glanced at Michael; she would let him answer.

"Gina, I just asked her last night."

His sister reached for the pitcher of orange juice. "Well, it was taking you so long, I thought she might have asked you."

Cheri met Michael's eyes. Gina wasn't far off base.

Mrs. Stone merely hugged Cheri and whispered, "I know you'll be happy and I welcome you into the family."

Everyone oohed and aahed over the ring, and for

several moments Cheri basked in the warmth of their affection. Then she remembered the reason she had been invited for the weekend and looked across the table toward Michael's father.

"But it's your birthday! Happy Birthday, Mr. Stone."

"Do you think you could manage to call me Robert?" There was a soft gleam in his eyes, so like Michael's.

"Happy Birthday, Robert."

"He'll have you calling him Dad in no time," Gina promised as she began to clear away the dishes.

"Only if you want to," Mr. Stone reassured her. "Cheri?"

She turned toward him, half out of her chair on the way to the kitchen.

"Thank you." He glanced up at her over the top of his reading glasses, then picked up the paper. "I can't remember ever receiving a better birthday present."

I'LL KNOW IT WHEN I SEE IT, Cheri thought as she scanned the exclusive shop. She was about to give up when a piece of crystal in the back gallery caught her eye. Small and delicate, a beautifully formed musical note on a pedestal of white marble. The perfect gift for Robert Stone, a man who had devoted his life to bringing music to others.

Once the little note was safely wrapped in tissue and put in a gift box, Cheri spent another few minutes picking out wrapping paper, ribbon and a card. Then she joined Michael in the front of the shop.

"All done?" He sounded surprised.

"I was lucky. Let's go."

They arrived back in time to help Mrs. Stone with the final touches. The bar was ready. The food was in the refrigerator. The house was spotless.

Mr. Stone was swimming in the pool when Cheri and Michael joined him.

The older man shook his head. "I hate big parties. Every year I tell Francesca not to go to all this trouble, but she never listens."

Cheri looked away. She didn't want him to see the amusement she was sure was evident on her face.

He sighed, a sound of total resignation. "But it makes her happy, so I let her."

"You'll like seeing everyone, Dad." Michael gently splashed Cheri.

They swam until late afternoon, then Cheri excused herself and went inside to shower and prepare for the evening ahead.

She dressed quickly. The turquoise silk whispered down over her hips and she arranged the halter neckline until she was satisfied with the way it draped over her body. Taking her hot rollers out, she bent over and brushed her hair, then stood up and let it settle around her shoulders. Finishing her makeup quickly, she sprayed on some Chloe, perfume Michael had given her, then picked up the small silver package and headed toward the dining room.

There was a large pile of presents already in the middle of the gleaming mahogany table, so Cheri tucked hers in as unobtrusively as possible. Then she turned in the direction of the kitchen, where she heard voices.

The conversation stopped abruptly as she walked in. Cheri felt awkward for a split second before Francesca Stone leaned over and kissed her on the cheek.

"*Bellissima*. You are exquisite."

"Very pretty, Cheri." Robert raised his glass in a salute.

"Where's Michael?" Gina asked.

"Go check on him, *cara*, while I get dinner on the table." Michael's mother looked pointedly at Cheri. "It's the room next to yours."

Cheri walked away, feeling lighter than air, the whisper of silk and lightest touch of fragrance in her wake.

When she knocked, Michael said "Come in," but he sounded short-tempered. As the door swung open, Cheri saw he was in front of a mirror, struggling with his black tie.

"Let me help you." She went to him quickly, took the strips of material into her hands and began to work them gently into a knot.

He smelled of soap and after-shave. His white dress shirt felt cool to her touch as she laid her palm quickly against his chest. It was as if, in the midst of intense happiness, she had to touch him to reassure herself he was still here, with her.

The knot finished, she adjusted it against his throat, then smoothed his collar. "There you are."

He stood looking down at her with the strangest expression on his face, and as Cheri studied him she thought how lucky she was he loved her. She adored him, couldn't look at him enough. Michael looked dark and handsome as he put on his jacket, then ran a comb quickly through his hair.

"You need a haircut," she said softly, watching him. It felt very intimate being in his room during this last-minute grooming ritual.

"That's some dress. I haven't seen it before."

"I bought it with Rachel the day we went to Newport."

"I like it." He set the comb down on the dresser. "Is everyone else in the kitchen?"

"We're the only ones missing."

"They can miss us a few minutes longer," he said, smiling, as he pulled her gently into his arms.

"Now who is this from?" Robert Stone asked as he extricated a blue package from the enormous pile.

"Robbie," Gina said. "He picked it out himself."

There was a small ripple of laughter around the table as Robert tore open the wrapping and took out a jeweler's box. Opening it up, he admired its contents for a minute, then said gravely, "Thank you, Robbie. I needed another pair of cuff links. I'll probably lose these, too."

When he reached for the small silver package, Cheri felt her throat go dry.

Opening the card, he read it. The stern expression on his face softened for an instant, and when he looked up, his gaze was directed at her.

"Thank you, Cheri." He slid the card back in its envelope and, instead of passing it around, put it in his jacket pocket. Peeling the tape off the paper with the greatest care, he slowly unwrapped the package. The outer gift box gave him no clue, and he opened it, taking out the tissue-wrapped object. Unwrapping it, he held the tiny crystal note for an instant, then set it in front of him.

Michael squeezed her hand underneath the table.

"Cheri, it's gorgeous!" Gina exclaimed.

But all of Cheri's attention was focused on the older man. It was as if this were her final moment of acceptance, and only he could give it to her.

"I've been admiring this note for a long time," he murmured. "The little gift shop on Ocean Avenue?"

She nodded.

He directed his next words to Michael. "You've got yourself a prize. Not only is she beautiful, but she has excellent taste as well." He glanced back at Cheri. "Thank you. This will go in my study."

She hadn't realized she was holding her breath until she slowly let it out.

"MICHAEL, I WISH you'd bought more ice!" Francesca waved her hands in an agitated manner as she scanned the crowded living room.

"I'll go out and get some more later, Mom. Cheri can come with me." He tightened his grip around her waist.

"No, I want to show her off. It isn't every day my son brings his fiancée to visit. I want to make sure all your father's friends meet her."

Michael raised his dark brows in inquiry. Cheri nodded. "I'll stay. I don't mind." She liked Mrs. Stone's fussing. If she was proud to show her off, then Cheri felt she must measure up to whatever invisible standard applied.

Gina brushed by, radiant in a silver-and-black harem pantsuit. Her long hair was pulled back from her face and cascaded down her back in shimmering waves.

"Cheri, come to the kitchen with me. I need some help."

Cheri glanced at Mrs. Stone, who nodded. The party had been going on for about an hour, and even though Michael had told her all of Mr. Stone's friends were invited, she had underestimated the number of people the large living room could hold.

Michael had introduced her around at the start, and Cheri was astute enough to realize she'd make several very helpful contacts in the music industry. She had also tried not to stare as a few of Robert Stone's famous clients had come through the door to throw their arms around him and wish him a happy birthday.

"I'm sorry I had to rush you away." Gina's voice was muffled as she knelt in front of the refrigerator and piled crudités on the large silver platter in her other hand. "But Mother gets crazy if the littlest thing runs out. She's been telling Michael to get her more ice for the last half hour."

"I know. He just left."

"He'll probably come back with twelve sacks. He hates it when she doesn't get enough in the first place. Hand me the other tray, would you?"

"Sure."

When Gina finished, both women walked back out into the party, threading their way through the crowded room to the low table filled to capacity with all sorts of delicacies. Cheri had come to respect Francesca for her talents in the kitchen, but Michael's mother had truly outdone herself tonight. Cold pasta salads, platters of vegetables and cheese, a basket of breads, a fruit plate, a torte, caviar—the list was endless.

Cheri felt at loose ends without Michael, so she went back to the bar and asked for another glass of tomato juice. She was contemplating fighting her way back to the buffet when Gina touched her arm and whispered in her ear.

"Another business acquaintance." She grinned. "If I were you, I'd be sick of all this. But I guess Michael's worth it." She linked her fingers with Cheri and led her toward the far side of the living room.

"Cheri, Gregory Bradford. Gregory, this is my brother Michael's fiancée."

Cheri dropped her glass, her fingers suddenly nerveless.

"Cheri, I'm sorry." Gina was all concern. "Did I bump you?"

"Let me." Cheri knelt down quickly, her head buzzing, her hands shaking.

What was he doing here?

She didn't look up as she collected the fragile glass, piece by piece, off the hardwood floor. The juice looked like blood as it seeped into the nearby Oriental carpet.

She couldn't look up. Cheri knew what she'd see—

dark-brown hair, shot through with auburn, dark-blue eyes, all so like her own. But his face had haunted her through countless nightmares, and when she'd thought of him, it had only brought back the old familiar pain.

Quite deliberately, feeling nothing, she cut her finger with a piece of glass. *Get away from him.* When she stood up, she avoided his eyes.

"I'm so sorry—I must have had too much to drink." She directed her apology to Gina, glad she had an excuse for the tears in her eyes. "I'll be back as soon as I clean up." She hurried out of the room without a backward glance.

When she reached the bathroom, she was almost hyperventilating. *Easy, easy.* Throwing the broken glass into the wastebasket, she gripped the sink and lowered her head, taking deep breaths to quiet the pure rage coursing through her body. It made her want to vomit, the sensation was that strong.

"Cheri?" She heard the quick knock on the door.

When she looked up, she saw the tears streaming down her face. She wiped her hand across her face, smearing a bit of blood across her cheek. Keeping her voice as steady as possible, she answered. "I'm all right, Francesca. I'll be out in a second."

"*Cara*, if you need me, I'm in the kitchen."

Cheri washed her face and hands slowly, then got a Band-Aid out of the medicine cabinet and bandaged her finger.

You're out of control. With a passion she'd never suspected she possessed, Cheri had a sudden urge to run into the living room and start beating him, tearing at his face with her nails, punishing him for what he had put her through, what it had done to her relationship with Michael.

Michael. She had to tell him now.

He had to be back from getting the ice. Opening the

bathroom door slowly, she peered up and down the long, silent hallway.

No one.

If she could make it to the kitchen, she could find Mrs. Stone. She could leave the house through the back door, and meet Michael in the driveway, tell him before he walked back inside.

She began to walk slowly down the hall, as if her body didn't belong to her. Away from the lights and laughter, toward the sanctuary of the kitchen.

One of the guests, a big, burly man, burst in through a side door. She covered her mouth, tried to hold back a scream.

"Sorry. Which way's the bathroom?"

She pointed, then turned back toward the kitchen and began to walk rapidly.

Pushing open the swinging door, she stopped. No one was there. Where was Mrs. Stone? Michael?

Feeling sick, she leaned her forehead against the cool white surface of the refrigerator, wishing she could crawl inside the frozen interior and shut the door forever.

She couldn't seem to stop the tears. *I'm not as strong as you think, Michael, really I'm not.*

When she heard the door open, all her muscles tensed. It had to be one of the Stone family. What would they feel toward her when they knew? There was nothing she could do now but tell them.

But before she had a chance to turn around, she heard his voice. A voice that had followed her to hell and back. A voice she always heard before she fell asleep at night. A voice she had never been able to make go away.

"Hello, Cheri."

Chapter Thirteen

Robert Stone was an observant man. It was part of what had made him so phenomenally successful in the business. Even at his age, there wasn't much that passed him by.

He had seen Cheri drop the glass, seen her flee the room. And he had seen his daughter introduce her to Gregory Bradford seconds before.

Something didn't fit. It niggled at the back of his mind, made him inattentive as one of his guests rambled along, telling him about her house in Mexico. He couldn't get the quick glance he had seen of Cheri's face out of his mind.

She's scared to death of him.

Gregory was cool as always, surrounded by people near the bar. A fine attorney and a specialist in entertainment law, he'd been a professional acquaintance of Robert's for years. But now Robert wondered if he'd ever known the man at all. He decided to watch him.

Within five minutes, he could see Gregory was paying as little attention to his company as Robert was to his. All his attention was focused on the doorway to the hall.

The doorway Cheri had taken.

And then he saw her, saw her pass by the opened hall door with a flash of turquoise skirt, saw Gregory set down his drink and excuse himself as he walked smoothly toward the kitchen.

"Excuse me just a minute," he said to his guest. "I've got to see what my wife is up to."

Robert Stone now knew whom Cheri resembled.

SHE COULDN'T ANSWER HIM.

"Cheri."

She heard him coming closer, but her legs wouldn't move. Suddenly, she felt like a child, back in her bed at home, hiding behind her stuffed animals.

"Turn around, Cheri."

She gripped the counter as if it were a lifeline, digging into the Formica so hard it hurt her palms. She knew she had to look, had to keep him from touching her again. If he did, she'd never be able to stop screaming.

"Stay away from me."

"Can't you even look at me?" His voice had that high, pleading quality she'd always detested.

He touched her bare shoulder gently and she jerked as if he'd applied a live flame. Taking a deep, shuddering breath, she swallowed the urge to scream and faced him.

"Leave me alone." She tried to sound strong. But her lips were trembling.

He smiled then and she looked away.

"Get out of here. Please."

"You don't really want me to." That high voice again. She couldn't look at him.

"So you're going to marry Michael Stone." There was a possessive quality to his voice.

She didn't move.

"You should thank me, you know."

"*Thank* you!" Her voice broke. "For *what*?" She knew she was dangerously close to breaking, but she didn't want to be incoherent. She wanted to make him face what he had done to her. "For destroying a part of me I can never get back? For making it so hard for me to feel anything I have to—" she took a deep breath, sick to her stomach "—that I have to have therapy twice a week, *just to be able to look at myself in the mirror*?"

His face was smooth. Composed. Unemotional.

Cheri knew she was out of control now, knew her voice was rising, knew she was becoming hysterical, but she didn't care.

"For making me feel like some screwed-up, worthless piece of— You were *wrong. You were wrong to do what you did to me*!"

They faced each other, locked in battle. Neither heard the kitchen door open.

"I didn't hurt you. I *taught* you. You would have learned sooner or later. Stone will thank me after you're married."

He doesn't feel anything. He doesn't think he was wrong. She could feel herself breaking out in a cold sweat, starting to tremble. Pure, animal fear. He even smelled the same—expensive cologne and tobacco.

"I won't bother you after you're married. Then you'll belong to him. But I thought maybe we could—"

"No. Get out."

"Cheri, that's not like you. I remember—"

"Get out!"

"I think you—"

"Get out of my house." Robert Stone's words were measured and even. "Don't ever come back. And don't come near her again."

Cheri couldn't meet Robert's eyes as Gregory Bradford walked quickly out of the kitchen, pushing the door open with more force than necessary. She stood looking down at the counter. Numb. Nothing mattered anymore.

She felt him standing next to her. The tightness in her throat was unbearable. She swallowed once, twice. All her weight was supported by the counter, her legs were trembling violently.

He touched her shoulder gently.

"Please don't," she whispered. Just saying the words seemed to loosen the tight ball of pain in her chest. Without looking at him, she slowly knelt down, put her face into her hands and started to cry.

"SHE'S ASLEEP. I stayed with her until she couldn't cry anymore," Francesca whispered to her husband.

"Go back to the bedroom. I'll catch Michael when he comes in the door."

Robert Stone looked around the crowded living room with distaste. Now, genuinely, he wished his wife had never decided to give him a birthday party. He was sure it wouldn't be over for at least another hour.

He turned his head and set down his glass as he saw his son come in the front door, two grocery bags balanced in his arms.

"I bought enough for an army. Now she'll probably have leftovers," Michael snapped as he pushed open the kitchen door. "Where's Cheri?"

"She wasn't feeling well, so she went to her room to lie down."

"What's wrong?" He headed for the door.

Robert reacted with the reflexes of a young man, blocking Michael's exit. "Come with me. I want to talk to you before you see her."

Inside the den, Michael paced impatiently, like a wild animal confined in its cage. "Dad, what the hell is going on? I leave the house for half an hour and come back to—"

"Sit down. Here's a drink. I don't want you making a damn fool of yourself."

Michael stared at his father for just a second. Then force of habit took over. He sat down.

"Drink that."

Michael swallowed the liquor with one fluid motion, then sat on the edge of his chair impatiently.

"How well do you know Cheri?" The old man's voice was gruff.

"I think I know her pretty well."

"Have the two of you ever had problems?"

"What the hell do you mean?"

Robert smiled sadly. He'd found the answer in his son's defensiveness.

"She met a man tonight. A man who upset her a great deal." He watched the color slowly drain from his son's face, not liking to impart this kind of news. "That's all I know."

Michael was already out of his chair and starting toward the door.

"Michael!" He stopped for a second, looked at his father. "I don't know if she'll want to see you. Be easy with her."

But Michael was already out the door.

Robert sat back in his chair and poured himself another drink. As he set the glass down, he caught sight of the crystal note on his desk. He picked it up and turned it over slowly in his hands, allowing the facets to catch the light and shimmer.

So fragile. So beautiful.

Setting it down gently, he got up and walked out to join his guests.

WHEN MICHAEL OPENED THE GUEST-ROOM DOOR, his mother motioned for him to be quiet. Shutting it slowly behind him, he walked over beside her chair at the head of the bed.

The only light came from the small lamp on the dresser, turned to the lowest setting.

He pulled up another chair and sat down.

"What happened?" he whispered.

His mother shook her head. "I don't know. I heard some shouting in the kitchen and when I came in, she was curled up on the kitchen floor and crying as if her heart had been broken."

"Who was the man?"

She stared at him. "What man?"

"Dad said someone upset her." In the mood he was in, Michael wanted to track him down and beat him so badly he'd never come near Cheri again.

"I don't know what you're talking about."

"Dad said—" He stopped talking as Cheri made a small sound of distress and rolled over.

They were both silent for a few minutes, watching her, then Francesca touched her son's shoulder gently. "I'm going to talk with your father and try to bring the party to an end. You stay here with Cheri."

As soon as Michael was alone, he pulled his chair up as close to the bed as possible. Then he waited and watched.

She seemed lost in the large bed beneath the knitted blanket. Her hair spread out over the pillows gave her an innocent, almost virginal quality. His eyes examined every part of her, his mouth tightening as he saw the bandage on her hand.

What the hell had happened?

MICHAEL WATCHED CHERI sleep for a long time, until he noticed light outside the window and heard birds calling softly. Everything in the world was caught up in the gentle rise and fall of her chest. And he began to think back over their relationship, over everything he should have done. Everything that should have been different.

He must have dozed in the chair for a short time, but he woke to find she still hadn't moved. Rubbing his hands wearily over his face, he sat up straighter and yawned, then resumed his vigil.

For the first time, Michael began to wish he'd never met Cheri on a professional basis. How much easier it would have been to have simply met her on the beach, at a party, in a bar. They could have started a relationship in a normal way, without any outside pressures.

Had he pushed her too hard? He knew he was a relentless taskmaster when it came to the people he managed, but he'd thought she'd been able to separate their personal and professional lives. Maybe she hadn't.

And what had been left to tell him? Michael lowered his face back into his hands and sighed. If he was honest with himself, that was what hurt the most. He had wanted to give her everything, had tried so hard.

He hadn't even been able to win her trust.

She stirred and he lifted his head. He was looking at her when she slowly opened her eyes and started to focus them. She seemed disoriented. She slowly sat up in bed, and the covers fell away from her bare shoulders. Michael moved toward her, wanting to touch her, reassure her.

She jerked back sharply, instinctively, her eyes clouded with fear. Michael had the sensation she didn't know who he was for just an instant. Then her face cleared. She tried a tentative smile. Her eyes filled with tears and she looked down at the bed.

"Cheri?" His voice was barely a whisper.

WHAT COULD SHE TELL HIM? *How much did he know already? What had his father told him about what he'd seen in the kitchen?*

Cheri pushed back her hair with her hand, kept the other at the blanket in front of her chest.

She couldn't lose more than she already had.

"I met a man..." she started. Her throat closed up.

He remained silent.

"I met the man who . . . raped me." There wasn't any other way of putting it. She looked up into Michael's eyes, so soft and caring, and she remembered the first time she had met him. If she had known then what lay in store for them, she would have run away as fast as she could.

Michael moved very slowly. Standing up, he came over next to her.

"Can I sit on the bed with you?"

She nodded.

They were silent for a while. She didn't want him to touch her, and he seemed to sense her mood. He just sat on the mattress, barely a foot away, saying nothing.

She looked up at him through her hair. "Did your father tell you?"

"Tell me what?" When she didn't answer, he said softly, "He didn't tell me anything except that you met a man in the kitchen who upset you. When I came back with the ice, you were in bed."

He didn't know.

Michael stood up then, slowly. "Do you want me to get you anything? Maybe we could sit out on the patio for a while." She wasn't going to trust him, and he felt something inside him die a little.

"Michael, sit down for a minute."

He did.

"If I tell you something, will you promise to stay until I finish?"

He nodded.

"I lied to you. I guess I've lied all along, letting you believe—" She reached over to the nightstand and took a tissue, then blew her nose. "My parents aren't dead. They live in San Francisco."

He stayed perfectly still, not understanding why she was telling him this.

"I ran away from home when I was thirteen. I didn't run away for good until I turned fifteen. I hitched a ride to Los Angeles and took any kind of job I could get to stay alive."

He didn't say anything, and she continued.

"It was easier for me to think of my parents as dead. It was too painful to remember what living at home had been like."

"Cheri—"

She held up her hand. "I guess I really lied to you when I wouldn't trust you and tell you the truth about why I was so afraid for you to...touch me. But each time with you, it got a little easier. What we had was so special to me.... I'd never felt that way before, Michael. I didn't want to ruin it by telling you anything."

"Nothing you could tell me—"

"I know how you think you'd feel, but what you may feel is something different. I really like your family, Michael."

"What?"

"They're good people. I've never been around a family that just likes one another so much. I was always afraid at home, wondering what was going to happen next, never feeling I was good enough, just for myself. The first night I spent here, I lay awake in bed and pretended I was a member of this family and I'd always been loved and protected as much as you and Gina. It's hard for you to understand, Michael, because you've always had it."

"Cheri..."

She looked up at him, and he was startled by how old she suddenly appeared, as if all the energy had been drained out of her body and she didn't have any to spare.

"The man who raped me was my father."

HE STARED AT HER for what seemed like a long time, but it couldn't have been more than a few seconds.

"Your father?"

She nodded, slowly, wearily.

"You were—thirteen?

"Yes." She sounded tired.

Her voice was flat and dull as she continued, and it seemed to Michael all of what had been held in check for years came tumbling out, as if she were trying to push him away from her with a barrage of words.

"It started... when I was so young I really can't remember. Just the way he touched me. Even as a child, I knew. When I was little, he used to come into my bedroom at night and... play with me. He told me all fathers played that way with their little girls. I trusted him. I was so stupid."

He reached for her hand, but she pulled it gently from his grasp.

"The older I got, the more he made me do. He laughed at me because he knew I had feelings, and sometimes—sometimes it even felt good. That's always the hardest part for me to live with. Sometimes, Michael, when you and I made love, I'd feel so good and then I'd remember and feel so awful." She pushed a lock of hair out of her face and picked at a loose piece of yarn in the spread.

"The evening he... made me... he followed me through the house and... I locked the door to my bedroom but he broke it and—"

"Don't Cheri. You don't have to tell me." He hated hearing her pain.

She went on as if she hadn't heard him. "My mother didn't even ask. A broken door. She didn't ask me what happened. I ran away to my grandmother's and she took care of me. She believed me."

She cleared her throat, and he saw a shimmer of tears in her eyes. "She died when I was fifteen. I knew I had to get away. She was the only person in my entire life who gave a damn about what happened to me. She'd given me some money, but my father took it out of my purse when he took me back. I ran away for good that same night."

He thought of her as she must have been. Fifteen, alone and frightened in a city like Los Angeles. He couldn't bear to think of it.

"I had a lot of different jobs until I turned eighteen. One year it seemed like I had a job a week." She met his eyes. "But I never went out on the street."

"I met Rachel when I was twenty; she heard me singing on Hollywood Boulevard in front of the Chinese Theater. She got me a job at the bookstore. I didn't meet her there like I told you." She sighed. "Sometimes I lied so much I used to stay awake at night and wonder when I was going to give myself away."

"Cheri, none of this—"

"I gave the ring back to your mother last night. I told her to keep it for me until I felt better. I don't want it back."

His throat hurt when he spoke. "I still want to marry you."

She laughed, a harsh sound, and he watched her composure break completely. "Why? So you can help me the same way you helped Nancy? Why don't you find a woman who's whole?" Her blue eyes were dull with pain. "What is it with you, Michael, do you like rejects? Do you like playing the Good Samaritan?"

Even as he felt the color leaving his face, he knew she was trying to push him away. But he didn't know what to do. "Honey, we'll talk about this when you feel better."

"Don't patronize me, Michael. I mean what I say."

He opened his mouth to reply, but she cut in before he could.

"Just leave me alone, Michael. Please leave me alone."

MICHAEL FOUND HIS FATHER out by the pool, reading the paper.

"Dad, I want you to tell me something."

Robert Stone glanced at his son over the top of his glasses.

"Who was he?"

His father remained silent.

"Tell me."

"Why? So you can do some damn fool stunt like go blow his brains out? In the mood you're in, I wouldn't trust you with that kind of information."

When Michael didn't reply, he continued: "You should be in there taking care of Cheri."

"She doesn't want me anymore." His words were short. Bitter.

His father folded his paper and set it down on the table in front of him. "For someone who's so damn smart in business, you have a way of completely missing the point when it comes to personal affairs."

"Then why don't you fill me in on what I'm missing?"

"She needs you. She threw you out of that bedroom as a way of testing you. Before you drive her home, you make sure you find a way to tell her you love her no matter what's happened to her."

"Dad, where the hell do you get off telling me all this?"

Robert Stone picked up his paper and adjusted his glasses. "It's called having perspective. I'm not the man who's in love with her."

Chapter Fourteen

Cheri pulled on a pair of shorts and a T-shirt, then began to pack. More than anything, she wanted to leave this house. She practically tore her clothes off the hangers, took them out of the dresser in great clumps. The black dress here. The rose dress there. The turquoise silk she stuffed in the wastebasket. She knew she'd never wear it again.

Snapping her case shut, she made the bed, then collected any stray tissues and threw them away. She washed her face until it hurt and pulled her hair into a tight braid down her back.

Now all she had to do was say good-bye to the Stones, thank them—and endure the ride back to Los Angeles with Michael.

Well, you got what you deserved all along, she thought as she hoisted her suitcase off the bed and carried it down the hall.

The house seemed strangely deserted, devoid of all family sounds. The kitchen had been cleaned, the living-room rug vacuumed.

She must have slept through it all.

When she entered the family room, she saw Michael through the sliding glass doors. He was sitting on the far side of the pool, his back to her. She stepped down into the room, then crossed to the sliding door.

Opening it slowly, she walked out onto the patio.

It seemed impossible she could feel so bad on such a glorious day. The sky was such an intense blue, it hurt her to look at it. There wasn't a cloud in sight. Sunlight bounced off the surface of the water in the pool.

She shut the door behind her. Michael turned around. His face was drawn, the muscles in his jaw tight. His eyes were squinted against the bright light.

"Michael?" she called tentatively. She really didn't want to hurt him anymore.

He remained where he was.

She walked up to him, her sandals tapping briskly. "What time do you want to start back?" She carefully didn't use the word "home."

"Whenever you want."

He seemed distant. Remote. For just an instant she wanted to reach out and touch his shoulder, but she stifled the impulse. *You don't have that right anymore.*

"Where are your parents? I'd like to say good-bye." Cheri felt awkward, as if she were carrying on a conversation all by herself.

"They're out by the garden. Mom's trying to figure out what to cook for supper."

"Do you want to stay?" She didn't know what to do.

He looked at her for a long moment. And at that moment she had the same sensation she'd had a long time ago in the bookstore. He was looking at her and seeing beyond everything superficial. He was seeing inside her soul.

"I want you to give me one week." His voice was so low she barely heard it.

"What?"

"One week." When she didn't answer, he bent his head and stared at the surface of the water.

She focused on the back of his head, on the dark hair she'd loved to touch, on the strong neck and shoulders.

He had carried all their problems for so long. Couldn't she give him this?

"Please, Cheri." He was whispering now, as if his throat were too tight to let a louder sound out. "Trust me."

Slowly, very slowly, she set down her suitcase.

HE TOOK HER BACK to Maui. They caught a flight out that same Sunday evening at six from San Francisco, then slept over in Honolulu. He didn't go near her. Their room had twin beds and he was scrupulously careful not to touch her as they moved about the suite.

By Monday they were in their original cabin. Cheri lay back on one of the small beds and listened to the booming of the waves through the lava formations. Michael had made up their bedroom to look like their room at the hotel, but there was a little less space between the beds.

They spent their days outdoors, hiking and swimming, sunbathing and eating. Cheri began to relax again. And Michael was always there. Close, but not too close. He never touched her—except with words.

At night, she listened to his gentle, even breathing and wondered why it was so hard to find happiness with this man. She still loved him—she'd never stopped. There were no secrets between them anymore, so she was surprised he still wanted to be with her.

On their third evening at the cabin, after a day spent in Hana, Michael began asking her questions.

"Tell me what it was like, Cheri." His voice was soft in the darkness.

She couldn't speak.

He seemed to be able to sense her emotions, see the fear inside her mind. "I don't mean that actual evening, I mean, what did you feel, all that time? From the time you were little."

When she didn't answer, he reached his hand slowly between the two beds and held hers, his fingers warm and strong. A lifeline.

"It wasn't your fault," he said quietly.

Something in his expression broke part of the frozen wall of emotions separating them. Closing her eyes, Cheri reached deep inside for old, frightening feelings she'd never shared before.

"I...I always felt different." She gripped his hand harder. "For a while, I thought everyone knew. I thought there was something about me, something they could see. I...I tried to be as perfect as I could be. I guess I believed if I was perfect, no one would suspect."

He squeezed her hand gently and she found his presence in the darkness comforting.

"Did you have any friends while you were in school?" Michael's voice was lazy and relaxed; he might have been asking her if she wanted to go for a swim.

She shook her head back and forth on her pillow. "My father...he seemed to like to keep my mother and me isolated. I think he knew, if anyone came too close they would sense something was very wrong."

They were silent for a time, until she spoke again.

"I had one boyfriend. I remember I went to a homecoming dance my sophomore year. My grandmother made me go. We went out with his friend and his friend's girl friend. We stopped at this restaurant, and afterward I was in the bathroom with this girl and she began talking about how she wanted to make love with her boyfriend but she wasn't sure because she didn't know what to expect and she didn't know what it would feel like."

She blinked her eyes, determined not to cry.

"And I felt so old, Michael. And then so angry. I just

kept wishing, all the way home, that I could feel the way she felt, but I knew I never would because he... he took that away from me and I can never get it back."

He squeezed her hand, gently encouraging.

She took a deep breath, let out a long, shaken sigh.

"I'm so tired, Michael."

THEY TALKED a little each night, and by the end of the sixth day, Cheri felt she had told him everything. There was no fear in her revelations: They had one day left together; then she was sure she'd never see him again.

Michael arranged for them to have a picnic out on the lava formations. After they'd finished their meal, he wrapped his arms around her as she sat in front of him and they watched the sun set over the island. Cheri looked up at the stars and remembered wishes they had made. It seemed like a long time ago.

That evening, he talked to her.

"I know I can never... understand what you went through, but I want to try. I want us to start over again. I want you to come back with me to our house and see how things go." When she didn't answer him, he rushed on. "I didn't *know* before, Cheri. It makes all the difference in the world. It'll be better this time, you'll see."

It was always the best. She gently disengaged her hand from his, slowly moved it underneath the cotton sheet on her bed. As much as it hurt, she couldn't let a man as special as Michael spend the rest of his life with someone like her.

"No."

THE WIND PLAYED through the palm fronds as Michael lay in his narrow cot, staring unseeing at the darkness. It would rain tonight; the weather would mirror the turbulence inside him. He could hear Cheri's even breathing. She'd fallen asleep quickly, exhausted from giving him the story of her life in one week's time.

Careful not to wake her, he got up out of bed and pulled on a pair of faded jeans. Slipping on a pair of tennis shoes, he walked quietly out of the cabin and headed for the ocean.

The waves were high that night, booming as they swept up underneath the pebbles, shot through small openings. He climbed up on one of the bigger formations and sat looking out over the ocean.

He hadn't cried when Nancy died. Though he'd never forgotten the look on the doctor's face when she'd told him. He'd simply driven home and locked himself in his house. Two days later, Gina had come to the door, wondering why he wasn't home for Christmas.

By then, he'd buried all his feelings.

Years of work had followed. He'd been relentless in pursuing his goals. So easy, when that was all you had.

Until he'd seen her. How had he known, from the very first moment, that she was going to play such a part in his life? As he thought back over the months they'd been together, every last piece fell into place. There were no more secrets.

She'd told him everything, he was certain. He'd made her tell him, had pushed relentlessly against her reluctance. Because he'd known he had to catch her at a vulnerable moment. Before she shut it all away.

They were alike in that respect.

He knew she'd only told him because she was convinced she'd never see him once they flew back to Los Angeles. But he knew better. He'd keep her here a month if that was what it took. He'd go through therapy with her, listen to anything she had to say, walk through hell and back.

But he wasn't going to give up.

He leaned back on his hands and watched the surface of the water, remembered everything she'd told him. He thought of her, the child she'd been, the woman she was, how much had been taken from her.

As he tasted salt in his mouth, he realized he was finally crying.

CHERI WASN'T AWARE she'd drifted to sleep until she woke up and sensed she was alone in the bedroom. She couldn't hear Michael breathing.

Moonlight spilled over her bed as she threw back the sheet and reached for her cotton robe. Shrugging it on, she slipped her feet into thongs and went in search of him.

She expected to find him out on the porch, so she was surprised to discover it empty.

The waves boomed over the shore with a primitive rhythm. A slight breeze had come up, and it whipped her robe around her thin legs as she walked quickly around the cabin, calling softly.

No answer.

Had he left her? The minute the question formed in her mind, she rejected it. Michael would never leave her. She knew that now.

She set off toward the beach, her feet moving lightly over the moonlit trail.

He was up on one of the higher lava formations, looking out over the ocean. Without a sound, she began to climb up to him. He wasn't wearing anything but a pair of jeans. He'd catch a chill.

She was almost to him, still behind him, when she saw him pull his knees up against his chest, and bury his face in his hands.

Cheri stopped. She sensed she was a witness to an intensely private moment, nothing she should see. Yet she couldn't move.

His shoulders shook slightly, and she thought for a

moment he was trembling with cold. Then the shaking slowly became deeper, his body rippling violently. Michael's hands came up over his head, his fingers ran through his hair, then pressed against the side of his face. Then he clasped his arms around his knees and bowed his head, still shaking.

He's crying. Cheri felt her legs start to tremble and had to lower herself slowly to the ground. She closed her fingers around the rough rock and anchored herself as she watched him.

She couldn't hear anything, and it made it more awful to watch. As if he were keeping all sound inside.

Go to him. She stood up, started toward him, then stopped.

Leave him alone. You already told him you didn't want him. And what would he want with you?

She couldn't stop looking at him. The silent shaking of his shoulders, the tightness of his body. This wasn't Michael. Michael, with his quick smile, his soft brown eyes and tender heart.

She slowly lowered herself to the ground, her hand gripping the rock until it hurt. His hand came up again, then his head, as he quickly wiped his face with his fingers.

The gesture caused something to shatter deep inside her. Cheri stood up, started to run toward him. And then she was there, kneeling beside him, enclosing him in her arms.

"Michael?"

He turned away from her, trying to hide his face. "I'll be in in a minute. Go back to bed."

"But you're crying—"

"No. Go back to bed."

She pressed herself against him, touched his hair with her hands, tried to turn his face toward hers.

"No, Cheri. Don't, please."

She had thought she'd made her choice back in the darkness of their bedroom, but she knew she had to make it now.

"Michael." She took his hand and put it gently over her left breast. "Feel how fast my heart is pounding. I'm scared to death."

"Cheri..."

The last of the silent wall that separated them began to crack as Cheri told him what she'd never thought she'd be able to say.

"I want to stay with you. I don't know how I'm going to do it, but I want to." Her words tumbled out, faster and faster. "I thought I was doing what was right for you, but I was such a fool to think I could make decisions like that."

His hands came up and framed her face, and the reassurance of his touch slowed her words, filled her with warmth.

"Michael, I never meant to hurt you. That's why I thought it was better if I left you."

"Oh, no." His thumbs caressed her cheekbones, and the beginning of a smile touched his face. He gently tilted her face closer to his. "I never wanted you to feel like that."

She swallowed. Then she forced the words out, words that laid her heart on the line and made her vulnerable. "It's just that—" *Say it.* "I've never loved anyone the way I love you, so I don't know what I'm doing and I get scared because I think whatever I do is going to be wrong."

He laughed then, a sound of exultation, pure joy. Pulling her toward him, he held her tightly against his chest, and she could hear his heart pounding. Her tears came then, and she was glad she'd wiped away his pain, made him happy. Made him feel the way he'd always made her feel.

They stayed wrapped in each other's arms until the first drops of rain touched them.

"Come on." Michael stood up, pulling her with him. Putting his arm tightly around her waist, he began to climb down to the black sand below.

They were silent as they walked through the warm rain, letting it flow over their bodies. There was no need to hurry, no need to come in out of the rain when they had each other.

"I'm holding you to this, you know," he said teasingly. She looked up at his face, at the dancing light in his brown eyes, and felt as if her spirit were breaking loose at last, as if she really had a chance of leaving everything behind. Of starting again, with Michael.

He pinched her side gently and she nodded her head. "Okay with me."

"No backing out in the morning, all right?" There was still the tiniest bit of anxiety in his expression.

"Never." As the tension left his face, she hugged him more tightly with her fingers, his skin wet and slippery from the warm tropical rain.

When they reached their cabin, he helped her take off her clothes and tenderly dried her off. She laughed as he tried to remove his soaked jeans, then reached for the towel and began to massage his smooth muscles.

They didn't bother to push the beds together, simply climbed into one of the twin beds and curled up underneath the light cotton sheets. The sound of the rain drumming against the roof was soothing.

Held tightly in Michael's warm embrace, Cheri remembered the words he'd said at his parents' home. She shifted her head on the pillow until their eyes met.

"I'll make you happy, Michael. I promise."

He threaded one of his legs through hers, then tilted his head so his lips came down over hers.

When he broke the kiss, he breathed softly against

her lips. "You already do." He kissed her again. "We'll get married in Hana. My parents can fly in."

She nodded, feeling her body slowly begin to fill with warmth. "You aren't taking any chances, are you?" she teased.

"Damn right." He traced her cheekbone with a finger. "We can go to one of the outer islands for our honeymoon." His dark eyes deepened. "I want to see you lying in bed, covered with nothing but flowers."

She caught her breath as his hand moved lower, gently capturing her breast.

"Can Rachel fly over?" she asked, her voice breathless.

"Only—" he gently rolled her onto her back in the small bed, until he had her pinned to the mattress with his hard body "—if she promises to wait until we're hidden away before she phones the *Enquirer*."

"You knew!" Cheri gasped as he started to laugh, and she felt his stomach quiver against hers. She tried to keep a straight face, bit the inside of her mouth, but his laughter was contagious. He buried his face against her neck, nibbled her skin until she shrieked for mercy.

His caresses changed, became less playful and more erotically charged. When he kissed her the next time, she deepened the kiss, opening her mouth slightly. She moved her hand until her fingers were laced through his hair, held him gently. When he raised his head, he looked down at her flushed face with the beginnings of a smile.

I'll never get tired of looking at his eyes, she thought as she smoothed her fingers over his cheek. She felt her body soften as he moved over her. And as they started to make love, Cheri knew deep inside her soul the rest of her life would be touched by love.

Epilogue

"Mommy! Mommy, watch me!"

Cheri sat up on the chaise lounge and smiled as she saw Michelle, her three-year-old daughter, balanced precariously on Michael's shoulders. He was standing chest-deep in the pool and was holding each of her hands with his.

"Watch!"

"I'm watching, sweet pea," she called out, shading her eyes against the hot summer sun. She and Michael were house-sitting for his parents while they took a six-week vacation in Italy.

"Okay, Daddy, you let go now," Michelle commanded, and Cheri put her hand over her mouth to hide her grin. There were instants when she looked so much like Michael. They shared the same determination.

"I'm watching you," she called out again, and Michelle screamed with delight as she leaped up and hurtled into the pool like a cannonball.

As the water splashed up, Cheri caught Michael's eye. He was grinning. Seconds later, their daughter's tiny dark head surfaced and she began to swim toward Michael.

"That was wonderful, Micki!"

"Did you see me jump, Mommy?"

"I sure did."

"You jump now!" The strong little jaw thrust out determinedly.

Cheri stood up and ran to the edge of the pool, then leaped in next to Michael. Michelle laughed as Cheri surfaced and caught her daughter up in her arms.

Michael's eyes were mischievous. "Micki, would you like to see Mommy jump from my shoulders?"

As soon as Cheri saw the look in her daughter's dark eyes, she knew there was no escaping that one. She stuck out her tongue at her husband but took the hand he offered.

THAT EVENING as she lay in bed beside Michael, her thoughts drifted.

What a distance to have traveled—in less than a decade.

When she remembered that night on Maui, Cheri considered it the moment her life had begun. She'd married Michael within the week.

Robert Stone had been right. "More Than Destiny," one of the songs from Tough Cookie's first album, hit number thirty-one on the charts like a bullet the first week. She'd been driving home from the Valley with Michael when she'd first heard herself on the radio. He'd pulled the car over, and she'd sat very still, not believing her voice, her band, on nationwide radio.

In six weeks, the song was number one, and held its position for two weeks. By that time, "Dream Lover" was already climbing the charts.

Michael had made it a point to meet Glenda the first week they'd returned to Los Angeles. Her therapy had resumed, twice a week, with Michael attending every other session. And he never missed.

Two years into their marriage, Michael convinced her to go back to school. She'd always been secretly ashamed of her lack of education, so receiving her high school diploma set some feelings of inadequacy to rest.

As her marriage prospered, so did the band. All three albums they recorded went platinum, selling over one million copies each.

And Micki. At thirty, Cheri had become restless. Touring with the band, recording, was no longer enough. She had known Michael wanted a family when she married him, but she hadn't been sure she did. As she attended friends' showers and played with Gina's children, she became more sure it was a part of life she wanted to experience.

Micki was born two weeks after Michael's thirty-seventh birthday. Michael had stayed with her throughout labor, breathed with her, never left her alone. And he caught his daughter when she was born. Cheri had been exhausted, childbirth harder than any concert she'd ever given. But she'd managed to look over at him and catch the expression in his eyes as he looked down at the tiny red face.

And in her heart, she finally made peace with herself. She'd given him something of real worth.

Within six months after Micki's birth, she'd been restless again. It had been Michael who'd pushed her gently back into a tour. "Take Micki with you," he said, as if it were the most natural thing in the world. Then he surprised her, took on a partner at the agency, and accompanied them.

Her thoughts were interrupted by the squeak of the door. It swung slowly open, and Cheri squinted her eyes. She could barely make out the shape of her daughter in her long pink-flowered nightgown.

"Mommy?" Her tone was so different from that afternoon at the pool. Tremulous. Afraid.

"What's wrong, Micki?" she whispered, not wanting to wake Michael.

"I saw the monster under the bed again." She stood in the doorway, hanging onto the knob and swinging the door slightly.

Cheri patted the king-sized bed. "Do you want to stay here for a little bit?"

"Yes!" She rushed for the bed, clambered up and crawled between Cheri and Michael. He was sleeping on his stomach, and Micki reached over and patted his head gently.

"Don't wake Daddy up. I'll sing you a song and we'll see if we can chase that monster away, okay?"

"Okay." Micki snuggled against her as Cheri started to sing a lullaby she'd written while she was pregnant. Micki closed her eyes and tucked her head underneath Cheri's chin.

She sang all six verses, and by the fifth, Micki's breathing was relaxed and even. Cheri touched her daughter's hair gently, smoothed it back from her delicate face.

"I'd love to put that on an album someday," Michael said softly.

She glanced over and saw he was awake. He reached for her hand and she laced her fingers through his.

"The monsters again, huh?"

She nodded. "The one under the bed."

"We'll have a monster hunt in the morning," he said.

She loved him for taking Micki's fears seriously. "I have a better idea."

Michael slowly sat up in bed and propped his pillow beneath his shoulders. "Is it something I can help you with?"

She grinned. "I think it's about time we gave Micki a real live monster she can play with. Do you think you can survive another one?"

"Oh, I think so." He leaned over and kissed her,

then gently slid his hands underneath his sleeping daughter. "And getting there is half the fun."

He carried the sleeping Micki to the door, then looked over his shoulder at Cheri.

"You aren't going anyplace tonight, are you?"

She smiled. "Nope. I'm right where I want to be."

ANNE MATHER

Anne Mather, one of Harlequin's leading romance authors, has published more than 100 million copies worldwide, including **Wild Concerto**, a *New York Times* best-seller.

Catherine Loring was an innocent in a South American country beset by civil war. Doctor Armand Alvares was arrogant yet compassionate. They could not ignore the flame of love igniting within them...whatever the cost.

HIDDEN IN THE FLAME

Available at your favorite bookstore in June, or send your name, address and zip or postal code, along with a check or money order for $4.25 (includes 75¢ for postage and handling) payable to Worldwide Library Reader Service to:

Worldwide Library Reader Service

In the U.S.
Box 52040
Phoenix, AZ
85072-2040

In Canada
5170 Yonge Street, P.O. Box 2800,
Postal Station A
Willowdale, Ont. M2N 6J3

HIF-A-1

Share the joys and sorrows
of real-life love with
Harlequin American Romance!™·

GET THIS BOOK
FREE as your introduction to
Harlequin American Romance –
an exciting series of romance
novels written especially for
the American woman of today.

Mail to:
Harlequin Reader Service

In the U.S.	In Canada
2504 West Southern Ave.	P.O. Box 2800, Postal Station A
Tempe, AZ 85282	5170 Yonge St., Willowdale, Ont. M2N 6J3

YES! I want to be one of the first to discover
Harlequin American Romance. Send me FREE and without
obligation *Twice in a Lifetime.* If you do not hear from me after I
have examined my FREE book, please send me the 4 new
Harlequin American Romances each month as soon as they
come off the presses. I understand that I will be billed only $2.25
for each book (total $9.00). There are no shipping or handling
charges. There is no minimum number of books that I have to
purchase. In fact, I may cancel this arrangement at any time.
Twice in a Lifetime is mine to keep as a FREE gift. even if I do not
buy any additional books.   154–BPA–NAZJ

Name	(please print)	

Address		Apt. no.

City	State/Prov.	Zip/Postal Code

Signature (If under 18, parent or guardian must sign.)

This offer is limited to one order per household and not valid to current Harlequin
American Romance subscribers. We reserve the right to exercise discretion in
granting membership. If price changes are necessary, you will be notified.

AMR–SUB–1R